THE
DINNER
PARTY

By the same author:

THE NEW LITERATURE
(1959)

Claude Mauriac

THE
DINNER
PARTY

TRANSLATED BY MERLOYD LAWRENCE

George Braziller, Inc.
New York
1960

28605

Seating arrangement at
THE DINNER PARTY

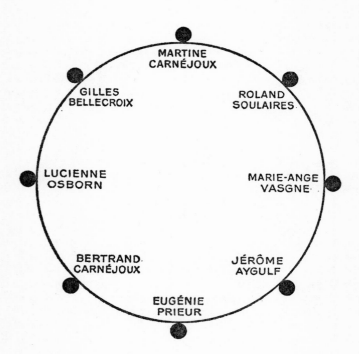

MARTINE
CARNÉJOUX

GILLES
BELLECROIX

ROLAND
SOULAIRES

LUCIENNE
OSBORN

MARIE-ANGE
VASGNE

BERTRAND
CARNÉJOUX

JÉRÔME
AYGULF

EUGÉNIE
PRIEUR

THE
DINNER
PARTY

"... JUST TO FINISH OUR CONVERSATION ..."

"But of course, Jérôme my boy. Not another word. I assure you that ..."

"... allow me to add this: a nation which is struggling for its liberty, wherever and under whatever conditions, is always right."

"Thus the paper which I was telling you about was written in 1844. In it Joinville demonstrated that only a fleet propelled by steam could be effective, in both the offense ..."

"In 1844, steamships, imagine!"

"But my dear lady, there were at least sixty ships of mixed propulsion in our navy at the time. And as for the actual invention of steamships, why in 1780 ..."

"Eugénie, do me the favor of sitting over there, across from me. Wouldn't you like to take off your shawl? No? Gilles on my right. And you, Roland, excuse my interrupting, here. Your dinner partner is our ravishing Marie-Ange. All the rest of you will find your names written on ..."

"As early as 1780, a steamboat cruised up the Saône. The real innovation was the propeller. That same year, in 1844, Joinville was made a member of the Admiralty Council where he played a significant role in the special Commission formed to institute a steam-propelled navy. And he was even more instrumental, along with certain eminent individuals, in a particular sub-commission, so much so that one wonders if the paper in question were not the joint creation of this group. Credit must go to the Prince for opposing the bureaucratic routine and, with Dupuy de Lôme, a young engineer whom Joinville himself said was twenty years ahead of his time, proving that a steam-propelled fleet, this I must emphasize because it is the heart of the matter, a steam propelled fleet was just as worthwhile for the offense as for the defense . . ."

. . . M. Soulaires is posing and looking at us as though what he said were particularly intelligent. With his fat bald head and falsetto voice, his tics, and his sleepy eyes, I wouldn't be surprised if the fellow were something of a bore . . .

"Even, he added, as a reinforcement for operations on land."

"A round table is always so much more pleasant!"

"A friend of mine has a round table that is so big . . ."

"Eight is a very bad number. I had the hardest time seating everyone."

"Martine made it clear, you know, that it was impossible for me to sit at the head of the table without having two men, or two women, I don't remember which, sitting next to each other. All the same, my dear Eugénie, you are on my right, and that is the important thing."

"There should have been ten of us, but Mr. Osborn telephoned that he was unable to come. An important conference to discuss his new film. His charming wife tells me, however, that he will join us after dinner . . ."

. . . Not all that charming, although still rather lovely, with her tan complexion, and the gentle expression in her grey eyes which may be just nearsightedness. Nor does she know anyone here, with the exception of Gilles Bellecroix. We certainly have had bad luck with this dinner. Two more people dropping out at the last minute and having to replace Zerbanian, who had already regretted yesterday, with Jérôme. Jérôme who started talking politics before we even sat down to dinner, and worried us half to death. He looks calmer now, but it bodes poorly . . .

"As for Bénédicte, my dear Gilles, I told you, didn't I, that she was sweet enough to call me from the depths of her sickbed . . ."

"If you only knew how disappointed she was! When I returned from Marseilles, just this afternoon, for you know I've been travelling all day, I could see as soon as I got off the train and found her waiting for me, that the poor dear was not herself. You know how she is . . . Well, I had to insist that she take her temperature. Can you imagine, it was 102.6°!"

"Let's hope it is nothing serious."

"There has been a lot of flu around this fall."

"That friend of mine has such an enormous table (actually he lives on your island, but on the other end, on the Quai de Béthune) that it can seat eighteen."

"Eight is plenty, you know. Almost too many. The vidame de Pamiers, unless maybe it was the chevalier de

Valois (they are very much alike) said, and I must get this exactly, for quoting Balzac is like giving a telephone number, there can be no more-or-less about it, just let me remember . . ."

"Oh, but take your time, Eugénie, please . . ."

"Here we are '. . . was extremely contemptuous of any dinner at which there were more than five or six guests, for, said he, such a dinner could provide neither conversation, nor a memorable cuisine, nor wine tasted in complete possession of one's faculties.' "

"Charming!"

. . . Charming indeed. She is giving us a little lecture. And there were supposed to have been ten of us . . .

. . . Eugénie is so superbly cultured. Of course *La Comédie Humaine* is one of her specialties . . .

"Champagne! We are having champagne! How perfectly wonderful . . ."

. . . Roland is all excited. It must be well over twenty years that he has been drinking champagne and still he is not tired of it. The frivolity of these people always amazes me. Martine was right to insist that we serve champagne right through dinner. It should be livelier this way . . .

. . . That fat gentleman certainly has bad manners. Grandmother always taught me that a well-brought up person never makes the slightest mention of what is being served . . .

"Then I will have to have some sugar. Fortunately I haven't yet begun my consommé."

"Antoine, did you hear M. Soulaires? He would like some sugar."

"Sugar?"

"Of course! You gave us scotch before dinner and I didn't exactly skimp on it, so . . ."

"Sugar . . ."

". . . allows one to go on drinking with complete impunity. Didn't you know that?"

"I would like some sugar too . . ."

"So would I . . ."

"Thank you. Here, one piece is enough . . ."

"Well then, Antoine, still spry?"

"Madame is too kind. I mustn't complain. And Madame, has she been in good health?"

"Things could be worse, as you can see."

"I can see that Madame is as susceptible to the cold as ever, if she will excuse my saying so, but Madame has never looked better, it is always a pleasure to serve Madame."

"Susceptible to the cold, my good Antoine! Nothing escapes you, does it?"

. . . dear old Antoine. The Carnéjoux must have known about him through me. It is so pleasant to be waited on. My new maid seems an energetic sort. But she doesn't arrive until nine o'clock and leaves at five, leaving me alone in the morning and the evening, and alone at night. I did have to cut down, but it is no fun, at my age. Antoine had raised his rates again last time I gave a dinner. The day may come when I won't be able to entertain at all. Zerbanian will suffer the most; he enjoys my scotch so. Whiskey gets more and more expensive . . .

. . . Eugénie Prieur, recognizing the butler we hired for

tonight, exchanges a few words with him, in one of the elated, falsely contented moments of triumph which money makes possible for older people: a brief *marivaudage* in which a servant is forced to play at flirting. Though our presence cramps the butler's style, Gigi, for her part, seems quite at ease, simpering away coyly at the trumped-up compliments of a servant who makes her feel, with his casual but faintly suggestive little speeches, in which impertinence and respect are carefully blended along with apparent spontaneity, that for the moment she is, once again, the pretty young woman to whom even the servants could not help but offer their discreet homage. Lucienne Osborn's sober, preoccupied expression . . .

. . . under my sign of Capricorn yesterday's horoscope in *France-Soir* predicted a pleasant encounter will help you spend a good evening away from home since I didn't go out last night and anyway the newspaper is dated for the following day it must have meant tonight and most certainly Bertrand Carnéjoux he has a fine position now editor-in-chief of *Ring* he did marry well those horoscopes in *France-Soir* are really amazing also those of *Paris-Presse* though they are not quite as good I was wrong actually to have been angry with John it is lucky that he is not here it wouldn't surprise me either if he called again to say that he couldn't come after dinner . . .

. . . Little oblong cards with gold borders. Since the one belonging to my enormous and ancient partner on the left has been turned over, I can't read the name on it. Pilou didn't choose to introduce me. It's just as well. What would I say to such an old fossil? Imagine coming to dine wearing a grey wool shawl. On my right is the fair and lovely and well-known Marie-Ange Vasgne, with her ash-blonde hair drawn straight across her brow. And her huge, gold-flecked eyes. Frightening. On this other card, how impressive, my name, *Jérôme Aygulf*, carefully written out by Pilou, who is sitting at the other end of the table smiling at her husband. She is the same and yet different. A face that has grown opaque as the features have become more symmetrical. Her soul, which once showed through the translucent surface, is no longer perceptible. Her soul! How Raymond Frôlet would laugh, if he could hear me. The ravishing soul of Martine. Somehow I am all worn out, even though I did nothing today but read twenty pages of *Political Economy* and go to the movies. As tired as if the number of years which I have lived . . . She can't be much under eighty, that old bag in the yellow wig whom Pilou so thoughtfully put beside me and who is looking at me surreptitiously. She may even have the crust to say something . . .

. . . Bertrand and I exchanged knowing glances when Gigi, swathed like an onion, spoke to the butler. That would be all the masculine attention she could count on nowadays, if it were not for her little court of homosexuals who, by some fluke, and the unavoidable absence of Zer-banian, have sent us no representative tonight. They can be as frivolous as they like in the presence of this old lady who tolerates a vice which she chooses not to regard as such. Because they are incapable of making her jealous, she invites them to her house, the old couples and the young ones, listens to their troubles, takes part in their

scenes and reconciliations, and in return enjoys the favor
of their compliments, which they can dispense all the more
liberally to women since it commits them to nothing . . .

. . . Joinville's report was interesting, just the same. But
they are all so frivolous. I must find a lighter subject. I
feel like talking tonight, I want to be brilliant and enjoy
myself. What a tiresome walk that was this afternoon,
from Montmartre to the Grands-Boulevards. The same
places and the same thoughts as twenty years ago. Though
I have become rich, I am still poor. On the board of so
many corporations, president and director of the Loubski
mines. But my heart stops beating when a prostitute stops
me and says: "How about it, you fat sweetie . . ." I'm not
fat. And I've never dared become her sweetie . . .

. . . I've always been sensitive to mirrors and their effects.
It is one of the themes in my book, *Sober Pleasures*. The
mirrors which cover most of the wall in our dining room
reflect a host of candelabra around which the guests seem
to be multiplied in a radiant twilight. All the dinner
parties I have ever been to since I started going out over
twenty years ago are reflected here—in my own house, too,
it *is* pleasant to be settled at last in my own house—distilled into one exact, simultaneous image. I must persuade
Martine to find another place for those two blackamoors.
Their pedestals are too high. The plant we bought yesterday at the flower market has the tallest, most elegant . . .

. . . Bertrand is looking at our philodendron. It shouldn't
be watered too often, the florist said that was very important. Nearly everyone has finished his consommé. They
are in too much of a hurry. The fish will never be ready in

time. The butler, fortunately, is pouring champagne. I must keep an eye on the glasses. Bertrand really should be the one to take care of that. But he is not exactly what one would call a good host, nor even a good husband, the poor love. I must say something, anything to fill in this silence . . .

". . . Have you seen Tristan Bernard's new play in which . . ."

"Of course!"

"It is one of the funniest plays that I . . ."

"There is nothing in it to compare with the lines which made him famous, like the great definition of an intermission in his crossword puzzles!"

. . . "Empties the loges and fills up the lounges." We know, you old walrus, we know. Don't think that you are going to get me out of my lethargy with those hackneyed quotes of yours. If I did come out of it, it was just to enlighten you on a few points, to show up your ignorance, and I'm not the least bit sorry . . .

"You probably know that Tristan Bernard once had a theater of his own, I don't remember quite where, but in some peculiar part of town. It was even named after him. Very few people ever . . ."

"Ah! yes. If anyone asked for a seat, he used to say: 'Impossible, I have only rows' . . ."

. . . Polite smiles. Only the very young man on my right laughed heartily, as he kept an eye peeled on the all-too-slow progress of the champagne bottle. Now that I've taken my shoes off, I feel a lot better. I mustn't let them get out of reach. Tristan Bernard is amusing enough, but he is not one of my topics. The Orléans dynasty, on the other hand, which Roland began talking about . . .

"You know what Tristan used to call his theater? The Sahara Bernard!"

"How perfect! But since we are on the subject of Tristan Bernard and the theater, there is always his definition of an intermission . . ."

. . . It never fails. Sahara, that *is* a gem. Champagne, finally. It's about time. I should have waited and not grabbed my glass so quickly. Such tingling, icy effervescence, such dry but gentle astringency, so clear, so brisk . . .

. . . He also used to say as he pointed at the perpetually empty orchestra: "My theater always has the best disengagements." But that is not funny enough to quote here. Instead . . .

". . . The other thing Tristan used to say about his theater, don't you remember, was: 'Knock three times, once for each spectator.' "

. . . The royal box in the middle of the theater. Lined with red velvet. There you are, Marietta, greeting the audience which rose to its feet when you entered. All those faces turned towards you. Cheers from every side. Tomorrow at dawn you leave by plane for Hollywood and tonight Paris is bidding you farewell, with all its love. You throw kisses to Paris. Your dress is pale pink, irridescent. With lace inserts. For a French-Canadian girl the road to Hollywood is by way of Paris.

. . . I am not worried about Bénédicte. There is no reason to be. Just a simple case of flu. Am I worried about Bénédicte? I miss her, that's all. Here we are, just the few of us, observing a ritual that promises no surprises, even though we all anticipate a certain amount of pleasure. A dinner party, just like every other dinner party. Unless something quite unexpected happens, it will fade into our memory of the many other dinners we have attended. The same faces, picked from the same supply of eligible choices. (Though I haven't ever met this beautiful young woman before, a Canadian, I gather.) The same cups of consommé, the rest of the menu being predictable, with a few set variations. The same candelabra casting a scalloped pattern on the tablecloth. Dark green candles, obtained from shops as familiar as the caterers who supply the inevitable petit-fours which will appear at the end of dinner, only three possibilities: two old and respected establishments, or the new one that came into fashion this year. The butler himself, helped by the Carnéjoux's pretty chambermaid, is on loan from the same menagerie which supplies all the people here with extra help, when their turn comes to entertain . . .

. . . Notre-Dame, illuminated and crouching at the end of the quai. One can see it clearly through this window where the curtains haven't yet been drawn. Before I could bring myself to enter, I leaned for a long time on the parapet where Restif de la Bretonne carved his cries of love, now worn away, but still unforgettable. Thinking of Pilou whom I love and Bertrand who stole her from me just because I was born a few years too late . . .

. . . How many times have we met again like this, since we began dining out? Before the Carnéjoux moved to this house on the quai d'Orléans, I often came here, on other floors, and in this same second floor apartment, where the

Meilleuses once lived. Bertrand and Martine will move away sooner or later and we will still meet, in this apartment or another, Gilles Bellecroix, Roland Soulaires and I, indestructible old Parisians. The tenants of these beautiful apartments on the Ile Saint-Louis change more often than their guests. I think I have found a way of bringing the conversation around to the Orléans . . .

". . . When one is as old as I am, yes, alas, old is the word, one is somewhat like, it's hard to express. Not Asmodeus. It's not a matter of evil curiosity, prying, but a way of seeing things all at once, do you see what I am trying to say? Take this dinner, for instance. Well, just as it becomes more and more brilliant and delightful, I can see others taking place, in this same building, even in this same room, dinners which I once attended. The Meilleuses used to live in this apartment . . ."

"The Meilleuses?"

"Yes. Doesn't that mean anything to you? How young you are! They have disappeared, of course, in the flesh, and with all their worldly goods. The worldly goods first, unfortunately for them, and for us too. They really knew how to entertain, in their day. You must remember, Gilles. And you, Roland . . ."

"Yes, I remember . . ."

"As for the flesh . . . no use dwelling on that. Anyway, I can still see, in this very dining room, just about where our Martine is sitting, the old Princess . . . But I think you must have known her too, Bertrand. Martine won't be angry, will she, if I say that she had a little weakness for you? In the most honorable sense, of course. If you could have seen the poor soul . . ."

"She struck me as someone, how can I describe it, who might wear puttees . . ."

"But she did, my dear, she really did. Do you remember what Zerbanian used to say? 'The Princess? Why I did my military training with her.' That gives you an idea of the sort of person she was . . ."

"He also used to say that her eyes fairly sparkled with stupidity."

"I always thought that was your expression, Roland."

"Thank you. It's not so hilarious that I must claim . . ."

"My dear, unto him that hath, it shall be given . . ."

. . . They are looking at each other and laughing. There is a kind of conspiracy between Gilles Bellecroix, Roland Soulaires, and Bertrand Carnéjoux, even under the sarcastic little thrusts which they exchange in this seemingly casual manner. They are among peers, initiated into the same secrets of wealth and fame; friendship is only possible for them above a certain level of success. I can hardly believe that I am here, a young nobody, admitted by some oversight into the Holy of Holies. And suddenly, with the help of the champagne, it seems to be the simplest thing in the world to become a successful screen writer like Gilles Bellecroix, or make as much money as Roland Soulaires, or even to have written a book like Bertrand Carnéjoux and thus acquire the right to invite whomever I want to dinner, for instance a lady as pretty as Marie-Ange Vasgne. An intoxicating daydream, which I indulge with calm poise, as though it were not just a temporary privilege that I am taking part in this freemasonry of success. I can go on building these castles in the air, playing the magnate, the arrogant, self-assured "businessman," who steps lightly under his burden of responsibility as he dines between planes with the prime minister and the latest winner of the Nobel prize. But the humiliating sensation of being excluded from all this intrudes itself once again . . .

"What I meant to say about the Princess is that, contrary to what she gave one to believe, she hadn't a drop of Orléans blood, not one drop . . ."

"But her grandfather, though . . ."

"Her grandfather! Let's discuss her grandfather, right here and now. The marriage of Louis-Philippe and Marie-Amélie produced eight children. The Duc d'Orléans, he was the one who was killed in an automobile accident. Nemours. Aumale. Montpensier. That makes four. Then the youngest, the Prince de Joinville, whom Roland was just talking about. That leaves three . . ."

"Didn't she have ten children?"

. . . How boring they are but if John could only die in an automobile accident driving as fast as he does that would really be interesting it's too bad horoscopes don't tell you about things like that . . .

"Eight. That's not doing too badly, either! But anyway, the five sons, actually six, because we forgot Penthièvre who died in infancy. Then three girls, am I right? So that makes nine . . ."

. . . Eugénie has a daughter and several grandchildren, but she never talks about them. Bénédicte Bellecroix has a son (it would be polite to ask Gilles about them later on), but she is not here. Who else is there, then, who knows the greatest of all mysteries? No one but me, since, as far as I know, not one of the other women here possesses any

22

children, nor is possessed by them. When I think of Jean-Paul and Rachel, a warmth goes straight through my body, a kind of joyful melting of my whole being. And these poor souls think that they have lived! Without the fundamental, the primordial experience of motherhood, they think that they know the meaning of life . . .

. . . The same child, my son, born under Louis-Philippe, or in Louis XIV's place and destined to his reign, which his personality would have made entirely different. No one at Saint-Germain was ever astonished when a baby wasn't the real one. My Rachel wouldn't be a bit surprised to learn that it was now 1660, in the days of fireworks and a king called Louis XIV . . .

. . . If they stay on the subject of Louis-Philippe's children and if Eugénie allows me to get a word in edgeways, I may have a chance to shine. On my left, Marie-Ange Vasgne, the young Canadian model in such demand, with her picture in all the magazines. And those huge eyes which made her famous. (Grey, blue, brown? It's hard to tell. They are variegated, flecked with gold.) That picture of her with the deep décolletage (even more revealing than the one she has on tonight) should be very exciting now that I haven't been looking at it for a while. Where could I have put it? . . .

. . . He is sneaking a sly look at my breasts as he rolls that bit of bread between his stubby fingers. Yes indeed, old boy, I'm a nice little morsel. With you it should be easy. If Bertrand put you on my right, with John Osborn not here, it's because you can be of more help in my career than Gilles Bellecroix, even if he is a screen writer. I should have been on the right of the host, though. After all, I am from abroad. Bertrand is very thoughtless. He is only interested in me when we are in bed, like the day before yesterday in that cheap hotel where he takes me now. The place we used to go is sanctified in his eyes, ever since he found out that Stendhal died there . . .

"What a lovely view you have from here, Martine!"

"It's so much prettier in the daytime . . ."

"But it's very fine at night, too. Believe me! There is certainly no reason for you to feel uprooted, my dear."

"Still overlooking the Seine, of course, Eugénie. But living on the Ile Saint-Louis is like nothing else, really a world of its own."

. . . Not so savory when you come to think of it, Bertrand marrying Irène's daughter . . .

. . . Eugénie is breathing deeply, with a kind of rasping sound. Glancing at Martine, and then at me, but avoiding my eyes. As far as I can remember, it was because of a dream that I married Pilou. Almost a child. Always around us, at the edge of our lives, closer to her brother and little sister than to us, somehow distant, indifferent. Not judging us. Out of reach, if only in thoughts. And suddenly, in this dream, taking advantage of a moment when we were alone to bring her face close to mine. The effect of her mouth, under mine, was extraordinary. It was as though there were nothing in the universe but the lips of a young girl, and through the lips of this young girl I possessed the whole universe. The reality did not live up to the promise of the dream. But without the dream there would have been no reality. Pilou confessed that she had been hoping for a long time for the kiss which I gave her, not long after the night when I imagined it. It was at her mother's, one Sunday evening when the servants were out and we were in the kitchen together getting dinner. In this way Martine's desire, which I never would have suspected but to which I unconsciously reacted, revealed itself, thanks to a dream, to be urgent and demanding . . .

. . . From the day I was born to the day I was married I lived in a house that looked out, just as this one does, over the Seine. Tonight the river is behind my back. My parents' apartment overlooked the arcade on one side, and on the other, the quai du Louvre. Bertrand often came to see Mummy. He paid no attention to me, but was sweet to Luc and Simone, making up stories for them, all about the colored prints that decorated the nursery and the hall: *One day, after a long walk, as he rested in the shade of a grapefruit tree* . . . Now that we are married, Bertrand still doesn't pay much attention to me. My only joy is from the children, a daily earthquake of pleasure. My little girl brings me the most happiness, because of the fleeting miracle of her age. Marie-Ange's eyes just caught mine. Neither of us wanted to give in, so we kept on with this contest of smiles until both of us silently agreed to put an end to it . . .

. . . Martine put the red roses which Roland sent her in the dining room. I hadn't noticed until now. She and Marie-Ange just smiled at each other in such a friendly way. Who would believe that Marie-Ange could be so two-faced and Martine so innocent? Now she is looking at me. Little Pilou. I am not worthy of her love, which is some-

how so forbearing and so protective of me. I hope she remembered to thank Roland. But who sent those other
roses which I saw in the salon? Marie-Ange, your name
appealed to me before your face and your body, because it
reminded me of the only woman whom I ever loved and
whom I lost forever, Marie-Plum . . .

. . . Martine is still too young to show the signs of her
marriage. One shudders to think what Bertrand will do
to her. Imagine the life of one woman and all the different
destinies which might be hers. She could be shown with
each of the six suitors among whom she had to choose as
a young girl, blooming with one, withering with the next.
Transformed by each one of them. But remaining essentially the same, though even that isn't certain. Paula,
say her name is Paula, would be an entirely different person
depending on the character of the man she married, rich or
poor, stingy or generous, according to his good traits and
his faults, a rake like Bertrand Carnéjoux or a faithful husband like me . . .

. . . Don't hold back, go to it, man. I suppose I should
call him *maître d'hôtel* but I can't bring myself to do that.
Fill it right up. So icy on my palate, already deliciously
warm in my body. I feel such a kid, with all these people
who have been drinking together for years; I have the same
feeling I used to have as a child; a desire to grow older, to
understand the language of grown-ups, their secret code,
to share in their corruption, for that is what it is, after all.
Pilou and I, innocent together, are of another race. Genuinely young. As for the rest of them. Except of course for
Mademoiselle Vasgne . . .

26

. . . My partner on the the left, a callow youth, with slicked-down red hair. In the absence of John Osborn, fortunately only temporary, I should concentrate my charms on his colleague, the screen writer Gilles Bellecroix, who is unaware, like everyone else here except Bertrand, that the dinner was planned especially so that I could meet the two of them. My other partner, this bald fat man with such nasty hands and puffy eyes, Roland Soulaires, is actually very rich and might be even more of a help to me . . .

. . . So satisfying, when I find an attractive woman, after one of my long, distracted walks, and sit next to her, without expecting anything, or even looking in her direction, as though all I needed were the radiating presence of a body near me. But when it is no longer just an anonymous girl sitting beside me, but a young lady to whom I have been introduced, such as this Marie-Ange Vasgne, I feel nervous and uncomfortable, *because then and then only* . . .

"The Prince de Joinville and his sister Clementine once went in disguise to a ball given by the Duchesse de Berri. And what disguises! Utterly ravishing, both late eighteenth century, you can picture the effect. It was not long, as you might imagine, before they were noticed by old Charles X, who, like the tutor of Victurnien d'Esgrignon, was one of those old men who are 'astride two centuries, adorning the present with the dried roses of experience and the withered bloom of the customs of their youth.' Balzac. Who else? Then Charles X, whose youth was personified there, in the form of a charming young girl, reminding him of all the others he had loved, said to the future Louis-Philippe, (I find this kind of gesture so endearing): 'If I were forty

years younger, sir, your daughter would be Queen of
France.' Isn't that a lovely story? But to get back to the
Duchesse de Berri . . . More champagne! Well then, just a
drop . . ."

. . . Bertrand gave this dinner in my honor; he invited
a few friends just for me. In honor of my new face. No one
seems to have noticed. Only Marie-Ange Vasgne, who
said, in a slightly nasty, impertinent tone of voice—she has
always hated me, I can't understand why, after all,
shouldn't I be the one? She said, looking at me with a
genuinely surprised expression, as she came into what she
calls the *front room* (how quaint these Canadians are):
"You look so beautiful tonight!" Everyone else does seem
a bit surprised, but they don't want to stare at my new
features. Only that idiot, Jérôme, keeps looking at me.
Poor soul, that enormous bunch of roses must have cost
him a fortune. If Zerbanian hadn't called up on such short
notice, we never would have invited him. Gilles, who also
found out, was more discreet . . .

. . . Drunks. Maybe even drug addicts. They all seemed
so glamorous to me at first, the youthful-looking men at the
table, laughing with women who are still pretty, but if I
look objectively they are nothing but a bunch of fops and
old crones. (Mrs. Osborn's skin is too sunburned; it looks
creased, like cloth . . .) How sad. I don't seem to exist for
these people. To think that I have sunk as low as this;
fretting about not being accepted by such decayed old
creatures. I'll never change, always trying to excel, whether
in good or in evil, imitating whatever is before me. To
please these people, one has to be handsome. Or talented.

28

A name, that is. Or else notorious for a particular vice. I am not a fairy; I am not famous; I am too red-headed to be handsome; and too young, too young . . .

. . . All women are too female for me. The beauty in a photograph is more reassuring, with all the ugliness suppressed, and only the magnetic charm of sex showing through. I always feel slightly dizzy as I look at the delicately touched-up nudes in magazines. Smooth, polished women. The rounded flesh of Marie-Ange Vasgne's bosom, which I can see out of the corner of my eye, the living curves of her small breasts, were much more attractive in her photographs where their graceful proportions and cool brilliance aroused such overpowering emotions in me. There they seemed to come alive, to rise and fall and then suddenly to crystallize again into a two-dimensional image. How odd Martine looks tonight . . .

. . . One universe joined with another, worlds sealed together, mouths making love, so perfect was the unison of those lips: nostalgia for an imagined kiss. A kiss forbidden and then allowed. The impossible which proved to be possible. None of our real kisses, Martine, ever approached the burning perfection of the dream. I have waited for the revelations of eroticism all my life, and always in vain, except in this dream and a few others. The surprise and thrill of violating a sacred taboo, as with Edwige; the unexpected discovery of something I had always unconsciously sought; the kind of enjoyment that is no less voluptuous even though it is sublimated, more intense than the sharp climaxes of pleasure; a state of innocence regained in sleep, a kiss purified of all ugliness while it kept the savor of the forbidden; the joy of imaginary embraces: none of that could survive the reality of possession. Today not even Marie-Ange satisfies me. But what woman has ever satisfied me? Not even Marie-Plum . . .

. . . I may be nearsighted but I noticed immediately that our young hostess has had her nose operated on I wonder if noses that have been remade tan as well as the rest of one's face my nose is small it is a pretty nose and I have such a magnificent suntan . . .

. . . For instance, according to whether or not he had collaborated during the occupation, whether or not his wife was forced to take any responsibility. Both happy and unhappy at the same time, with all the contradictions of life itself. With certain inflexible traits of character. Her will power. Her flirtations. Traits more or less pronounced according to the circumstances. Six different stories with a single opening: the surprise party where Bénédicte, no, not Bénédicte, Paula as a young girl decides to choose a husband among the six boys who are courting her. Six fine stories. Six sketches. For once again, of course, I have been thinking of an idea for a film and not a novel. The occupational disease of a calling which I had no choice but to accept once I had failed so demonstrably in the world of letters. Anyway, film or novel, the key to the story will be the lingering doubt about which was the right choice. *The Lingering Doubt*, that would make a good title. Paula marries only once. The rest of the scenes, which show what she would have become living with the others, will be daydreams, hypothetical unrealized possibilities. Register the idea and the title tomorrow.

. . . It is now up to John Osborn, who fortunately will be here after dinner, to make you, Marietta, the international star that, sooner or later, you are bound to become. The trouble is that I won't be able to make love tonight. Maybe it's all to the good. I invariably give in too quickly, not out of desire but out of sheer indifference, to get it over with, for it always ends up the same way, lying in the clover, or somewhere else.

. . . Valromé, this afternoon. The radiant light of autumn. Many leaves still on the trees. A softly glowing auburn sky. A few seconds that were brief and fleeting, but also somehow infinite and timeless, when the world was anchored in one splendid moment of the present. In the evening, along the river, the last tiny gold leaves rustle on the poplars, whose ancient limbs now so often end in stumps as the branches die off one after the other. As the day ends, the light of the tugboats and the beacons on the little houseboats make the Seine into a quiet lagoon where even the musty atmosphere has something of Venice. Together, Bertrand and I experienced this almost painful, evanescent happiness. Jean-Paul looked like a little Spaniard. Rachel's serenity evoked the eternal wisdom of the child-god. A happiness that was almost unbearable in its brittle poignancy. It was only by chance that Bertrand was there with me. And the children, the children. Rachel was not feeling very well this evening . . .

. . . A little while ago, at Valromé, as I hunted for nuts with Jean-Paul, letting him smell their aromatic perfume and that of the apples that lay on the ground, my cousin Thomas came back to me. It was not just a memory of childhood, the kind which returns whenever I crush a leaf of that same walnut tree or a magnolia between my fingers to snuff it, but the actual childhood itself which materialized, both in me and outside of me. I was comforted by the thought that my son (perhaps I don't spend enough time with him, but he is still so small) will have some of the same memories, set in the same places and at the same time of year; I was watching him live through his future reminiscences. No one is listening to Eugénie but she goes right on talking, regardless. What is she saying? . . .

"People get set ideas about things like that, but they are all wrong, these princes were very prolific. Joinville, Nemours, and Aumale may each have had only two heirs, but Montpensier, I want you to know, had no less than seven children. Four sons and three daughters. Or was it the other way around? It doesn't really matter. But even more astonishing is . . ."

"Eugénie, you amaze me. Your knowledge is perfectly extraordinary."

"Oh, come now. Everyone knows that!"

. . . Eugénie Prieur. The famous Eugénie Prieur. Right next to me, in a yellow wig, all wrapped up in shawls, is the well-known Gigi; for that is what her close friends and those who want to pass themselves off as such call her. There couldn't be more than one Gigi in Paris, an aged creature who was once beautiful, probably in the days of Poincaré, who knows everything, and whose erudite monologues are a deadly bore. I will have to tell Raymond Frôlet that I sat next to Eugénie Prieur at dinner. He will be flabbergasted . . .

. . . What a feeling of relief, of accomplishment, after it is all over and he has had his money's worth, the disgusting old man. Then, for a while at least, I won't have to bear his skin next to mine, nor to make believe that I love him and experience pleasure with him (poor unfortunate Breillac), dessicated, that's the word, Bertrand said it was from a novel by the great Colette. He always calls her that to distinguish her from his secretary, little Colette. Colette, I've never had any doubts about her. What if she was once his mistress?

. . . Of course he will have to go back again and again to that same tree before the poetry of this hunt, with the sweet nutmeats encased in their smooth, precious wooden shells, hidden under the black leaves, takes shape in his imagination. The polished chestnuts, the late, slightly tart raspberries, the exhilarating air of autumn, together we felt its enchantment. When I am gone, a part of me will come to life in him as he tastes them, perhaps with his own son . . .

. . . There are cars going by along the Tournelle bridge, but our quai is silent. If I had left Rachel behind, even for the short time that I went to Valromé with Bertrand and Jean-Paul, I would have missed her presence acutely; I need to feel the weight of her hand in mine. When I come home to her my joy and wonder are even stronger than the indescribable sensation which now comes to me as I think about her. Every time I look at her (which will be very soon when I go to tuck her into bed) her irreplaceable little face surprises me all over again, as though it were impossible to remember her exactly, even after so short an absence. Right now, the picture of her in my mind is probably only a feeble, hazy image, in spite of the intense way it obsesses me. But she is still present within me when I am not near her. I see her, my little girl, I see nothing but her, without having to think about her, without forgetting my little boy, but I had forgotten him just then, although he is very dear to me. A break in the continuity of my love, for which I will not forgive myself, in my love which is just now reborn in all its violence, its abundance . . .

. . . A mild evening for this time of year the shutters and curtains have been left open it looks sloppy just so long as there is sun tomorrow the waters of the Seine must seem very close from this second floor window behind the long balcony and the trees which probably still have a few leaves but I can't see anything except the muddled reflection of bright lights it is so long since I have seen Bertrand over twenty years he didn't recognize me and I feel lost among these people if only I could wear my glasses luckily I haven't brought them with me for otherwise I would certainly succumb to the temptation and goodbye beauty and with John not here who knows he may even beg off again after dinner the diamond that young woman is wearing is smaller than mine her dress is from Rémon Castillo is just as good in any case my nearsightedness doesn't keep me from seeing what is interesting my gold necklace must stand out nicely against my suntan these candles are very restful a pleasant light when one is no longer a young girl excellent for Eugénie Prieur I haven't quite reached that point yet but this lighting doesn't improve my eyesight . . .

"You have more room here than when you were on the rue de L'Abbaye."

"But, my dear lady, how did you know . . ."

"Oh, by chance. Someone, I can't remember who, was just talking about it."

"I was amazed!"

. . . He obviously has forgotten me no use reminding him I am slightly ashamed of how provincial I was then . . .

. . . I seem to interest this well-tanned lady whom I hardly know even though she is my guest. Osborn should either have arranged to be here or else not have sent us his wife. If she would make a little effort, conversation shouldn't be too hard. At the moment, Eugénie is going full steam, so there is no need to worry. Thick lips but lovely ones, with the lipstick applied just inside the real outlines. The pale pink border that is left over accentuates rather than disguises the natural shape of her mouth. What is usually a vain and silly affectation on most women has a rather attractive effect on Mrs. Osborn, emphasizing in a paradoxical manner the undeniable existence of what she was trying to erase . . .

. . . It is not out of vanity that I automatically keep looking in the mirror. It is just that I am trying to pass the time with the help of the only person at this table, other than Pilou, who interests me and whose features I find rather pleasing at a slight distance and from this angle: myself . . .

"If he hadn't been deaf, Joinville would have been what you might call one of the blessed of this world. He had sailed under all the latitudes; he was courageous, (this was so clearly brought out in the Fieschi and Meunier conspiracies); and, if I remember correctly, he was equally successful in his love-life. As if this were not enough, he was a gifted writer and an even more gifted painter . . . I saw some of his work at the Saint-Palpouls', you must remember, Bertrand, now just listen a little, won't you? You must have seen, as I did, those watercolors which belonged to poor Edward, I certainly would like to know what happened to them, charming watercolors by the Prince, saved after the sacking of the Tuileries in 48 or perhaps a part of his *Mémoires*, I don't remember any more. One of them was called *Game of Billiards at Neuilly Castle* and underneath was written in pencil: "A Winning Hazard by the reverend Abbot Labordère." There was also one called *Ball at the Palais Royal* which showed Charles X, dressed to kill, greeting from a safe distance the hostile crowds assembled in the gardens. While we are on the subject of Joinville's taste for the arts, there is a lovely anecdote. It was when Louis-Philippe lost his temper at his youngest son, and not without reason, as you will see . . ."

"But this is terrible, all this waiting. What are they up to in the kitchen? I am heartbroken, absolutely heartbroken. And what we are having, if it ever comes, is not worth all this . . ."

"I'm sure it will be delicious . . ."

"Anyway, I adore toast . . ."

"This couldn't be more pleasant . . ."

. . . And, strange as it may seem, that is perfectly true. No one is the least bit impatient in spite of the way the dinner is dragging on. Thanks to the champagne, we are all well on our way. If I were not so unhappy (so unhappy!) I would be quite content here. *My sadness*, after all this time I should be accustomed to it . . .

. . . Being a covergirl is not enough, no matter how famous, admired, or well-paid. Mrs. Osborn's ultramarine dress isn't at all bad. Lanvin-Castillo. In this half-light it blends nicely with the pale blue wallpaper. Martine looks almost pretty in her dress, which is sort of a Veronese green, not quite emerald, and must be from Rémon, but from last season. Something is different about her. Maybe a new hairstyle. Pushing his bicycle, which bounces over the uneven ground of the corn-fields, a redhead, he comes towards me, suddenly cutting through the crimson clover and I look at him, more curious than afraid . . .

. . . I don't know what Rachel was thinking. But I know what it was that I felt as I held her against my heart: a bewildered love, as desperate and fleeting as any love although it will last until I die. And though it dies with me, it is eternal. Belied by its very intensity. Indescribable. Deceptive, but magnificent . . .

. . . And what have I done with Bénédicte, who was also very young when she was given to me? When I was lucky enough to marry her, ten years ago, I was already thirty-nine and she was nineteen. For some reason she still feels jealous about my past, although never, not once since we have been married, have I been unfaithful to her; fidelity has become second nature to me, so that now, if I wanted to deceive her, it would be painful for me, while at first, it was difficult not to deceive. Martine's large nose did not detract from her beauty. That could be the first line of a novel. I must write another book, try once more, after such a long silence. *Her large nose* . . . call her Mélanie, to cover up the tracks. *Without her large nose, Mélanie would have been beautiful* . . .

. . . Anxiety. In spite of profit-taking as a result of the settlement, the market should have stabilized its recent rise. But of course, why didn't I realize it before, Martine has had her nose operated on. A very subtle change, hardly noticeable. Now that I think of it, my friend Odile, who has been going around recently with a nose very similar to this one, must have had hers redone too, and probably by the same doctor, Chanuz. There are now in Paris a few types of noses (always the same) with only two possible creators. These two bear the unmistakable signature of Chanuz. It was such a surprise almost not to recognize Odile the other night at the theater; I should have realized from the deliberately casual expression on her husband's face that she had just had an operation. Exactly what was needed, Martine, but was it really necessary?

. . . I am here as a childhood friend of Pilou's, or more exactly, of her younger sister. What an idea, to have had her nose operated on. Her face is prettier, but not as nice. No one is paying any attention to me. I would not like any part of it, if I were Bertrand Carnéjoux. It is not his wife any more. The face he married was stolen from him. Too young, yes, I am too young and these girls are too beautiful. So what, though, since Pilou hasn't looked at me once . . .

. . . *Without her large nose, Mélanie would have been beautiful.* Such a sentence is so much more interesting to polish than those which are destined to become images on a screen. Literature is my real calling. *It was not only her old-fashioned name which took away her glamor in the eyes of her friends. Her features were said to have elements of beauty. This was only a polite way of pointing out, or emphasizing, her ugliness.* Martine was not ugly before her operation. She was rather attractive to me. I remember a certain dance we had! But now she is even more charming. What a fine writer I could be if people only would read my books. *With Tears in Her Eyes*, of course, was not very successful . . .

. . . Marie-Ange Vasgne. Your name, Marietta, in huge neon letters all along Broadway. Your name in Japanese on the movie-houses of Tokyo. Lying down in a bed of crimson clover, with the sun in your eyes, a stone digging into your back. On top of you is that brutal, determined man, who has no idea who you are, who you will be, or who you still may become. But this dinner tonight may be the beginning of the last lap, the one that leads straight to Hollywood, to Broadway. It's a bore, all the same, that tonight I won't be able to. One never knows, but sometimes opportunities don't knock twice. I didn't have a chance to take a bath. What a nuisance! . . .

. . . Her weight and the feeling of her body in the hollow of my arm, her warmth, her smell, her baby hair against my cheek, the clear, open, but profound look in her eyes, full of thoughts from another world, the world perhaps from which she has only just emerged . . .

. . . And Gigi who goes right on talking. What a chatterbox, as my grandmother would say . . .

"For you mustn't forget that he was exiled. Imagine, a

39

son of Louis-Philippe, exiled! But that didn't keep Join-ville, I think he was then called the Duc de Joinville, these princes have a sense of duty, of honor, of patriotism, and everything else, you can't take that away from them, that didn't hold him back from joining the troops at the front, the first army of the Loire, if I remember correctly, where he served under the name of colonel, or was it general, no colonel, Colonel Lutterod . . . Now, remember, there had been for a long time among Joinville's entourage a certain Mr. Lutteroth, whose wife was the sister of Count Bat-thyany (executed in Hungary in 1848, you know) but I am getting off the subject. What I meant to say was, it is quite probable that Joinville's *nom de guerre* was inspired by his friend Mr. Lutteroth. As it turned out, Gambetta ordered him arrested at Le Mans and he had to go into exile again, in January or February of 71, I don't quite remember . . ."

. . . Mme Prieur stops talking, finally coming out of that long tunnel where no one tried to follow her. Deep in our own thoughts we paid no attention to what she was saying about that duke or whoever he was becoming colonel what's-his-name in the resistance. But Roland Soulaires, with his little eyes squinting inside large, sepia circles, takes up the challenge . . .

"Among Louis-Philippe's children then, the only ones left are the princesses. Marie, who was every bit as artistic as her brother Joinville, also a pupil of Ary Scheffer, but she did mostly sculpture. She became a Würtemberg . . ."

"By marrying Alexander of Würtemberg. Am I right? With Marie that makes seven. The Queen of Belgium, eight . . ."

"The Queen of Belgium?"

"But of course, Roland. One of the daughters of Louis-Philippe, Louise, married Leopold the 1st. And apropos of them, if you will forgive me, there is a charming anecdote. First I must tell you that the king of Belgium had the reputation, how can I say it, well, of having led a rather wild life up until then. Romantically speaking, of course. And so, on the occasion of his marriage with Louise, a play by Dupaty was being given in their honor at Compiègne castle and the leading actor had to recite these lines which, as you will see, gave rise to a flood of barely-muffled hilarity:

> *Oui, c'en est fait, je me marie,*
> *Je veux vivre comme un Caton,*
> *Il fut un temps pour la folie,*
> *Il en est pour la raison."*

(I'm married now, the days will fly
In peace and quiet leisure.
Like Cato will I live and die,
Gone are the days of pleasure.)

"Two children were born from this marriage."

"Three, Roland, three. Leopold, Duke of Brabant. Philip, Count of Flanders. And finally Charlotte, the future wife of Maxmilian of Austria."

"Aren't they sensational?"

"The champagne is sensational!"

"How right you are, dear Mrs. Osborn. I have been in France for a long time, but this beverage is still marvelous to me, and not just as an appetizer . . ."

"As a what?"

"*Apéritif*, then. Don't you call it that in France?"

"'Appetizer?' 'beverage?' Well, not exactly. But you are charming . . ."

"I would be more charming if I spoke correctly, wouldn't I?"

"But you speak beautifully, Mademoiselle, and without a trace of accent . . ."

"You are just saying that to be nice . . . What is your name? I certainly don't plan to call you 'Mr.' . . ."

"Jérôme. My name is Jérôme."

"Mine is Marie-Ange."

. . . Marie-Ange the lucky one, Marie-Ange who would be a chore-girl on some farm if she weren't so clever . . .

. . . Pretty Marie-Ange Vasgne so pretty the little Canadian girl if I were Martine Carnéjoux I would watch out of course my nearsightedness does make women seem prettier I have often noticed it the way I answered her no one could be better brought up than I am and I married an American oh well Bertrand is older his face is dried out hardened when the last traces of youth have faded this shabby mask is what is left and those errands that kept me from taking my sunbath this morning one of the last ones this year but I had to go to the hairdresser he really did a sensational job this time but what a shame really Louisette was just saying to me poor Madame . . .

. . . My dazzling beauty. Leaving a wake of silent admirers, faces turned towards me in awed silence, wherever I go. My entrance into Maxim's just last night, in my beautiful dress of red on red, vermilion, scarlet, red ochre.

Wearing an air of cool indifference, so graceful, so care-free, but knowing very well that I am considered the most beautiful woman there and that all the men think so, to the great annoyance of their companions, and that they ask the headwaiter who I am, those who haven't recognized me already, that is, for you are famous now, Marietta my dear, little country girl who got raped. You have come a long way from that field of trampled clover on the outskirts of Quebec, on your way to Paris and Hollywood . . .

. . . Other than flowers, which don't cost him anything since they can be put under the heading of miscellaneous expenses, the only thing which Roland Soulaires is generous with is his sharply distilled supply of words. He has the reputation of being rather funny. Unmarried, no children, who is he saving up all his money for? Is it to avoid taxes that he spends a part of the year in Geneva? He has some business there, it is true. No one knows just what, though. Even his activities in France, epecially those in France, are obscure. His personal life is supposed to be rather mysterious. But I've heard . . .

. . . *Gilles was never unfaithful to Mélanie and had no desire to be. The faults of his wife were dearer to him than the qualities of all other women, for he was not under their spell. He was himself surprised; he did not understand how one woman who was not even beautiful* (Bénédicte is beautiful, but this is where the subtle transpositions of the imagination, of Art, begin to intervene.) *could thus take the place of all others, without his feeling in the least deprived.* Such felicity of expression, impossible to translate it into the broad images of the screen. Bénédicte takes the place of all other women for me and I do not feel in the least deprived. *Gilles discovered that a person who is truly loved risks nothing; the charm that he bears robs the enchantment from everything but himself.* This waiting is interminable. Martine keeps looking at the pantry door . . .

. . . The strange virtuosity of Eugénie Prieur and Roland Soulaires. Intoxicated with their own knowledge, they shame us in our ignorance. Futile learning. I am interested, not in what they are saying, but in how they say it. So many forgotten dialogues could be superimposed on their conversation, dialogues that are just as pointless. So many other Parisians who are not here tonight could be the ones reflected in the shadowy depths of the mirrors. In this way the prosaic novel of society could turn into a new experiment in fiction, the kind I have already published, in which, during a dinner such as this one, space and time would be temporarily obliterated. There is a light breeze coming through the half-open windows. Maybe we should have turned off the heat. Outside, behind the black, mutilated trunks of the Caroline poplars, the dark shimmering waters of the Seine. Consommé finished long ago. Plates changed long ago, and still nothing comes. I mustn't forget to point this out to Martine after our guests have left. Everything will have to run more smoothly next time we entertain . . .

"Ah! There you are! Where is the butler? I've never known anything to take so long!"

. . . Very successful dinner party we are having tonight! Martine just sits back and tries to be philosophical. I will have to take matters in hand myself . . .

44

"My little Armande, would you please go back into the kitchen and hurry things along . . ."

"Armande? What a funny name . . ."

"Shh. You might at least wait until she is out of the room . . ."

"Her real name is Martine, like mine. We thought it might be confusing. So Bertrand decided, I really don't know why, that we would call her Armande."

. . . Armande, that was the name of the unforgettable chambermaid at the Peagsons. I rather like the idea of having my own Armande. My own . . .

"At home, in the days when I had servants, all the cooks were called Marie, that is I called them all Marie, and all the chambermaids were Bertha. You can't imagine how convenient it was, believe me!"

. . . How low can you get. Robbing a woman of her Christian name just because she is working for you, and then calling her something else, as if she were some kind of domestic animal. Domestic, that's the word, all right.

"She looks to me like a good one, that girl . . ."

. . . A bit saucy but one settles for anything . . .

". . . Even if you take whatever comes along it's still difficult . . ."

. . . Poor Mme. Prieur, she is about to say, it is inevitable, that it is impossible to be waited on properly these days . . .

"We have been rather lucky, I must admit."

"Just an ordinary maid, do you know what you have to pay one of them these days?"

"Don't tell me about it!"

"And what is more, you should have seen the look of

surprise on the face of the one I hired when I told her that she would be waiting on table, not very often, either; I am hardly ever at home, and besides, I live alone . . ."

"Not really! It is incredible. The so-called 'maids-of-all-work' do no work at all!"

"And this is only the beginning. Look what is happening in Sweden!"

. . . Yes it is the beginning of the end for you, and for us as well, and it is none too soon. Mme. Prieur said it just then, she said it was impossible to be waited on any more . . .

"None of them ever stay with us very long, I never know why. They probably just like the change, but it doesn't matter, we find others very easily. Bénédicte, who is easy to work for, very understanding you know, has excellent marks."

"What do you mean, marks? From whom?"

"Why from the maids, of course. At the employment bureau. Don't you know that today, not in Sweden, my dear, in France, it is the servants who choose their employers?"

"You know, just between ourselves, it is only right . . ."

"One can see, young man, that you live with your grandmother, and that you don't have to worry about running a household!"

. . . Pilou looks furious. What I said didn't go over very well. Maybe I should keep quiet . . .

. . . The domestic situation. Always fascinating. But the time has come to change the subject. Rémon's new collection, maybe, and that very successful yellow and mauve dress which Lucine de Brouges wore to the Dusselières the other night. It was really beautiful, more beautiful than the pretty ultramarine affair in which Mrs. Osborn is decked out. . . .

". . . I just adore the cut of your dress, Mrs. Osborn. I've never seen anything so chic! It reminds me slightly, although yours is so much more effective, of the one which Lucine de Brouges was wearing the other evening at the Dusselières, or was it at the Mallemorts . . .?"

. . . Where has she been all these years? You would think that it was the first time that she had ever heard Lucine's name . . .

. . . Mallemorts. Dead and gone. Well, almost. What next? To think that Pilou lives among that kind of people. Of course with a mother like hers she was well-prepared. I'm hungry. It's not so much the slowness of the courses, but the way the talk goes on and on . . .

. . . These women who think you know all the same people they do but she is perfectly right about my dress it goes without saying that it is superb all the same it is nice to hear her say it especially since I'm sure she didn't mean to she just couldn't help it and tried to take it back but it was too late pretty girl that Marie-Ange Vasgne very inviting a bit of a broad more than a bit luckily John isn't here the old fanny-pincher he would have mortified me . . .

". . . Oh, no, no you are too kind but I know perfectly well, I've seen the new collections, that my poor old dress isn't at all in style, no not at all, not the least bit. This just isn't being worn any more, it just isn't."

. . . We have seen the collections too, so why try to pretend? False modesty which only appears to be polite, but actually shames me, because my own dress, and it is all Bertrand's fault, is really from last year . . .

"What magnificent fish!"

"It's about time! Such a fuss over a simple dish of red mullet . . ."

. . . At last! That odd pinched feeling in the middle of my face . . .

"And look how beautifully the platters are decorated!"

"It's sensational, really my dear, sensational!"

. . . Everything is "sensational" for Lucienne Osborn. I can see why John would rather be with Ivy Luck. The fish lying on that sand-colored purée look as if they were left ashore at low tide. Or as if the ocean had evaporated. The Deluge. For fish. Noah, an old Dolphin, is warned by Neptune and builds a huge aquarium to save two members of each species. Bit by bit the ocean dries up and the transparent Ark sits alone on the sands of the deep, with darting patterns of round eyes and shimmering scales behind the glass walls. One day, a flying fish arrives, bearing a wisp of algae in its beak. Idea for an animated cartoon. When I get back to writing again, the problem will be to forget all these graphic modes of conception, these techniques peculiar to the screen. Lucienne Osborn has a sudden look of concentration. Almost serious, when you think of her usual vapid expression. What could she be thinking about?

. . . Probably at least half a pound of mushrooms for the purée then 10 or 12 caps cooked separately for the garnish eight eggs two lemons try to remember the recipe I'm sure Léon-Pierre would like this but for all the attention he pays me he shouldn't be the one to be indulged odd kind of chambermaid and think of poor Zip who is all alone in the house I can take just a tiny bit more no second helping and I won't touch the main dish what was on television tonight I would rather not know then I won't feel so badly about it fish like this must be very expensive . . .

". . . The market is still the best place to shop . . ."

"If one can bear getting up so early . . ."

"Oh, I send my cook. But everything is so expensive . . ."

"The local stores are even more expensive. The workers will pay anything!"

. . . Swine. Just plain swine . . .

. . . They shouldn't be talking like that in front of the servants. Definition of paradise: living off the income of one's income . . .

. . . Workers have far less worries than I do I'm sure John is such a cheapskate and Ivy Luck is expensive . . .

. . . *Genital butchering*, whatever could that mean, where could I have picked up such an absurd expression?

"I don't mean to say anything against them, but it is a fact that the workers always buy the choicest items. Nothing is too expensive for them . . ."

"How right you are! The prices these days are entirely out of range. As I said to my cook, at the end of last winter: "250 francs a kilo for spinach! 1200 francs for string beans! Henriette, we simply can't afford such things . . ."

. . . Swine, yes swine. The ephemeral complicity of a dinner party augmenting the permanent conspiracy of class preservation. How can we call ourselves human beings? We are members of a bourgeois society, well-brought-up men and women sharing a meal, in other words nothing but absurd phantoms. I am just as much to blame. Even though I try to exonerate myself by sarcastic observations, it is still a game in which, alas, I am participating . . ."

"We need one more . . ."

"The prettiest part was the design. You can't imagine . . ."

"There is at least one Orléans princess whom we have forgotten."

"Who could it be?"

"Tiny green, blue, and yellow flowers . . ."

"Clementine! But I thought I had mentioned her."

"It was covered with little blue, green, and yellow flowers . . ."

"Marie-Clementine of Saxe-Coburg, but of course . . ."

"Yes, it must have been very pretty, with all those little flowers . . ."

"Of Saxe-Coburg and Gotha, please!"

. . . Great satisfaction, Eugénie's snobbery, for the want of any immediate application in the society around her, fastens itself onto matters of history and genealogy. But I may teach her a thing or two. I now remember . . .

". . . Exactly. Wasn't she the grandmother of Ferdinand of Rumania?"

"But no, Roland darling, her mother . . ."

. . . I am not her darling Roland. (Of course it was inevitable that the speculators who had waited for the split should wish to realize their profits.) Now that she is prettier, I am even more afraid of Martine. It is not just that women scare me. They also disgust me, in a way. Alibi for my cowardice. (Up to this point, the market has been rather favorable.) The rest of the women are not even pretending to listen, and are talking about clothes, while Eugénie goes right on trying to prove that she knows more history than I do . . .

. . . Marie-Ange is slipping her rings up and down her thin fingers. It seems to be a habit of hers. The jewels, the flowers, the champagne, especially the champagne, nothing is missing from this fashionable decor which is the most banal, if not the most outdated and mediocre of settings, not at all suitable for the transformations and transfigurations of art . . .

. . . *He couldn't even expect, as he had in the past, to find pleasure in a kiss. The lips of strange women no longer attracted him, and sometimes the thought of their strange saliva even disgusted him slightly. To kiss Mélanie's soft, smooth cheek, to linger on her cool mouth, gave him a voluptuous sensation that was inconceivable with other women. A subtle kind of pleasure, deeper than it seemed, calm even in its exhilaration. With Bénédicte not only the pleasures of love-making were transformed into happiness* . . . My heroine has become my wife, I have reverted to my own life, as it always happens when one tries to tell the story of an imaginary character. Bénédicte's fever is annoying. And to think that she came to fetch me at the station, the poor darling. Just so long as she didn't catch cold. Excellent fish . . .

"There is only one thing wrong with going to Paul. You

have to wait. But I've tried them all; no one else knows how to do my hair."

"Now wait a minute! Not of Rumania, of Bulgaria. Ferdinand of Rumania was the son of the Infanta of Portugal, Antonia."

"All these Ferdinands are rather fun."

"I don't go to Paul anymore. He never cuts hair with a razor. If I told him once, I told him a hundred times: unless you use the razor, my hair . . ."

"They all do it their own way."

"The Ferdinands of Spain, first of all . . ."

"And those of Portugal . . ."

"Luigi always takes me the moment I arrive; I gain at least an hour that way . . ."

"It takes so long to get to him . . ."

"The Ferdinands of Italy."

"But my dear, I live in Neuilly . . ."

"Two Ferdinands in Naples. Isn't that amusing?"

. . . A Ferdinand who makes yellow wigs would be even funnier. This conversation can't be very amusing to Mme. Prieur, or to Roland Soulaires, either, bald as he is, if by some chance the socio-historical debate which they are having allows them to hear a word of what anyone else is saying . . .

"I tell my hairdresser again and again, but he is so stubborn, 'Why do you insist on not using a razor? With hair like mine,' I said, 'there just isn't anything else that will do.' This time, I must say, he didn't do too bad a job, but I still would have liked him to use a razor!"

. . . They all, including Mrs. Osborn who is no more

talkative than the next person, have a way of saying the same idiotic thing three or four times in succession, in exactly the same words . . .

. . . In the mirror in front of me, all I can see are the flowers behind my back. My own bouquet of eighteen red roses and three white ones (always the same) which my secretary sends whenever I dine out, a reassuring reminder of my power (my potency!), a special item of protocol, like a flag raised for a visiting dignitary . . .

. . . Would a bourgeois setting be a drawback? One can only write about what one knows. Lunch in any middle-class restaurant would do just as well. Ordinary red wine creates a euphoria identical, in quantity if not in quality, with that of champagne. The human mind has the same patterns of thought and emotion, regardless of social class, and the organs of the body throb and contract in their ruddy inner darkness according to the eternal rhythms of yesterday, today, and tomorrow. After *Sober Pleasures* my next piece of fiction, which I will have to go back to soon again, will be called *Lunch at the Bistro*.

. . . Little Martine is looking lovely this evening. Was it last night, or a few months, or even a few years ago when I had that dream? An automobile accident? Or unsuccessful plastic surgery? I forget which, but I came back from the hospital with my face disfigured. In despair that I had not taken one last look, while I still could, at the beauty which I had lost. Rejoicing when I discovered that it was only a dream. The feeling lasted for a few seconds after I woke up. For those few seconds I felt secretly pleased and proud of my looks, an emotion I never feel when I am

53

awake. Then at last I realized that the image which I cherished in my dream had not existed for a long time. The beauty which I lamented was itself a dream . . .

"Our hairdressers. Of course it is not as interesting as what you are talking about! Two Ferdinands the First in Naples? How astonishing, really sensational!"

. . . Nothing can astonish Mrs. Osborn, since she knows nothing. Nor do I. "Sensational," everything is "sensational.". . . What an idiot. Soon I will be making a movie in Naples. With the Americans, why not . . .

. . . Two years ago in Capri those marvelous sunbaths by the swimming pool at the Canzone what a shame to have missed my sunbath this morning but I couldn't I had to go to the hairdresser's . . .

. . . That trip to Italy last year as a reward for having passed my law exams. How astonishing to find the Neapolitan countryside just as described by Goethe, with the same grapevines clinging to the same poplars. And Naples itself not so different from the picture Duclos drew of it a few years before. The beauty of the gardens around Sorrento: oranges and lemons glowing in the shade under the high, shiny leaves of walnut trees, as though in an aquarium. If I had been with Martine and if Martine had been my wife instead of marrying this older man with the fine, worn face, this Bertrand Carnéjoux, without whom, I must admit, I would never have discovered Duclos, and whom I admire, I admire . . .

. . . Pompeii was too different from what I had expected, for I unconsciously compared it to the pictures I remembered from childhood, when my grandfather, at Valromé,

54

told me of a buried city which I believed to be almost perfectly preserved, and which I continued to imagine in just that way, although I knew it was nowhere near intact. But the only reality which matters, and which eclipses all others, is the inner reality of the mind. While I visited these ruins with Martine, toward the end of our wedding trip, I indeed found a buried city, a Pompeii buried not in lava, but in memory, from which it emerged, exactly as I had imagined it in childhood . . .

. . . In Naples I was able to relax, in Naples we began to understand each other. Bertrand's book, which he was then correcting in proof, dampened my joy; in *Sober Pleasures* he maintains that through physical love one can commune with the unattainable in women, the eternal feminine. What then becomes of me, of Martine? But in the long-extinguished ashes of Herculaneum, love was still burning . . .

". . . Herculaneum, Bertrand, do you remember?"

. . . The look in Martine's eyes is even more revealing than the appeal which she so indiscreetly sent me across the table, out loud, in front of everyone. Fortunately they are all either preoccupied or indifferent. Roland Soulaires, overjoyed at having illuminated us about the two Ferdinands of Naples, is temporarily posing in order to savor his triumph . . .

". . . And the museum in Naples, Martine, that museum in Naples . . ."

. . . This was even more dangerous, but no one seems to have paid the slightest attention to my rash, twice-repeated allusion. Just as executions apparently arouse the desire to make love, in the same way this encounter with a town that has been buried for two thousand years, but whose inhabitants left such a piercing impression of their presence that they seemed to be carrying on their existence all around us, kindled the basic instincts of life and reproduction. A protest of the body against death. Pilou broke the silence first, to speak of the emotion she felt at the sight of so many rooms in which men and women had made love, of the public baths where they had undressed. After the morning spent at Herculaneum and then the visit to the museum in Naples, we made love more passionately and with greater desire, communing with the lovers of the past, recreating rather than merely imitating the eternal gestures. And Martine said, referring to the posture suggested by an erotic painting on one of the ancient vases, "I am the one who is lying there like that," the "I" being herself and also the Roman woman pictured on the vase. The "I" being, above all, the nameless eternal feminine which I held in my arms as I embraced my own wife and mistress, twice-dizzied, once by the vertigo of blind, impersonal passion, and then again, by the love of a single, unique being without parallel through the ages . . .

. . . So many celebrations must have been reflected in these ancient, lightly-speckled mirrors, with their fine perpendicular joinings. Perhaps they have retained something of all this. Where did I read that solids may be endowed with potential memory? Not only the mirrors but the walls themselves could be screens from which the past will one day project itself. A televised record of the endless spectacle of time. I'd better not have anything more to drink for a while. I feel better, really very well, much too well. Besides, my glass is empty . . .

. . . Bénédicte is so pretty! Getting back to Bénédicte, I mean Mélanie. An excellent subject. *Although she was perhaps less beautiful than some, Mélanie was nevertheless without the flaw which disturbed Gilles in all other women, and which might be called* Roland once said this in front of me *an excess of femininity, something too incarnate, too much of the flesh. If the temptations, the nearness, and the possession of a woman* remain indispensable to my equilibrium, I have nonetheless become more fastidious in the object of my desire. Once again it is myself, and Bénédicte . . .

. . . Simply a materialization of all the confused and super-imposed images which we thought were erased forever. An infinity of simultaneous scenes in which we are not the only actors. We are surrounded, crowded, and smothered by mobs of rich men and beautiful women. The silent film of the centuries, the moving picture of life on the Ile Saint-Louis, in which the voices themselves, why not, will eventually be rendered . . .

. . . I had to force her to go to bed. She didn't want to, because of Nicolas. She said she had to help him in his homework, some arithmetic problems, I think. Arithmetic, why she doesn't even know her multiplication tables, the poor darling! *Gilles felt disgusted at the thought of another body. It was not that he had become less passionate. On the contrary, he had never been more obsessed by desire for a woman.* For instance that attractive chambermaid. *But no longer could it be just any woman. Only Bénédicte could satisfy this craving because only she was delicate enough not to disappoint him.* What a pity! I produce nothing but fine, classical prose, and I have to write for the movies. No one appreciates fine, classical prose any more . . .

. . . And among the crowd of resurrected dead, on the carved panel of this wall, is the image of a very young girl who would have appealed to me and to whom I would have appealed in the year 1600 or thereabouts. A young girl like other young girls, at once honest and perverse, with her subtle supply of venom. Believing herself to be irreplaceable, when she is constantly and universally replaced. Anonymous and marvelous, the eternal young girl. Pilou was even more innocent and poisonous. But Pilou is no longer a young girl . . .

. . . If I had been Bertrand, I would have opposed the operation. By changing her natural appearance, Martine rashly interfered in the realm of the supernatural which is the source of all love, whether one believes in it or not. I am a believer. A husband could refuse to agree to an operation like this for reasons that are not stupid and selfish, and find it hard to forgive his wife if she went ahead without his permission. Even if Cleopatra's nose had been too long, and had then been changed, love could have fastened on the original. Love is less aesthetic and more mystical than one might believe . . .

"There was one who died just before the invasion of Charles VIII, around 1495. And then, much later on, another king of Naples, Ferdinand IV, called himself Ferdinand I when the Kingdom of the Two Sicilies was created . . ."

"Oh this is very funny, you must pause a minute. Our conversation has made a complete circle, and, if I may use the expression, is biting its own tail. Marie-Amélie of the Two Sicilies, if you can believe it, Marie-Amélie of Bourbon, the future wife of the Duc d'Orléans, himself the future Louis-Philippe, is the daughter of this very same Ferdinand whom we are talking about . . ."

. . . I've got him this time. I've won . . .

. . . Eugénie scored another point. Racking my brain for some additional detail. It shouldn't be that hard to win this contest of erudition . . .

. . . Eugénie and Roland are often very brilliant, but what bores they can be when they compete against each other in these pointless exercises of memory. I like stories better than history. If only they would let me write a scenario that was a little less hackneyed . . .

. . . Take your time; we've got all night. Having said that, how I envy them, knowing nothing about all this, never having known about it. And law school won't be the place to acquire such knowledge, either. Fortunately in literary and scientific matters . . .

. . . That sunbath which I missed will not be too serious if only it is a good day tomorrow *but this vague distress, this blind fear.* . . .

. . . Crimson clover. Red mustache. Stale breath. Clammy hands. A big green grasshopper sitting motionless on a blade of grass inches from my face. The stone hurting my back. Fourteen years old. Ten years have already gone by, only ten years. And the clear, bright blue of the sky . . .

. . . Pilou was right. She looks much prettier. It was an odd impression to feel that I was deceiving her by sleeping with her. And the other day, of deceiving Marie-Ange by thinking of Martine whom we were both deceiving. With my eyes closed, I thought of the pretty shape of her new nose. I'm really rather tired of Marie-Ange. And of Armande, and Colette, and all these other monotonously interchangeable girls . . .

. . . Extraordinary child, busy, talkative, preoccupied with her own little world, in which we also play a part. When I hold her to me, what an abyss of sweetness, a dizziness of love. She will be asleep when I go up soon to see her; I will not be able to hold her in my arms. I hope we are not making too much noise. She did not look very well this evening . . .

". . . Bertrand . . ."

. . . He didn't hear me, lost in his thoughts. What could he be thinking about?

". . . Bertrand! Oh, Bertrand!"

. . . Marie-Amélie, what could that mean to him . . .

". . . Is this interesting to you, Jérôme, Marie Amélie?"

. . . Finally, she deigned to speak to me. I'll tell you what I think about Marie-Amélie . . .

. . . Jérôme is very amusing. What a face he is making . . .

". . . Bertrand, I am talking to you. Rachel, Rachel!"

. . . Poor Pilou. She will never become what her mother is, to such a degree of perfection, a *hostess* . . .

". . . What about Rachel?"

"Ah! I knew very well that I could get your attention by mentioning your daughter's name!"

"Your little girl, what a darling . . ."

"She must be learning to talk by now. How old is your little Leah?"

"Rachel. Rachel is two. She babbles . . ."

. . . Leah! And Eugénie thought she was being so nice! When you don't know, it is better to keep quiet. Yes. Rachel is beginning to babble, as the expression goes. I had to have children of my own to know what a good description it is . . .

"And your grandchildren, Gigi dear?"

"They are well. But I must confess, they don't interest me very much. I was too much of a mother to be a good grandmother . . ."

. . . Marie-Thérese thinks otherwise. The poor thing suffered terribly, never being fondled or pampered by her mother. Her mother loved no one but her lovers. *Like mine.* A silent cry from the depths of my heart. When a girl becomes a woman her body separates her from her mother. Physically, it is impossible not to struggle against one's mother. *Is there really a chance that I will slowly become like that, growing hunch-backed under Bertrand's very eyes!* There is a prurience about that aging woman which makes me feel uncomfortable. Fleeing from the confession which she so eagerly, although silently, seeks, one carefully hides one's secrets. Mothers are always obsessed by the intimacies of young couples. Bertrand's mind is wandering again . . .

". . . She looked a bit peakéd this evening, didn't you notice?"

"How charming, a young mother worrying about her

little daughter! You haven't by any chance any pictures, have you?"

. . . Photographs? Of course, in my purse. But tonight I have only powder and lipstick in my gold evening bag. Right behind me, within reach, is that frame full of old snapshots, and among them . . . But she will have to ask again, I mustn't seem too eager . . .

". . . I assure you that she was not feeling very well this evening."

"You are imagining things. Besides, no one is interested."

"Now wait a minute; we all know how Martine feels. I have a daughter of my own and even though she is no longer a child . . ."

. . . Nor even a young woman. To think that I could have had a little boy . . .

". . . Are you sure you haven't a single photograph?"

"Why yes, Eugénie, right here. Please don't get up, Jérôme, I can reach it."

. . . I was already standing. Now I am in my seat again. My body is better brought up than I am and it makes all the decisions. Pilou turned around in her chair to reach the frame which was on the table behind her. She moved only from the waist. The well-shaved hollow of her arm-pit. As the shoulderstrap was pulled aside, one could see the beginning of a round breast. So graceful and poised. Her unfamiliar profile was a surprise, like a statue with a broken nose, or the image on a worn coin . . .

"Here is Rachel this summer, at Pyla. But she has changed a great deal since. She is even more adorable. You should see her! Behind her is Jean-Paul. He is handsome, don't you think?"

"Very handsome . . ."

. . . My little boy, the little boy whom I . . .

"Maybe she ate too much candy."

"And I didn't make her take a nap. With dinner to pre-pare . . . This other picture is better . . ."

. . . How close I feel to Bertrand when we are talking about the children. He tries to look unconcerned, but I could tell that he is worried at the thought that his little daughter might be sick. But she is really all right. Just a little tired, that's all. Tomorrow she will be herself again. Eugénie is sweet to be interested in the children . . .

. . . Martine thinks I am looking at her children, but it is the beach at Pyla, behind those uninteresting babies, which fills me with such delight, which brings back memories of that glorious summer with Jean-Jacques Lim-her . . .

. . . If I only dared show them the photograph of Nicholas in my wallet. In it I am sitting crosslegged along a path in the Bois de Boulogne. My little boy is sitting on my left thigh and his rounded profile is outlined against my heart. It is the same Nicholas as now, and yet a different one; the proportions, which are the key to all works of art and to that masterpiece of masterpieces, a child, are changed. As he grew, he became someone else. He is no longer the same, round, bouncing, clumsy and adorable little being . . .

"Do you wear glasses now, Gigi? That's something new."

"I have been wearing them for quite awhile. Since I am farsighted, almost any glasses will do. I even buy them, don't laugh, in antique shops. It's true, believe me! I do think I will take off my shawl now . . ."

"May I help you? . . ."

"Thank you. These were left to me. They belonged to Cecily. Or to poor dear Edward, I forget. I've lost my memory."

. . . And your heart as well. The little grey jacket which she is wearing under her shawl may be of slightly finer wool, but it is just as dowdy . . .

"Anyway they are enough to help me read my program or look at a photograph, like now, you see. That's all I need!"

. . . Dead, both of them, poor Cecily Peagson and her husband, whose invitations to dinner were so sought after, and who are now nothing more to their friend Eugénie Prieur than the original possessors of a useful object. The dead were never more conclusively cut off from life than by these few words spoken by a woman who is essentially ruthless, as they all are, as we all are: "Cecily or Edward, I don't remember . . ."

. . . Pure, unspoiled delight, joy endlessly renewed, every evening after work when I come home to Bénédicte and Nicolas. Three violently joyful beings. One immense happiness. Complete harmony, incredible bliss, a triumphant blending of pride and humility. And I know Whom to thank, gratefully, but also in sorrow . . .

. . . One of those moments when Pilou and I are alone, although in the presence of others. When the everyday monotony is slightly glorified by our idyllic understanding, and the usual expressions are put away in their casket of silence; moments when we say nothing, even when we are alone, because we are together and because we are happy. The dunes of Pyla were splayed against the sky and my violet and yellow kite vibrated in the wind. Oh no, not now, the telephone . . .

. . . The telephone, how annoying. Coming home from Dr. Chanuz's clinic. Jean-Paul still in school. Rachel appears in the doorway, looking both calm and delighted, a little scared, but above all trying not to hurry, to make her mother understand that she couldn't abandon her just like that, without being punished. In the end, showing me how happy she is, apparently not even noticing my bandage, "looking at me with the tips of her fingers" as mother would say, asking for a doll, which of course was there for her, bought as we came home along the Champs Elysées, then making little sounds of admiration (pretty dress!) but also very objective, pointing out a defect (her eyes don't close). Then thanking me, as I hug her, so soft and trusting in my arms, with the moist traces of forgotten tears still on her little cheek for me to see, and to kiss . . . Then I finally put her down and tear myself away from this vain embrace, patting her on her round white behind before she disappears like a little animal which has just been set free. But why doesn't Armande answer? . . .

. . . Flower of a smile, phosphorescent star, motionless, blooming flower of a smile. When she smiles like that, I know that my chickadee is not thinking of me any more, but of her children. Not too much of a mother to be a wife, as Irène hinted the other day. It is not that I occupy a lower level in the hierarchy of her affections, only that we reign at different times. But I couldn't hope for a smile like that one, although there is tenderness in her love for me . . .

"Please answer, Armande. Can't you hear the telephone?"

. . . The day I got home, Jean-Paul looked at me with a ravishing but unusual expression. A stranger who was my own child. A little boy born of my own flesh, but outside of me. Belonging to me in the most terrible way, but also far from me in space. Very near and very far. This only lasted a few seconds. Then he became Jean-Paul again, a little more grown up, but the same as always . . .

"You have another daughter, haven't you?"

"No, a son, Jean-Paul."

. . . Nicolas, my son. I always return to him with such poignant happiness, smothering him with affection, unreasonable in my admiration of his beauty, nearly faint with love for him. It doesn't matter that he is no longer the child he once was, the child whose very weight and shape imprinted themselves on my being, through my senses, and also through the secret, extra-sensory channels of love . . .

"How old is it? One can never tell, they change all the time."

. . . Not quite as bad as that old cow the other day who had the nerve to ask me: Who does it look like? It, it. Speaking of these marvelous little creatures as though they were objects. Marie-Ange looked so casual and facetious when she asked me that question, as if Bertrand hadn't already told her . . .

"Almost five."

"Already! But that's impossible. You turn around and they've grown. They shoot up like sputniks . . ."

. . . Gilles Bellecroix looks a bit astonished. Obviously

surprised at what I just said, one, two, three, four, which wasn't all that clever, five, six. He didn't think me capable of even this faint spark . . .

. . . That little Vasgne number is not quite such a pea-brain, after all . . .

. . . That's right, my dear sir, no more stupid than the rest. And I would be a fine actress if only, six, five, four, three, two, one . . .

. . . Utter indifference, worse, utter impertinence, for she knows perfectly well that we have a girl and a boy. Just wait though . . .

". . . And you, Marie-Ange?"

"Oh, no! I haven't any children . . ."

. . . Children! That's all I need. I was a bit worried again this month. But I'm not in the family way yet, thank goodness . . .

. . . And mine, how old would he be, or she, if I had allowed him to be born? Instead, I have only these indelible memories, and remorse which grows more terrible with age, which obsesses me. If Jean-Jacques had wanted it, we would now have a forty-year-old son.

"Who was it?"

"It was for . . . Monsieur . . ."

. . . Armande hesitated, imperceptibly (but perceptibly) between for and Monsieur, as though it were difficult for her to say monsieur, or as a hint of some ulterior purpose of her own. Would Bertrand deceive poor Pilou with the chambermaid, too? What an old rascal, but with something insidiously attractive about him . . .

"I told the . . . lady who called that . . . Monsieur . . ."

"Fine, fine, don't bother to tell me . . ."

. . . Probably Lisa. The idiot! But I told her . . . Or Colette. But of course, she did it deliberately. Fortunately, Martine . . .

. . . A woman? Some nerve. I'm not as stupid as Martine. You'd better watch your step there, old boy. Just you wait . . .

. . . *Don't bother to tell him,* or me either. That sentence is a kind of magic formula for Bertrand which he uses again and again and which he has used once more without realizing that it gives him away every time, an open sesame which reveals all his secrets to me. But he can keep his secrets; his nasty little intrigues don't hurt me any more, not that I am resigned or indifferent, but I am beyond them, in a realm where I am happy with my children, and with Bertrand as the father of my children. Don't bother to tell *me,* if my husband has been deceiving me everywhere, and always, and with anyone, even with Marie-Ange; I couldn't care less. Marie-Ange doesn't seem to have caught on to him yet; she looked perfectly furious after this little telephone incident. Don't worry, my dear, it won't be the last time . . .

. . . I only regret my past for the youth which disappeared with it, and this is not in spite of my love for Bénédicte, but rather because of it. I owe what remains of my youth to her love, to my love, and to Nicholas. Bénédicte believes that I am nostalgic about the women who loved me or whom I loved, but they mean nothing to me. I only regret the years and years which I spent unattached, in aimless fellowship, which I can never recapture, with or without her, for these years were my youth . . .

. . . A childhood friend of the hostess. My only claim to
fame. Between the rest of them and myself, an abyss of
indifference. I do not exist in their eyes, being only real
enough to occupy one of the eight seats at this table where
I am less obtrusive than I would be if I had stayed home
and left an empty seat between two women. If I fell sick,
or were in an accident, or died, the news would make very
little impression on them; they would probably not even
remember that they had met me once at the Carnéjoux, or
else would have vague memories of a tall, red-headed
boy . . .

"May I see?"

"Of course."

"Oh look! There are some much earlier snapshots
here . . ."

"Why yes. A whole little family miscellany which Bertrand hates. He has no feeling for the family, my family,
that is. Over there is Mummy, when she was a young
girl . . ."

. . . Every time I mention my mother, Bertrand gives a
start. He looks suspicious, on the defensive, ready to
pounce on some mysterious words that must at all costs be
suppressed, lying in wait to smother them before they are
even spoken . . .

. . . Irène with her hunched shoulders, her nerve-racking
quest for pleasure, her jealousy, Irène who used to embarrass me . . .

"How much you look alike . . ."

"Especially around the eyes, it's uncanny . . ."

"But let me see, let me see."

. . . The frame is passing from hand to hand stopping

here and there for a moment there was dust on it you wouldn't see that at my house if I were the little Carnéjoux girl I would be ashamed . . .

. . . "Look at the one in the top left hand corner, Eugénie, that was taken in Bagnères-de-Bigorre while Mummy was expecting me . . ."

. . . She talks about her mother with such innocence; it is painful. And no one seems bothered by it. Bertrand barely raised an eyebrow. Nothing could surprise these monsters any more. My poor beloved Pilou, caught in such a corrupt world . . .

"Yes, I remember. I knew your father very well in those days. They were so happy then, he and Irène . . ."

"May I? Thank you."

. . . I look again at the picture of my parents, perhaps to take by surprise this lost glimmer of happiness, these traces of a joy that must have been very fleeting, judging by the way Eugénie spoke of it. But all joy is fleeting . . .

" . . . I kept that one because it shows my father as a young man. Do you see him, way over on the right of the group . . ."

. . . A dark figure silhouetted against the trees of the Tuileries gardens, in his bowler hat and short overcoat, more touching than ridiculous. Bertrand once pointed out how much this young bourgeois Parisian looked like Kafka, yes, like the little Jew from Prague who was then wearing the same kind of hat, and dreaming of the books he would someday write . . .

" . . . But I can't tell you who any of the other girls and boys were. Maybe Mummy would know. If my poor father were still alive, he could have told you . . ."

. . . Eugénie Prieur, lumped together into a heavy, de-formed kind of heap, seems to be warding off some fearful danger with her barrage of words. The gold necklace against Mrs. Osborn's tan skin. Large chunks of gold, strung in a pattern of twos and fours . . .

. . . That Vasgne girl is looking at my neck go ahead and admire it my dear yours won't be anywhere near so lovely when you reach my age there are already hollows behind your collarbones pretty breasts but tiny ones they are fine when you are twenty-five you are also much too pale of course you haven't the time to sunbathe although there is the beauty parlor in your line of work it would be a help no maybe she is looking at my bosom it is a beauti-ful one my figure was made to be seen naked but models like you for that is all you are a model models are nothing but skeletons underneath Léon-Pierre told me so . . .

. . . Bénédicte's youth makes her so demanding; she seeks perfection in her love. It is not enough for me to be faithful in the present; she tracks down my past, to which I am forbidden to make even the blandest allusion. A past in which everything that might incite her jealousy is com-pletely extinguished, alive only in the sense that it is a part of me, and that I am alive. Some day, later on, (but when?) after the years have mellowed her love, she will understand just how much she has made me suffer, and in vain, for my life is entirely hers, including the past which made me what I am and which I offered her ten years ago when I gave her the life I had left to live . . .

. . . Gilles is looking at my hand, at the one which is not holding the frame and which for some reason I am ashamed of. Still rather pretty if it weren't for those red spots. They are not bad for a woman who is no longer very young and who does her own dishes every night. Doing the dishes doesn't need to be hard on one's hands, if one knows how to go about it. I don't mind doing them, actually, it keeps me busy when I am alone at home, luckily not too often for I am always invited out . . .

"It is a maaaaarvelous photograph."

. . . This passing the pictures back and forth across the table is getting ludicrous. I have laughed at them enough . . .

"Let me see. This little boy who looks so noble was killed near Rheims in World War I. That young woman, a great friend of your father's, my dear, died of consumption at twenty-five. As for this solemn party in the boater and mustache, why it's poor old Edward de Saint Palpoul. How funny! Oh, but this one is even funnier. The one at the beach. Where could it have been taken? Unbelievable!"

. . . It is true that not one of them, except darling Pilou, means anything to me; they are just guests at a party, to which, though this kind of worldliness revolts me, I am impressed at having been invited, along with such pretty women and well-known men, each more glamorous than the next. If I were to see them any more often I would probably become quite bored by their problems, even by the life they lead . . .

"Those old-fashioned swim suits. How funny . . ."

"Those what? You are the one who is funny, Marie-Ange."

"Those swim suits, what's wrong with that?"

"Maybe nothing, in Canada . . ."

"It is a perfectly good expression, charming really . . ."

"Of course, Jérôme, when spoken by someone as pretty as Marie-Ange . . ."

"No, Pilou, that is not what I mean at all. The expression is perfectly accurate. One doesn't take a *bath* in a bathing suit, one takes a *swim* . . ."

. . . They are feeling so superior to this Canadian girl, when they don't even know their own language. I've heard them and their ilk confuse pine with fir, broom with gorse, swifts with swallows. That's the sort of thing I find it hard to forgive . . .

"And the little girl in front, is she your cousin Martha?"

. . . Cousin Martha whom everyone in the family finds so amusing, but whom I suddenly find rather appealing, no doubt because in this old photograph which I never look at, even though it is always there on the table, she is just a little girl, with little-girl dreams in her eyes and a little girl's nice fat cheeks. Could Rachel possibly become a ridiculous old woman, too? . . .

"Old snapshots are always touching . . ."

. . . Unknown lives, poor buried creatures whom I never knew existed, the dead who are forgotten. Attractive girls, dust unto dust (these girls, any girls). Be funny, Roland. I must keep in character . . .

"I just adore old photographs, especially the obscene ones, you know the kind, with big bozooms and enormous fannies . . ."

. . . Like Zerbanian, he can get away with the most outrageous vulgarity, just because he is so funny-looking with his round, innocent face and the mauve circles around his beady eyes . . .

. . . Roland Soulaires is going a bit too far. Even Raymond Frôlet wouldn't dare say things like that. But what poise! Society people don't seem as well-behaved as grandmother told me they would be . . .

"Oh come now! Let's be a little more serious. After all. The charm (in the original sense of the word) the charm we find in old photographs has a lot to do with the appeal that old movies have for us . . ."

"Motion changes everything . . ."

"It does, although no one has ever demonstrated this, on the contrary . . ."

. . . No one is listening to me. They would rather hear the smut that Roland Soulaires has to offer. But Bertrand understands what I am driving at. I can tell by his expression . . .

"It is a paradox, but only an apparent one. You are right, Gilles. I have often thought about it and of course it is your profession . . . It is a fact that the magic in still photography, contrary to what is generally believed . . ."

"Yes, it is even a kind of cliché . . ."

" . . . is superior to that of moving pictures, strictly speaking, although they use it, even go beyond it at times, but never attain . . ."

"The crystallization of time, old man, the crystallization of time. Nothing more, nothing less."

"Exactly."

. . . The rare pleasure of instantaneous understanding. Even though Bertrand is not a professional, he has thought about these problems. There is a poetry in still shots from old movies, an aura that is extinguished or at least dimmed when you see the same pictures moving on a screen. Could it be that the beauty of these photographs lies in the way the past is held at a standstill, while if they are set in motion, they again become life-like, and no longer have the quality of being at once preserved and lost forever? . . .

. . . Martine finally put the frame back where it belongs. I felt a pang, just the same, to see Irène in these seaside photographs. I had been too accustomed to seeing them on the little table ever to pay any attention to them. A young Irène, one I never knew. The poetry of dated styles and beaches that are no longer fashionable. Heart-rending little drops of time, solidified and preserved in these only slightly yellowed snapshots. Suspended motion, men and women unaware that they were being photographed, swimming and playing in the background of a family outing, and whose anonymous silhouettes, on this one day of their lives, are perhaps the only remaining traces of their earthly existence. Gilles is right. The magic which one credits to directors or to the primitive genius of the early moviemakers is here in these old snapshots; it is the magic of photography.

"And if I may say so, sir, your novel, *Sober Pleasures*, was influenced by the techniques of the cinema."

"Why yes, Jérôme. No one has paid sufficient attention to this fact. And since you are nice enough to show an interest in my work, it might interest you to know that I instinctively planned *The Metaphysics of Physical Passion*, which I ended up calling by the less pretentious title of

Sober Pleasures, as the screenwriters do their films, scene by scene, starting with the end, then the middle, the order doesn't matter, and finally checking it all for continuity, giving it a rhythm . . ."

. . . As I walked here, a little while ago, from the Saint-Paul subway station, I saw the deep, gutted foundations of a house that had been torn down. Against the tattered curtains and faded strips of paint, as though on a series of little screens, were couples endlessly making love. Ever since the days of Louis XIII, until now, when it was condemned and taken down, the grim struggles of love-making took place every night, in every room of this shabby building. Gesturing bodies, engaged in a marathon of love. A continuous performance. To think that Bertrand can do what he wants with Pilou's mysterious and sacred body . . .

. . . Jérôme is thinking of something else. Having been prompted to it, I dared bring up the subject that is more important to me than anything else in the world, the work which I never stop thinking about, which represents the very best that is in me, and no one, not even the person who seemed to realize what it means to me, bothers to listen. What's the use? The rest of them wouldn't understand anyway. Except perhaps Gilles Bellecroix if he was ever willing to think of anything but himself. There is after all such a strong relationship, at least Jérôme understood, between the literature of today and the movies. In my next novel, I may again confront the hero with a world that falls apart under his very eyes (and under ours as well) and then takes on a different shape, although one that is equally coherent. If in this book, I was about to say

76

this film, the streets can seem to have a strange, other-worldly charm, if the objects themselves can appear to be on another planet, if the faces of the men and women can be those which one has always imagined but never yet seen, then, and then only, will I be forgiven for whatever shallow story hides my true subject matter. The true novels and films of the future will show us, by means of the plots which they use as points of departure, but also going beyond these, that side of life which cannot be seen with the naked eye, but which alcohol, for instance, can magnify and illuminate. Volume, color, and sound will be put back into their actual relationships, into their precarious balance which threatens to give way at any moment but which this new art, acting as intermediary, as an instrument of revelation, will constantly renew. Bodies and objects, dignified and seen in their fleeting but eternal significance. The reader-spectator present in a world that is at once his own and *different*. Symbols to be interpreted on many levels. Minute details suddenly becoming the *essence* . . .

"And your new novel, Bertrand. Can you tell us . . ."

"I've hardly begun . . ."

. . . *The Rascals* is about to become *Lunch at the Bistro* . . .

"But what is it about? At least you can tell me . . ."

"It's not easy, Gigi . . . really . . . Please don't insist . . ."

. . . What it is about! As if that mattered in the slightest. One could write about anything. Everything is a microcosm. I have never been able to talk about my books, except with other professionals, and then only technically. One writes what one cannot say . . .

. . . *Keine Liebe liess ich aus* . . . the broken, rasping voice of that singer from Berlin whose record is the new hit in Paris can be heard from one of the floors above. It is the German version of *Toutes Les Femmes Sont Fatales* which was popular a few years ago and now, though uprooted and revamped, still has the same sultry and ambiguous charm. All women are dangerous, to me. Well-built, (though somewhat stout) rich, talented, and speaking three languages. *Keine Liebe liess ich aus* . . .

. . . Apparently this same tune, *Toutes Les Femmes Sont Fatales* is a hit again, with German lyrics. Now it is the very young who like it. There is not such a big difference after all, between these adolescents and an almost-old woman like me. What moves them moves me. They enjoy what I enjoy. In the moments when we find enchantment in the same rhythms, we are both outside of time, carried by the same emotions into the realm of eternal youth . . .

. . . I don't seem to be getting anywhere with either of my dinner partners Gilles hasn't looked at me once and Bertrand is the cad he always was he didn't recognize me rather he didn't choose to recognize me just as pleased with himself as ever I have a wrong to avenge the trouble is that Léon-Pierre is the only man who interests me right now what could he be up to in the bar with his cronies not all boys either one has to put up with these little annoyances the main thing is that he will be there at the usual time tomorrow Bertrand is paying just as little attention to the woman on his right . . .

. . . Gliding along the transparent surface of my champagne glass, which I raised to my lips not realizing that it was almost empty, the elongated profile of a crystal decanter and, behind it, the rosy cheeks of Roland Soulaires twist and turn in slithering distortion, caught in a trick mirror in which all things become melted and elastic. Describe the changes, superficial and in depth, which constantly disturb our apparently objective world. A world in which only our health, physical and spiritual, maintains a kind of equilibrium, and which the slightest indisposition can cause to slip and dissolve into confusion, leaving only the objects of our fear or our desire looming in absurd and outlandish isolation. Other shapes appear and disappear into the night. An exact reflection of what the eye sees, recorded as accurately as possible, with all the distortions brought about by the interference of both habit and reflection . . .

. . . Through this lull in the conversation (which I hope won't last!) one can hear the thundering footsteps of three boys chasing each other next door. Why aren't they in bed at this hour? It is too bad that the youngest is too old to play with Jean-Paul. At the same time, somewhere above, probably on Mme. Cloche's floor, a radio is playing a familiar song, though I never heard it in that language before. German, as far as I can tell. The music strikes a forgotten chord of nostalgia, putting all the objects and people in the room in a new perspective, lending a new atmosphere, as though this ordinary dinner party had suddenly been transformed into a work of art. It gives all of us present a heightened sense of enjoyment, the feeling that we are enacting new roles, heroic, erotic or romantic, especially romantic. Life is full of vast possibilities, with an infinite future, and our dinner party, Bertrand, our dinner party is a great success . . .

. . . This round table is a nucleus around which our temporarily intimate clan has jelled. For the length of one meal we will break through the indifference that ordinarily divides us one from the other, even those of us who call themselves friends, and commune together in a delightful, exhilarating, and flimsy alliance. At the edge of our circle begins the magma of the outside world. The world of the uninvited, including the butler, though not the chambermaid whose youth and beauty make her one of us even though she is not sitting down and. talking. Sometimes she takes leave of our group, assuming an air of distant detachment to wait on us. But her detachment does not apply to each one of us alike, judging by the intimate glances which pass between her and all the men present, including me, the youngest and shyest of them all. Thus it is not one, but several little secret and incompatible cliques, who have come together to brave the hazards of this party . . .

. . . She is not wearing a brassiere. I can see her breasts as she leans over to offer me a second helping of fish. An austere black dress with an indiscreet neckline. A surprising breach of etiquette in a household such as this. Immediate focus of my desire. Tonight it is not Bénédicte whom I need. I need an entirely different woman, one who is not wearing a brassiere. Perhaps Marie-Ange Vasgne, but Soulaires seems to interest her the most. Or Martine? But I know very well that I would never never deceive Bénédicte . . .

. . . The distance and (probably) some new interference make the German voice no longer intelligible. Only the music itself reaches us, and only its most piercing notes, so that the classical, old-fashioned melody of *Femmes Fatales* takes on a strange modern beat, a syncopated, staccato poignancy that anticipates the music of the future far better than the creations of any avant-garde composer. Though a born musician, and so talented, I am without a future. To all appearances fulfilled, I am hopelessly frustrated . . .

. . . I first heard *Toutes Les Femmes Sont Fatales* mixed with purring sounds from the engine of an outdated airplane, on the beach at Rio, as I watched that fragile creature emerging from the waves, Amelinha, the most vanished of the vanished. This music which I love, and the echoes of children playing, bring the past to life on several simultaneous levels; I am suddenly leading three existences at once: as a child, as a young man with certain unforgettable loves, oh Amelinha; and as this disenchanted witness to middle-age, the slightly anxious gentleman presiding here at dinner. Armande's bare arm glances gently off Marie-Ange's smooth shoulder, and her breast presses against my back as she serves me, reviving a desire which I have never been able to satisfy. Often, too often, driven by a longing for the impossible, I make a mad attempt to inflict my wretched strength on her, or on some other girl who is not indifferent but inaccessible. Just another warning (why another?) which I again read in reverse (why again?) only to find that the reality adapts itself to my desire: *Ladies, ready-made and wholesale* . . .

. . . 1950, that red-haired man who dragged his bicycle

across the fields, leaving a wake in the dazzling crimson clover. Brutal and determined, with a kind of horrible sweetness. "So they call ya Marietta?" The icy protruding eyes of a grasshopper right next to me. A damp hand on my body . . .

. . . The sensations that Léon-Pierre makes me feel are out of this world I must be careful it tires the facial muscles just so long as there is sun tomorrow and I can continue my sunbaths on the terrace like every morning except today it is really too annoying and with winter coming this unusual weather can't last I mustn't forget to order my ski outfit considering everything I have to remember it's a wonder how I manage Zig might like a new collar could anyone be more intelligent than I am or know how to so fully so marvelously so perfectly of course it took me a long time to learn and that dope John who thinks he is doing me a favor when once in a blue moon panting and incompetent that he is Ivy Luck must have a great time even without Bertrand there are some pretty good prospects this evening that is what is fun about dinners where you don't know anybody Roland Soulaires is a bit far away too bad I can't see him better . . .

. . . It is only because each one of them is completely indifferent rather than hostile to the others that they can thus take advantage of these favored moments to form a close, friendly, even clannish little conspiracy . . .

. . . Last night, before I went to sleep, I caressed Martine's slim hips and touching little bosom with chaste, wondering fingers. She was almost asleep. My delight, though it had nothing lustful about it at the time, was painful, nonetheless. A desire that was not physical but metaphysical, born of this gloriously deceptive caress. It was no longer the nude, anonymous woman, the unidentified creature of now and of always, but Martine as a single, unique individual, Martine to whom I am never as attentive and thoughtful as I should be, Martine who is forever escaping me . . .

. . . The music stopped and did not start again. Impoverishing a life that would be totally disenchanted without the presence of these young women. Especially the presence of Armande, the youngest of the girls here, with the most intense sex appeal. (So obvious that it is disturbing.) A chambermaid. A woman in a chamber. The nearness of these forbidden pleasures makes me dizzy, but they would be even more impossible to obtain if we were alone together and naked. Marie-Ange Vasgne, naked against my nakedness, what a mad daydream . . .

. . . Roland Soulaires, with his face suddenly distorted in a nasty twitch, avoids my eyes. He seems shy. He is rich. It would be fun to see how far I could go with him. And sensible. First because he is sitting next to me. Next because it would make Gilles Bellecroix jealous, and thus more vulnerable, assuming that he isn't already. Gilles or Roland, it really doesn't matter; I need a new mink coat, a blonde one this time and Bertrand, even though he is editor-in-chief of that newspaper, certainly isn't going to pay for it. And, above all, I must eventually get a big part in a big movie . . .

. . . What a disgusting appetite Eugénie Prieur has. Pilou's undeniable beauty is no longer entirely her own.

I would like her to be more real and less perfect. Maybe someday I will be able to forget this consuming, pointless, impossible love . . .

. . . That odd young man hasn't opened his mouth and seems to harbor a grudge for some reason . . .

. . . The young woman whose blurred image I seem to see reflected in the centerpiece is the ancient creature sitting on my left, Eugénie Prieur, who has turned her back on Bertrand Carnéjoux as if she wanted to see me or hear what I have to say. Pleasant, hazy reflections. Mirrors do not lie, but their truth can be that of a distant past . . .

"You are still young enough to tell me how old you are . . ."

"Twenty . . ."

. . . Here goes. I thought she would have the nerve to speak to me . . .

"Do you live with your . . ."

"My parents are dead."

"Please forgive me. I . . ."

"I live with my maternal grandparents. Except on vacations when my other grandmother invites me to . . ."

"Oh! I see."

. . . Father, grandfather, what is the difference? I may have to run the factory a bit sooner, that's all. Grandma is so anxious for my welfare that I can't even go out without making her worry. At night she waits to hear my key in the door before going to sleep. Just like any other boy growing up in a middle-class environment, ma'am. Nothing to get excited about . . .

. . . I hope it will be the chambermaid and not the butler who waits on me next time. My whole evening is going to be different because of this pretty girl. Armande is not wearing a brassiere. Gilles, who had no thought of making love, suddenly sees the free-floating outlines of an unknown bosom. Armande disappears from the screen and we see Gilles pondering, then deciding to find a prostitute. A difficult scene to portray. Perhaps it should be conveyed obliquely, and the camera could follow the girl until her next encounter. A new passer-by is about to approach her when he almost gets run over by a car, whose driver the camera then accompanies, and one transition follows another like a relay-race to the end of the world. In a good story each event would help determine the life of my wandering heroes. But what am I doing, writing a scenario, which couldn't be used in the kind of movies they make these days anyway, when all I need is to make love and there are no immediate prospects? . . .

. . . I have so many worries lately so many things have happened to me Louisette was saying the other night as she helped me get dressed poor Madame how right she is no one knows she is a good girl but stupid over-excited she gets carried away by anything my horoscope is much better I am about to enter a splendid period of my life wood quickly where can I find some wood here this polished cane with the rough edges my other hand on my lovely leg oh hell there goes a run in my stocking that will be charming after dinner everything happens to me but little misfortunes preserve me from greater ones *the great the terrible the inevitable misfortune of being mortal it is not possible I can't I can't I can't ever die ever ever* Bertrand there so pleased with himself his reputation as a seducer who has never failed his mortifying self-assurance when he deigns to look at me well you will get yours someday as far as you are concerned I am no longer playing the game the decanter has misted over the clear transparent flow of pure sparkling liquid being poured into my glass I really shouldn't have any more champagne . . .

. . . Bertrand's suave indifference. He is so dangerously masculine, and not once, not once this evening has he looked at me as though I were a woman. I who am so painfully a woman but whom no man seems to consider as such, any more . . .

. . . I loved Pilou the way she was; not beautiful in this peremptory manner that impresses itself upon you at first glance, but with an inner perfection known only to myself. And to Bertrand, too, alas, to Bertrand who stole her from me. True love always worships this higher perfection, even if the first impression is appealing, and the features ravishing. This is all the more true when some obvious fault hides the inner charm, not erasing it, but sending it deeper . . .

. . . It is not Mrs. Osborn, nor Martine that all the men here are looking at, or are not looking at, which is all the more flattering. Men have a way of not paying any attention to you and yet seeing no one but you! In that field of crimson clover—oh! that crimson—trampled in a small circle, with all the crushed stems and flowers and that field of corn through which I ran home crying, at sundown . . .

. . . He went into his father's business, just as I will soon go into my grandfather's. Or else he continued slowly along the regular academic channels. He disposes of his leisure in whatever fashion he wishes. At home, the table is always set. Everything is done for him, the cooking, the washing, the ironing. All he has to do is live from morning to night and then slip between the clean sheets of a carefully made bed. A beautiful bed, but an empty one; love has no place in such a house; although there are occasional oblique references to it, or casual witticisms, as though the problem had been solved long ago. Actually it was only suppressed: everything takes place as if the boy had never reached puberty. How does Raymond Frôlet manage to be so enterprising with women? How do they all manage? The problem would have been solved for me if I had been able to marry Pilou, if she had waited until I was old enough. These elegant gentlemen are so poised! The way Roland Soulaires is talking to his two pretty dinner partners, Pilou and Marie-Ange, as if they already belonged to him . . .

. . . *To the left of* my neighbor Marie-Ange, that adolescent (a friend of the hostess, I believe) is looking at me with (strange as it may seem) admiration in his eyes. (Admiration!) Inner rejoicing. Because I have nothing to be proud of, I can savor this real but unjustifiable pride all the more. A young man admires me. I mustn't disappoint him. Oh come now Roland, straightening the knot of your tie is too idiotic, even for a woman's benefit. I should try to look like a man who is completely fulfilled, a happy man. (I am not happy . . .)

. . . It is obvious that there is very little to expect from the young man on my right. So shy. Such red hair. Stubborn-looking. A child. Well, I might at least try. It is too bad that he is sitting by my bad ear . . .

". . . What are you studying?"

"Law, ma'am."

. . . The old frump. In her yellow wig . . .

"Is this your first year?"

"No ma'am. My third."

. . . How long is this interrogation going to last?

"Already! Congratulations. And you look so modest and unspoiled, believe me! . . ."

. . . *Believe me*, I would like to be left in peace now . . .

"Were you very young when you passed your baccalaureate?"

"My baccalaureate? Just like anyone else . . ."

. . . I still can't hear that word without a pang of revulsion. The bane of youth. The baccalaureate is the official entry into bourgeois life. Without it one could not rise in the hierarchy; one could not look eye to eye with the only people whom it would be suitable to have as friends; one would lack the confidence to give orders to one's "inferiors." Even if one never considered pursuing one's studies, one must have been in a position to do so; as if it were just as worthy to be eligible for a government position, as actually to run for office. The baccalaureate degree is thus the *toga virilis* of today's bourgeoisie; after achieving the right to wear it, a young man can relax with a good conscience. I don't recognize any such right. I have no good conscience . . .

. . . Little Jérôme Aygulf is a polite, well-behaved child. Even if he does pick his nose. When the Meilleuses lived here they had none of these antique mirrors. There was a Van Gogh, hanging on a background of yellow silk, lit indirectly to bring out the gleaming orange and dazzling greens. They had to sell it, along with everything else, before they died alone and penniless, within a few months of each other. The fear of losing the little I have, as my income shrinks and shrinks, and of dying alone and penniless. And an invalid, why not? A broken hip, at the very least. I must be careful going downstairs tonight. As I lean over, the reflections move along the three prongs of my fork. On the decanters, teardrops of light . . .

. . . That letter to my landlady will be so difficult I must write it tomorrow and tell her dear madam no madam you have no right to keep me from installing an antenna on the roof there is a law no I can put it better than that madam in answer to your letter of the permit me to draw your attention to such and such a clause in the code regulating the use of Léon-Pierre told me which law it was but it still doesn't sound right what a chore writing this letter my whole Sunday will be ruined *my whole life ruined lost it is not fair to have to die it's horrible I am so afraid how can they sit there and not be shrieking with horror* . . .

. . . It has been so long since I have written anything, except the scenarios which I write for a living and which are not bad as stories go; the films made from them are at least controversial. But after all! Mallarmé himself only wrote three poems during one twenty-year period of his life. Again that anguish. His works lasted. They exist today. But mine! It is not too late. The next time I find myself between films I will work on something other than a scenario. I will write a book. Like those I wrote between the ages of eighteen and twenty-eight. Novels which almost no one ever read. Which I never dared to re-read. But in which the undeniable talent revealed in my screenplays was already demonstrated, without being obscured by the compromises, the falsification, and the deception necessary to the screen. I am a success. I have made a name for myself. But in the movies, and that does not count . . .

. . . Rich as I am, and good-looking, although a bit (a very little bit) too stout, I could find happiness in the arms of a chambermaid. (Oh, how happy I could be!) Perspiring already. (One of my difficulties.) (Not the only one.) (Alas!) Try to wipe your forehead without being noticed. It is not because I am worried (What could I be afraid of?) that I am perspiring; it is just that I am too warm. This room is unbearably hot. (But why this panic?) . . .

. . . Still a faint soreness. Only slight. Not of mutilation, more like an inner transformation as if I changed my personality along with my nose . . .

. . . Silence. Martine is an abominable hostess. The conversation must continue. Pilou is really pretty now . . .

". . . Almost one hundred years have passed since Charlotte, the daughter of Leopold the First whom we were just talking about, married Maximilian. A hundred years, and yet, believe it or not, we all could have known her, for she did not die until about 1925."

"I couldn't have!"

"Nor I!"

. . . Not me, the youngest one here. Even Pilou, alas, is older than I am. Otherwise she would have paid more attention to me and today, who knows, she might even be Mme. Jérôme Aygulf . . .

"These young women are having a fine time making fun of us, Bertrand dear. You are right, though, as far as we are concerned. Believe me! It is a fact that in 1925, one could still meet the Empress of Mexico, insane, but alive just the same. She never recovered from the execution of her husband, poor soul. Of course it is understandable, believe me!"

. . . These "believe me's" with which Eugénie Prieur punctuates everything she has to say, when her noisy sighs are not enough, all mean the same thing although repeated in varied tones of voice: a firm conviction that there is no doubt whatsover about what she has just said, nor the slightest cause for discussion, it being an established fact, believe me, that . . .

. . . My inner equilibrium has just been destroyed. A parade of years suddenly marches forth from the vivid landmarks of my past, years which usually accumulate behind me without my noticing them. My awareness of my age is no longer abstract enough to be bearable. I find that my flesh is inextricably involved in the years which have passed. Shreds of me are caught on the steel spokes of time. Paris before the Great War. I was a little girl taking part in events which became gradually less blurred. My first ball, in 1910. In 1925 my son would have been six years old . . .

. . . The Charleston. Dresses above the knee. I've heard about all that. It gives me an awful feeling to think that Rachel, who already knows so many things, who loves the little world that is familiar to her, who has her little preoccupations, has her own habits and probably even her own memories, is still living her prehistory, and will be living it for a long time to come, a whole period of her life which someday she will have entirely forgotten. She is exactly two, the age I was in 1936. We remember a few fleeting images from our third year. None from our second year. To think that Bertrand was at least, let's see, eleven years old in 1925, while I had nine more years in what he calls, in the words of some poet, maybe Sully Prudhomme, *the nameless empire of the possible* . . .

. . . To think that in 1925 I was already eleven years old. When did my youth end? For it appears that I am no longer young. At approximately what date did I stop being young? Is youth really gone at forty-four? Even though I know that I am no longer young, I cannot admit it—since I feel just as fresh and independent, as weak and naive today as twenty years ago. Only the many different stages of life which lie behind me are a measure of the time that has passed. And the lines of age, not too obvious yet on my face, and this beginning of a paunch which I can't entirely ignore in spite of the power of illusion to deliberately deny things. I was probably no longer young when I made love to Francine during the occupation, for I was then already twenty-five. At twenty-five, though, one can still call oneself young. But at thirty-five, in the days of Amelinha? At thirty-five one is no longer young. And I am ten years older than that . . .

. . . 1925, eleven years before I was born. Touching, ridiculous years that are now ancient history. As he relieved me of my virginity, he kept asking me in a hoarse, panting voice, "What do they call ya, girlie, tell me what they call ya." I answered, "Marietta." And he said, "Marietta, eh, girlie, is that a fact? Me I'm a Montrealer myself." He was still for a moment, catching his breath, and then asked me again, "What's your name, kid, what do they call ya?" *Sick, like all men.* And I said Marietta and the clouds flowed across the deep blue sky and maybe it was true after all maybe he did come from Sainte-Hyacinthe . . .

. . . The ravages of time. Time which is belied and denied me by the youth of my sweet young wife, Bénédicte. A past which is now so far away that it is no longer out of style, in fact just the opposite. The decor of a future film. All conversation has ceased. The intensity of unspoken thoughts and their depth arrests time. Salt, that is what was lacking. The flavor of the fish is instantly heightened . . .

. . . *The gay twenties.* Dazzled by the marvels of '25 and those years which always bring me the same nostalgia, whether it is a tune or a book or a film that reminds me of them. Although I was very young then, I was old enough (at nine) to be aware of the world. So I am not like those scholarly fanatics who choose a certain era of the past in which to immerse themselves heart and soul. My memories are not figments of my imagination. I did not dream this past. I was there. My age, of course, kept me from participating but was able to observe from the outside.

. . . I am not so dumb I am not the slave of every whim of fashion since I still have a good figure why wear these dresses inspired by the twenties and furthermore as soon as they came out everyone imitated them why any little seamstress it is so important that I arrive at Megève with a perfect tan the other women will not be able even to attempt to make such an appearance am I as beautiful as Marie-Ange I am more beautiful than Marie-Ange and also more distinguished *but older older* . . .

. . . 1925, what can that mean to someone born in 1939? But even so, I know, yes, how well I know the anguish of growing old and how it makes me suffer. Carefree Raymond Frôlet, who never asks himself any questions. Old Soulaires is bald. Bertrand still has a comparatively full head of hair and it is still quite black. Gilles Bellecroix is white at the temples. But the women's hair is even more revealing. Marie-Ange's is naturally lustrous and ash-blonde. Pilou's is thick and black. While Mrs. Osborn's, carefully tousled, has something dead about it from having been bleached so many times. As for Eugénie Prieur, hers is definitely a wig. I am a redhead, alas, a redhead, though fortunately it is not frizzy or curly. Very fine hair, a bit long. I never manage to get to the barber. Lucky Raymond Frôlet. With hair like his, he can have a crew-cut . . .

. . . In 1925 I already had quite a past. It was between my two great loves, Jean-Jacques and Gilles. Only death proves the passage of time. Not one of us changes. Life slowly destroys us. Sickness and the death agony put an end to our activity. But the years which pile up one by one have no reality other than the noticeable, and suddenly final, wearing out of our bodies. The spirit remains the same; it is our true and invulnerable youth. At the moment of death, if my mind is still lucid, all my life will be gathered together as in a single day. Bertrand conveyed this in his book: time kills us but it does not exist . . .

. . . Yes, I was eleven years old. I can still see the arabesques of fire around the luminous fountains at the Exposition; I can hear the sound of the hunting horns—I will never stop hearing them—from the top of one of the towers of the esplanade; with the unforgettable racket of the roller coasters built on the banks of the Seine, not far from Paul Poiret's little houseboats. I can hear the whole symphony of 1925—*Amours, Délices, et Orgues.* The Eiffel tower with its neon CITROEN, illuminated with special little sparkling lights, stars of fire, pulsating in a fiery rhythm. The great writers of those years, in whom I was already interested, if I was not yet reading them: Valéry, Drieu La Rochelle, Mauriac. And Jean-Jacques Limher, then a leading light, to such an extent that I now find it hard to believe, but I can't deny the fact, that he is the same man when I meet him today . . .

". . . You know, the legend of 1925 is not entirely justified. Jean-Jacques Limher, whom I never knew at the time of course, I was too young . . . But I had the opportunity of meeting him later on at the . . ."

. . . Watch out there, don't put your foot in it. Eugénie Prieur lived for a long time with Jean-Jacques Limher, when she was a young woman. Their affair lasted at least ten years, if you count World War I, which of course separated them for a time . . .

. . . Jean-Jacques, the child, the child we didn't want, Jean-Jacques. The only cardinal sin for which I will never forgive myself. I confessed it several times. In vain. Never did I feel forgiven . . .

. . . Poor Eugénie is getting deafer. But it is fortunate that she didn't hear . . .

"Yes, what were you saying about Jean-Jacques Limher?"

"He maintained in my presence that the legend was not entirely justified, that 1925 was merely the public consecration, if not the vulgarization, of the years from 1917 to 1919."

. . . It was then, in 1919, in June 1919. Jean-Jacques took care of everything. But he refused to go with me; I had to go all alone to that horrible old man, near the Porte de Versailles. My child would be forty now. He would not be, nor would he have been for a long time, the little child whom I miss. But he would be a man of whom I could be proud and who would watch over me in my old age, unlike Marie-Therèse who has always been so aloof, so indifferent. There are names which obsess one, like this name. I could swear that someone has just mentioned Jean-Jacques . . .

. . . This unfamiliar face, my face. Am I more beautiful this way? It still hurts a little bit, but Dr. Chanuz assured me that in a few days I would feel nothing . . .

"Although I was born in 1916 (yes indeed, 1916, though you may not believe it) 1925 still means a great deal to me, you know. In spite of my youth, I experienced almost to the full . . ."

. . . Bertrand Carnéjoux looks so old already. Only two years difference between us. Luckily I am still blessed with youth and vitality. People are always surprised when I tell them the year I was born. It is my good fortune not to look my age. (My only good fortune.) Strange, though, and rather disturbing that tonight no one showed the slightest astonishment when I admitted to having been born in 1916. (It is true that I have put on a little weight.) I was foolish to lay myself open that way. Let's not be ridiculous, Roland. Some camouflage, quickly . . .

". . . But we all grow old, sooner or later. I've put on some weight, for one thing . . ."

. . . I have, but it becomes me . . .

"You haven't put on weight, Roland, you have just spread out a bit. Age does that. I feel free to say such things because I have, so to speak, crossed the bridge."

"And just what is the difference, Gigi?"

"One's features begin to disintegrate."

. . . The bitch. Insulting me like that and trying to look so innocent . . .

. . . Well done. How blind can you be? Hasn't Roland ever looked in a mirror? With that bald pate and big bags under his eyes. To think that he is two years younger than Bertrand. Of course my husband looks younger than his age. Not as much as Gilles Bellecroix, though; at nearly fifty he is absolutely amazing . . .

. . . He was asking for it. But I mustn't be mean to him. Instead I should try to seduce him; he isn't really so bad. Age means nothing, my children, someday you will learn this. Old as I am, as I appear to be on the outside, for it shows, alas, it shows, inside I am still only twenty, believe me! But I am the only one who knows this . . .

. . . Bénédicte is not so young anymore, either—almost thirty; soon she will understand. But why isn't she here this evening for me to contemplate her pink blond beauty, her sweet, beloved little face? Not as sweet as all that, not that sweet . . .

"You know, I was seven years old in 1925!"

"That would make me minus nine!"

"I would have been minus eleven!"

. . . Marie-Ange beat my wife by only two points while Mrs. Osborn is way behind with her plus seven. But Jérôme, the youngest, hasn't said anything. Why is he looking at us as though we were an exhibit of wild animals?

. . . Fossils! The last representatives of a dying race. They will soon disappear and the sooner the better . . .

"Well! What am I supposed to say, at forty-three?"

"Or me at . . ."

"I find . . ."

. . . Everyone is playing his solo in a score that has no unity other than its theme, and the I's that are called upon, one by one, to sing out calmly and without modesty. Whenever I run into other boys of my generation, or even ones a little younger, like Roland (whose obesity, and tics, and nasal voice have always made him unattractive), I am always surprised by their dry, withered and worn-out faces. Even though I am a bit older, I look considerably younger. Nobody could ever guess my age, could they, Martine? . . .

. . . John was born in 1880 eighty years old it can't last too much longer but with the new antibiotics these days one can't count on anything if Léon-Pierre left me I would have no trouble finding another lover no trouble at all why worry I am the one who makes love so well he does too of course but if I didn't know the way all his technique and good intentions would come to naught he is very young Léon-Pierre in 1925 he was not even born what a baby . . .

. . . Sometimes nothing is more difficult to believe than the facts themselves. To think that 1925 was only ten years after 1915, the year before I was born and which then appeared to be plunged in the depths of time, even more than it is now. 1915, legendary era of the Great War, almost contemporary with that era of prehistory: the days-before-the-war. Between 1920 and 1910, ten years (unbelievable), not one year more than the period between today and October 1950 (almost yesterday) which was itself connected to 1930 by a period of time that is long when compared to the last ten years but nothing when I think of the eternity separating 1915 from 1925.

. . . And suddenly I remember the enduring, but nevertheless momentarily forgotten memory of our love. The ravishing blonde with the shapely little breasts, the laughing girl who is still alive within me, how can I recognize her in that large old woman whose heavy features are plastered with make-up? It is she, however, Gigi, the one I loved at twenty. She was not yet married to that M. Prieur whom no one ever knew. Eugénie Valerbes, that was her name, Eugénie Valerbes. She was not young even then. But still so beautiful . . .

. . . One of those rare and brief glances which reassure me when we meet from time to time that Gilles has not entirely forgotten, that he remembers what was for me the last great happiness of my life. How handsome he was in 1932. Not yet a screenwriter, but a young novelist. How handsome he still is! . . .

"And the two of us, my little Gigi, what can we say for ourselves?"

"The two of us, my Gilles, the two of us . . ."

. . . He called me his little Gigi. Out loud. This public confession, so indiscreet, so tender . . .

. . . Your Gilles, Eugénie, is drawing attention to his age, in public, in front of everyone, for your sake, for them all to hear, although no one is paying any attention . . .

. . . They are too preoccupied . . .

. . . Indifferent to anything that does not regard them personally . . .

. . . The look in your eyes gives away our old, forgotten secret, but it doesn't matter . . .

. . . Even today, one can see that she was once beautiful . . .

. . . Gilles, my little Gilles, you are looking at me as a woman. I was and will always be a woman for you . . .

. . . And our dialogue continues in silence, more intimate and indiscreet than ever . . .

. . . The forest of Ermenonville and Senlis. 1932, you remember . . .

. . . The little inn in Mortefontaine. 1933 . . .

. . . A grand passion . . . the talk of the town . . .

. . . The love of three summers . . .

"Time does not exist. Bertrand wrote that somewhere . . ."

"It is true, Gigi. For us time does not exist."

. . . Once again we talked out loud. Once again we cried out, revealing our secrets. And the night at Fontainebleau, have you forgotten? . . .

. . . The same blue eyes in a face that has been ravaged. Time, Eugénie, time has destroyed us . . .

. . . Now we are cut off again. You are far away. There is no danger any more, alas, that anyone will catch our knowing glances . . .

. . . Even in those days she would sometimes look lost all of a sudden. Her lip would tremble, as now, in an empty face. Yes, she was very beautiful, but she was over forty and I was twenty-two. Under the worn lines of that poor face, there is still a trace of charm . . .

. . . As Martine and I did earlier in the evening, Eugénie

Prieur and Gilles Bellecroix have profited from the general lapse of attention to exchange a few revealing words, as though they were alone. Words whose blinding audacity protected them by making everyone even more dazed. And indeed, no one would have heard them, had I not been on the alert, even before my name was mentioned, hoping as always to discover between human beings that silent understanding which reveals so much. But this time, Eugénie and Gilles chose to say out loud what discretion would ordinarily keep to a whisper. In the presence of six (five) people, whom a kind of thrall kept from listening to what they certainly could hear, how beautiful, how deep and impregnable is their privacy. So they were lovers; who would have thought it? It must have been long ago and Gilles must have been very young . . .

. . . How I missed Bénédicte in Marseilles! I need her constant presence to feel completely myself. Far from her, unable to talk to her of what I saw, I felt crippled. Once in a while I even caught myself talking all alone, in the same tone of voice that I would use to point out such and such a funny detail, to amuse her. There she was, in her prim dress, at the station, before I noticed that she was sick. We both felt shy and had a hard time rediscovering the easy rhythms of happiness. And yet it was only two nights before that she had taken me to the train. Time varies according to the circumstances. There is a chronology of happiness that makes ten years of life together into one long minute, and two days of separation into a short year . . .

"The war is still the great landmark."

"Ours?"

"Theirs, Roland. The Great War."

. . . Jean-Jacques' war, and mine, for God knows how we suffered.

"Even for our generation which has only the vaguest memory of it, it remains the real turning point."

. . . 1926, at the Brouges'. A dinner such as this. After seven years without a letter, four of them terrible years, I saw Jean-Jacques again for the first time. The laughter of Paris, always the same. Whinnying. Guffawing. More gaiety and wit than today, it seems to me. He was wearing a dark grey suit and a red carnation. His beard, which I had never seen, and which he has since given up, amazed me. That evening you carried me away, Jean-Jacques, and I spent the night with you. All sensations were overpowered by emotion and all pleasure by joy. If you had kept me, if I had not let you escape, maybe we would have had another child . . .

. . . My son often asks me whether I did such and such a thing *before the war*. Of course he means the war which Roland Soulaires just called *ours*, the one we fought. It is all nothing but words to Jean-Paul, words which he repeats without knowing what they mean, but which prepare for the way these pre-war days will withdraw almost magically into a distant, mythological past when he is old enough to understand. The same thing happened to me with the days before the other war. Although I was much closer to them than he is—if he had been born around 1940, about the year when the tall young man here tonight came into the world, he would have had the same perspective on the second world war—nevertheless, those days seemed terribly far away to me, lost in the abyss of time. Having been born in 1914, I looked upon anyone born before 1910 as an ancestor. Even today I find it hard not to look upon those who are four years older than I am without a feeling of sympathy. As for the adults, I found it hard to believe that they had come so far, that anyone living before the great divide of the war could still be alive . . .

"I never knew the days before the war, either, for I was born slightly . . ."

. . . considerably . . .

". . . after you, in 1916. But 1925, though I observed it only from a distance, was, is still, full of marvels that were not only those of a child's imagination. Through my parents, I caught some of its reflected glory. Sometimes I even feel that I lived through it and loved it all, and become nostalgic about it . . ."

. . . Vague pangs of worry. I have so many reasons to be unhappy. The joys of 1925 may help me to forget them. How can they understand that I look back with longing on a period that I knew only at a distance, as a child. The paradox is that the most glorious era of my youth, my real paradise lost, was my tenth and not my twentieth year. My happiest memories are those of a little boy watching and admiring the wonders of adult life, from the wings. The secret affection and nostalgia usually reserved for memories of a triumphant adolescence, come to me instead when I think of those days between 1925 and 1926. (My adolescence was not triumphant.) That is my only real youth, for my other youth was rent by too many complexes, obsessions, and fears for me to remember it with anything but blinding revulsion. (No, my adolescence was far from triumphant.) But I must stop dwelling on my troubles. A little game will help distract me. Then it will be their turn to experience one of the many forms of anguish which torture me. Even if it causes me even more pain, at least we will all be in the same boat . . .

". . . Now listen, since you are all fond of history and since we are talking about our respective ages . . . I have made up a little game . . ."

"Bravo! Let's play . . ."

"I'm with you!"

"No, not you. This game is only for men . . ."

"Why?"

"Because each contestant has to give the year of his birth . . ."

"That doesn't bother me: 1934 . . ."

"Well then, Martine, you will have to find someone . . . say . . . like Vauban."

"I don't understand . . ."

"But it's simple: Vauban was born in 1633 . . . Taking into account any amazing examples of longevity, or on the other hand, of those who died young, and also considering that people live longer these days, all you have to do is to look through the centuries for as many as possible of your own "contemporaries," so to speak, and then make up an average out of the dates they died . . ."

"But that's horrible!"

"Realistic, though. May I begin? Let's try to find a few great men for me . . . They will be more or less the same ones that you are looking for, Bertrand. Shall we try?"

"It's rather intriguing . . ."

"I was born in 1916. So was Mary Tudor; I mean in 1516. She died in 1558. That doesn't count, then, I would have died two years ago. Marie-Thérèse of Austria, 1717-1780. Let's see, I can't seem to think. Offenbach, 1819-1880 . . . Soufflot, 1713-1780. Who else? Condillac, 1714-1780 . . ."

"Gluck, 1714-1786 or 1787 . . . Karl Marx, 1818-1883 . . ."

"Congratulations. You now know how to play the game. You can go on by yourselves."

"I don't like this game very much!"

"Gluck 14-87. Like a telephone number."

"Calling eternity, long distance . . ."

"Dialing heaven, direct!"

"And Vauban, when did he die?"

"I don't know, look in your dictionary . . ."

"Around 1707 . . . That leaves you plenty of time, my dear. Spinoza, give or take two years, might also interest you . . ."

"Only Roland could think up something like this!"

"Yes, we've had enough. Let's talk about something else . . ."

. . . I was born in 1893. Hm. Who else? I can't think of anyone, luckily. 93. My goodness. Gounod died in 1893. Born in 1818. He is for Lucienne Osborn, not me. To die in 1993, how fortunate she is. But it isn't all so simple, oh no, it would be too easy . . .

. . . I don't know a single date so this doesn't involve me there is no danger of dying that would be all I need death does not exist just a bad dream yes I am breathing *but no* not a dream *but yes* but no *alas yes* it is unthinkable I can't bear this abomination another minute but I have to there is nothing to do about it but yes *oh no* help help Léon-Pierre rescue me . . .

. . . So it happens that instead of looking back on my twenties (my ghastly twenties) like most men, I am nostalgic about my first ten years, though not about the little boy playing with marbles that I became at ten. I may not have been a happy child, but the worst was to follow, after puberty, as each year led me further and further into despair. My most intense suffering coincided with the beginning of the Phony War. It continued to plague me long after my adolescence was over; in fact my real youth began when according to the calendar I was no longer young at all, that is, when I was saved by Marie-Louise. (But was I really saved?) This constant feeling of embarrassment, as though someone has said something (or I have said something) that makes all peace of mind, even the temporary kind, impossible . . .

. . . The astringent fragrance of Armande. Eau de Cologne against fresh, very young skin. Her little breasts within the shadowy neckline of her dress . . .

. . . A world of trivialities, a vacuum from which we seek an impossible salvation, whose presence, and voice (or better still, silence) can bring us a fleeting but intense wonder: a girl . . .

. . . What a relief it would be to abandon Marie-Louise, if I could have one of the women here as my mistress (with the exception of Eugénie Prieur, of course). Armande, too, whose perfume I can detect even after she has moved away, attracts me. Who am I, after all, to be fussy? A lady or a chambermaid, just so long as it is a woman. No, the hidden anxiety that keeps oppressing me is not just my usual obsession. (It is both too piercing and too vague not to be some new, unexpected wound . . .)

. . . Madame I have the pleasure of bringing to your kind attention no why kind your attention the law concerning you have no right consequently I will and if you don't like it you know what you can do about it so there but that doesn't sound very dignified Madame in answer to yours of the no that is too business-like Léon-Pierre is mean not to jot down a rough version of it as for John his would be gibberish Madame I cannot postpone any longer we must absolutely come to a definite agreement you know perfectly well that my television does not work well with an inside antenna *and that we are mortal mortal* . . .

. . . Gigi took another helping of fish, and a big one. She really eats like a horse. But with elegant dispatch. Swift and sure. I'm not hungry any more; I'm never hungry. I haven't had an appetite for years. This morning, however, in the dining car, with the help of a little Listrac. But this evening I haven't the faintest desire for food, a complete lack of appetite . . .

. . . Strange anxiety. A vague oppression. A few minutes ago I knew why (but I have forgotten already). Something rather severe I'm sure. Not the same old worry, too familiar to be so disturbing. Maybe something financial? (Having to relinquish, or maybe even give away some gold mines . . .) Though the table and also the marble sideboard where they have placed a many-branched candelabra are brilliantly lit, the rest of the room lies in darkness.

Window panes like black mirrors. The glinting shadows of the Seine. Between the two, a street lamp and a tall, lopped tree. Beyond, on the other side of the river, a few lights in the far-away windows . . .

"We were talking a while back about the Kingdom of Naples. Well, the queen of Naples also died in 1925."

"The sister of the empress Elizabeth?"

"It doesn't seem possible!"

"But it's true. Imagine!"

. . . Here we go again. 1925 is beginning to be a bore. When was Herculaneum? In '79. Why did I think of Herculaneum? . . .

. . . Rachel and I understand each other most perfectly when I am holding her in my arms. As she nestles in the hollow of my neck, as I feel her soft little cheek next to mine, I experience a sense of peace and happiness that no kiss from Bertrand himself will ever be able to give me . . .

. . . So many different vantage points in my life, before and after 1925. I was then thirty-two. I am now sixty-five. Unthinkable. I am constantly surprised when I find myself surrounded by men and women who are not as old as I am: the young. The soldier who seemed to me, as a young girl, to be immoderately old, is now a child. Between this boy and me are all the possibilities of youth. I know babies who are grandfathers, and child-grandmothers. This crowd which grows younger as I grow older is a measure of time. One day, I will be the oldest of the beautiful young family of the living . . .

. . . The main thing is not to be pale to be very tan

when I arrive at Megève if only I could have brought Zig with me he wouldn't bother anyone the poor sweetheart all curled up by my feet it would have been so nice he would have *comforted me reassured me saved me* and at least I would not have worried about him all alone in the house I hope John hasn't closed the living room door I left it open in case Zig felt like lying on the couch instead of in his bed what on earth could they be up to at this hour John and Léon-Pierre I could easily have taken more fish but I must remember to watch my figure . . .

. . . Herculaneum woke me from my apathy. Martine was disturbed too. A giddy, intense feeling of reliving the past which had the most direct repercussions on our personal life. The abolition of time. The primordial secrets of humanity rediscovered at their source, in the ancient dead who were almost alive, and in ourselves, the living who are almost dead . . .

. . . The same vague feeling of anxiety, almost of panic . . .

"But who is it that you are talking about? Marie of Bavaria, the wife of poor François II? . . ."

"Yes, the very one. Proust wrote about her in *La Prison-nière*, you remember, at the Verdurins, the day when Charlus took care of the invitations . . ."

"You know what Barrès thought of Proust, don't you?"

. . . 1925. Like yesterday. Six years after that abortion which is still present in my mind, always more vivid and immediate, *as though there were still time to decide against it and to bear the child.* Yesterday, 1925? The same length of time as from 1925 back to my earliest childhood, so long ago that I have no memory of it. But if 1925 was only yesterday, I will die tomorrow. If I am still alive thirty-five years from now, I will be over a hundred. But I will not be alive . . .

. . . I feel the same happiness with my son but no longer in such a tranquil, secure way. He is almost five and is beginning to act like a little man, resenting too much tenderness. Even if the days of hugs and kisses are not entirely over, Jean-Paul is already too old for me to hope for more than a fleeting moment of abandon, or for him to allow it. So I am left, not knowing what to do with my burden of love. It is certainly very warm in here . . .

". . . Armande . . . Would you please turn off the radiator. We are suffocating in here. And open the window a little, too, would you. And Armande, our glasses, please, they are all empty. Everyone must be thirsty, I am so sorry!"

"What do you mean? We haven't once stopped . . . And this champagne, I have never tasted anything so good!"

". . . And Charlus said, don't you remember, it was so magnificent, he said to the Verdurins in almost these words: 'The queen of Naples, here? Why this is an historical occasion. When you think that she probably hasn't been out since the fall of . . .' "

. . . Be just as aloof and indifferent as you like, Martine, too confident in your beauty to have to test it on an insignificant young man, but nevertheless, if the eight of us were forced to live on a desert island, it would be me whom you would choose, whom you would guard jealously from all the other women. Small consolation. In this society in which a twenty-year-old young man simply does not exist, the beautiful Marie-Ange will not even bother to look at me . . .

. . . The little redheaded boy beside me keeps picking his nose. If it were up to me he would be wearing mittens . . .

. . . No one knows, no one could know that Marie-Ange is my mistress. My chickadee, especially. Little Pilou could never conceive of such a betrayal. For these things are called betrayals, though I could never understand why. "Diversions," would be a better word. In any case, it is something in the realm of the improbable, sometimes even of the impossible, as with Irène. Pilou must never know about that, not ever. Tonight there will be nothing to make her suspicious. Marie-Ange has eyes only for Roland Soulaires, saying little and wearing the fervent expression of a woman whose admiration makes it difficult for her to listen. A girl I once knew from New York, whose name escapes me, used to look at everyone like that, all the time . . .

"Gaeta, yes she referred to it later on, I mean Proust did; it was when she offered her arm to Charlus who had been insulted and humiliated by the Verdurins, and she said, about the arm that is . . now listen: 'In Gaeta, once upon a time, this arm kept the rabble at bay. Now let it be a rampart for you!' "

. . . That survey, called the *Ecology of Famous Men*, sent me by one of those official organizations. Two months later, when I hadn't answered, they sent me another copy, insisting that I tell them the reasons for my success. Their exact words (at the end of a long questionnaire) were: "What, in your opinion, is the essential factor behind your success?" How could I explain to statisticians that I do not feel as though I had succeeded, no not in the least, that my apparent success as a screenwriter has not made me forget my failure as a novelist . . .

. . . But the little bed I fixed up for him is quite comfortable really very nice for Zig there is no need to worry I have enough troubles already he is probably sound asleep by now the rascal but when John dies I will find a better place for him just the same . . .

. . . My mother was in Quebec for the day. Where were my brothers and sisters? I was by myself, in the field of crimson clover. The way he made me fall. His moist hand lifting my skirt. How wonderful it would be to eat all I wanted. To think how delicious all this is and how hungry I will be when I leave the table . . .

. . . I am the only one who can calm her tantrums. I take her in my arms (in moments like these no one else can even touch her) and hold her little head next to mine and, with my nose in her downy hair, I whisper gently to her and she lets me rock her slowly back and forth, in silence. Is that what they call a good up-bringing? Jean-Paul was and still is just as spoiled, but he is by no means an impossible child. One simply has to know where to draw the line, to enforce some discipline. Bertrand does this when he is at home—not very often—and so do I; it is not as if I let my children get away with anything, oh no! But aside from that, one can never love one's children enough, or give them too much happiness. Mummy never gave me enough happiness, or love. "Children must be prepared to face life, which is never very easy." Such an attitude is all wrong; they will exhaust their little backlog of happiness all too soon, even though I try so desperately to make it inexhaustible . . .

"When was *La Prisonnière* published?"

"In 1923 . . ."

"Proust had died, but the Queen of Naples was still alive. So she might have read the passage in which he spoke of the 'glorious sister of the empress Elizabeth.' "

"She did. I read or heard somewhere that when these pages from *La Prisonnière* were read to her, she said . . ."

. . . I doubt if Bertrand Carnéjoux received that questionnaire. He is not as famous as I am. But he is praised by the only critics whose opinion matters, and is admired by the young. And all because of one book, *Sober Pleasures.* An unpalatable, overwritten novel . . .

"Is it possible!"

". . . And she said, 'I do not remember having met Monsieur Proust. But he must have known me. For that is exactly how I would have acted under the circumstances.' "

"She must have been pleased! Proust spoke of her as the very soul of kindness . . ."

"That is right, my dear Jérôme, but I am not sure that it was intended as a compliment."

"We would have to see the remark in context."

"Just a minute, then. I'll get the book. Or no. Jérôme, would you be kind enough to go and fetch *La Prisonnière* from my library? It is right next door, you won't have any trouble. Thank you so much . . ."

"A propos of Proust, Barrès once had the audacity to say . . ."

"Jérôme is a very sweet young man . . ."

"Martine likes him very much. She assures me that he is intelligent."

"He does seem to know his Proust, anyhow."

. . . One, two, three, four,—five, six. That red-haired man was my salvation. If he hadn't taken me by force, I would have given myself to the first comer. I would have married and settled near Quebec. One, two, three, four,—five, six . . .

. . . I can continue with my tan at Harriette Ziem's under the sunlamp Marie-Ange is so pale under her make-up how dreadful but of course tonight is the night for *Tele-Faces* how stupid of me to have missed it when John wasn't even at home why did I bother when John dies and with the money he will leave me I will have a nice settled life with television sets everywhere at least in the three main rooms it will be far more convenient it's so very tiresome having to drag one around the apartment . . .

. . . Last time I saw Marie-Plum was almost two years ago, just by chance, in the lobby of a nightclub which she was leaving just as I arrived. I was alone. She was not. How surprised I was to find her just as pretty, after so many years. But I was even more surprised to find that it was not Marie-Plum herself, but a shadow, with whom I was still vaguely in love. She was there, in front of me, but she had never been more distant. She was alive, but for me she had died, leaving in my heart only an image of the woman she had been for a few, unforgettable hours . . .

". . . What is this? Oh, the Proust. Thank you, Jérôme my boy . . ."

. . . The heavy, cloying aroma of the roses. The same

114

smell will hover around my tomb. In the dark lobby of the night club, while the man who was with her talked to someone he had met inside, Marie-Plum did not flinch when I lit a match to see her face through the flattering shadows, —the bare reality of her face, which appeared in all its glaring defects . . .

". . . It must be around here somewhere . . . *I don't know whom you are talking about. There is only one queen of Naples who is sublime, and she has no carriage.* No, that is not quite it. Probably a bit further on . . ."

. . . My book, *Sober Pleasures,* was much read and talked about. A false success, based on misinterpretations. Very few readers even suspected what I was trying to do in the book. I failed, to be sure, but my intentions were not without interest. Only the colorful and erotic elements were singled out, while the essential aspect of the novel was neglected: my attempt to revolutionize the conventional forms of fiction by creating a dual point of view, at once objective and subjective, with the greatest possible precision and accuracy. What we think is as true, or as mistaken, as what we see. Our ideas are as valid as the evidence of our senses. Both are mechanical in origin; reactions to and interpretations of, a reality of which we will never have more complete knowledge . . .

". . . Here we are. Listen: *The queen was the very spirit of kindness, but kindness, to her, meant a resolute and unshakable loyalty to those she loved, to her family . . ."*

"You see!"

"Wait! . . . *To her family, to all its scions among whom was the Baron de Charlus, and to all those of the bour-*

geoisie or of the humble lower classes (now listen) *or of the humble lower classes* who respected those she loved, and who held the right political opinions. *Now this may be a rather narrow, conservative, and, today, outdated conception of kindness,* etc. What did I tell you?"

"She comes through in a rather bad light."

"I should say so!"

"The queen of Naples must have read the passage wrong."

"No one knows how to read anymore."

"Critics are no better than queens."

"Sovereign in their ignorance!"

"It is all too easy for writers to jump on the poor critics."

"Or for screen writers, my dear Gilles."

"Or for screen writers, why not? Although film critics, if I may say so, are a unique race. They have no idea what they are talking about . . ."

"Novelists face the same problem. But there is no need for me to point this out to the author of *With Tears in Her Eyes!*"

. . . He remembers *With Tears in Her Eyes* . . .

". . . But you must admit that everyone fancies himself a writer. It is a calling which . . ."

"Alas yes! This reminds me of a story. But first I must tell you . . ."

"Why *alas?* Is he afraid of the competition?"

"Be quiet, he will hear you. And why shouldn't he criticize . . ."

"Because the very least one can say about Bertrand is that he is not prolific. One book represents his entire career as a writer, and that was five years ago . . ."

"You are perfectly impossible, and besides, please talk a little more quietly . . ."

. . . So many young girls have said to me, in the same tone of pseudo-outrage, but actually delighted, "You are perfectly impossible!" It is one of the ploys of a harmless flirtation. But from this old party! Eugénie Prieur is playing the seductress, out of habit. The mechanical reflexes of an old woman who was once pretty; Bertrand described it in his book. Unless the old witch really has something in mind. That would be the limit. Silence. One can hear the noise of an airplane engine. Today that sound is almost outdated . . .

. . . Gilles is not paying attention to Eugénie anymore, but is dividing his favors between Marie-Ange and Martine. Mrs. Osborn, on his left, and not so young, is also being neglected. The elegant, slightly ridiculous gallantry of middle-aged men infatuated by pretty young women. What would the pure, aloof, and inaccessible Bénédicte think of all this? The male of the species does not age so fast as the female. The woman Gilles is married to is younger than Gigi was thirty years ago when they had their affair. And the women I have loved have seldom been over twenty-five. Have they all been alike? Was one more intelligent than another? Though the quality of mind is not very important in physical passion. Francine years ago, Marie-Ange now, all the Martines of today and yesterday have been the same woman, the Woman. There was Marie-Plum, however. And Amelinha . . .

. . . This airplane is flying at too high an altitude to have taken off from Orly. The noise of its engine almost deadens the sound of the traffic along the other side of the river on the Quai de la Tournelle. There are hardly any cars on our side. Maybe this plane is going to New York. To New York where Bertrand once had some love affairs. He confessed this to me. But it was before we were engaged . . .

. . . Sharks of the air, cast up on the beaches of heaven, on the flat shores of an airport, near the road which I took back from my grandmother's last Sunday. A frightening rocket with stubby wings. A young man, not much older than I am, graceful in spite of his flight gear, striding towards his plane. The pride of being twenty years old and the master of one of those slim steel killers. If possible, I will join the air force for my military training. My eyes, unfortunately, are not as good as they might be. Though he may actually be the slave of the machine, a pilot is not aware of this. Dedicated, consecrated to his instrument of death. Perhaps whoever created this airplane was in love with a young girl. Just as I am in love with Martine, with Martine who is no longer a young girl. I who hope to be as modern in my writings—for I will write someday, definitely, like Bertrand Carnéjoux—as these engineers are in their aeronautic creations. Men of the atomic age, the space age. In love with the days of the horse and buggy. Our emotions lag behind our capacities. So does our art. But I, at least, though I am young, am clear-headed. Or rather, because I am young . . .

. . . Maybe he came that way again the next year, through Longe. Who knows? One, two, three, four, five, six. I had already left. I was still in Canada, in Montreal, but not for long. It was too difficult, not being of age. One, two, three, four,—one, two. But I am a good daughter, I send money to my mother. One, two, three . . . I must stop

118

looking at Mrs. Osborn's necklace, counting the gold beads . . .

. . . He often takes the plane not to mention his reckless driving what an elegant funeral it will be with all his relatives and I will make a beautiful widow at last I will be able to relax I will be able to think about myself for once a sunbath is a very serious undertaking I mean a real sunbath you have to know how to concentrate luckily concentration has always been easy for me but it is tiring three sets might be a little extravagant maybe two would do one in the living room and the other in my bedroom young Marie-Ange is definitely admiring my bosom of course there is a lot to admire . . .

. . . In the end it matters very little who is thinking what. A red light and a green one blinking in sequence in the diffused radiance of the night. Our ideas, at least what we call our ideas, are not very different one from the other. All these sleepy, unknown people, embarked on the same ship, where do they come from, where are they going? The automatic gears of the mind, rotating in unison. Engines running patiently and rhythmically to the beat of an old Brazilian folksong. All that is left is our individual obsessions; mine is to be incessantly preoccupied with time. Amelinha, whom I betrayed so carelessly, with a stranger. Long ago, in 1947 . . .

. . . Always the same feeling, of something recently revealed to be final and absolute, but which left me only a vague, inscrutable impression. I know only that a certain event reduced my fondest and most confident expectations to sterility. (That is, whatever expectations I had left . . .)

. . . If the volatile course of our thoughts could suddenly

119

be crystallized, would we be able to acquire a picture of this dinner that is more accurate than the ones to be obtained by listening to our vain, guffawing laughter, and silence? A reality that would not be much more objective. How can one portray the presence of eight glutted, intoxicated bodies? What could they be thinking about, if they are thinking at all? Their own little preoccupations? *The answer is: we are all obsessed.* But the others do not have the same preoccupation as I do: a relentless drive to comprehend the inexpressible and to gather it in a book, in a book which I am always about to write . . .

. . . Bénédicte released me from the vain quest, exemplified by the hero of Bertrand Carnéjoux's novel, which plagues the majority of men, the hope for a revelation each time one takes possession of a new body. Another affair would only confront me with the great unknowable which I escape in my love for Bénédicte. Not that the delicious and terrifying mystery of her young breasts has been solved for me. But along with this wonder is a love which is simple and transparent, just the opposite in its pure violence from what we (for at heart we are all like romantic little shopgirls) could ever imagine. My metaphysical love is richer than its physical counterpart, which it embraces and outdistances, thus making all other women worthless (of no use) to me. I know how to use them, by heart (by body) but I no longer feel the desire to try. Little Martine is charming . . .

. . . Now I remember. This war, which I never fought, which I never had the chance to fight and which I called *my war.* ("Ours.") Relief. So it was nothing but this faint elaboration upon the truth; for after all, in 1940 I did participate, though at a distance. I may not have fought in it, but I endured it. Not courageously, oh no, but I was subjected to danger by the nature of things (once in a while, not very often), (like everyone else). So a little lie like that (a statement that was not entirely accurate) (nor entirely false, either) was enough to cause me such mental anguish . . .

. . . From that day on, (I was fourteen) I swore that it was the last time, the first but also the last, that a man would force himself upon me. And so I decided, as a young girl, to make use of men, instead of letting them use me. I have kept that promise . . .

. . . *The little things are great to little man.* Goldsmith, I believe. But was it so little? The way my thoughts could be so unpleasantly (painfully) (overwhelmingly) discolored by those few insignificant words which I spoke a while ago? Now that I know the origin of this anxiety, I will be able to escape it. Now that this mild annoyance is past, only my permanent sorrow remains. (The Bentzinger stocks came up for sale today, in an over-the-counter transaction. The buyers were assured of .03% interest, on 30,000 francs . . .)

. . . With only two or three exceptions, Henri, Paulo, Gaston, maybe Bertrand, I have never given in without being in complete control. No man, not even Henri whom I loved, ever got anything for nothing. Henri, the steward, thanks to whom I sailed to France . . .

. . . And in the den I was quite right I really do need three sets . . .

. . . So that is all it was. This dark shadow that fell over every one of my thoughts (and over that state of mind which replaces thought) was the result of such a trifling error. Trifling? I was ashamed to have been caught exaggerating. (Lying). *One must be fair all around.* Try to recover your self-respect. Correct the statement which you so imprudently, so impudently made a little while ago . . .

". . . I was boasting a bit, really, when I said . . ."

. . . No one is listening. But if I am to recover my self-respect and peace of mind someone must hear me retract the statement . . .

". . . As I was saying, during the war, though I shouldn't call it my war . . ."

"What do you think of . . ."

"Talk a little louder."

"Shh! What do you think of Martine's new nose?"

. . . I am despicable. I am tearing down my own love. A morbid, masochistic kind of enjoyment . . .

. . . Well that's what it was. Of course! And Bertrand, the louse, kept it a secret from me . . .

"What about you?"

"I don't think it's at all bad."

"Nor do I. She does look better. Don't worry, she can't hear us. M. Bellecroix is talking to her."

". . . Do you still go to the movies a great deal, Martine?"

. . . Enjoying her pretty face, though without being conceited about it . . .

"Oh, very often . . ."

. . . *Martine*, that gives me an odd feeling. Of course we know each other quite well now. But I would never dare call him Gilles. He is too old. Even after that evening, that unforgettable dance last January, I didn't dare . . . He may be old but he is terribly attractive . . .

"And what kind of films do you prefer? It would interest me very much to know . . ."

"Good ones."

. . . And mine, what about mine? . . .

"Of course. Have you seen *Circus Girl?*

"No, I don't think so. I don't remember all their titles, you know . . ."

"And *Caprices?*"

"Yes."

"Did you enjoy it?"

"So so. The actress was very good."

. . . She answers only yes or no, but one would not consider her ill-mannered or stupid. Her real answer is a gentle, fleeting smile, the nicest answer of all, not only because of its sweetness but also because of the genuine intelligence it reveals, the intelligence of the heart, which is never lacking in the other kind. Martine Carnéjoux is able to say the most when she is silent, but how could one ever express this kind of conversation on the screen? I can see a close-up of her serene face. She apparently does not know that I wrote the scenario and the dialogues of *Caprices* . . .

. . . Reserved, sheltered by her habit of silence, which is indifference rather than timidity, my wife is answering poor Gilles in words of one syllable. Dear Pilou, her silence is enough to discourage all attempts at politeness, even the most affectionate. Is it courtesy or affection that makes Gilles so interested in her? Whenever one feels like scolding Martine, her sweet, innocent smile suddenly beams forth as though it were a personal favor, and all grievances are forgotten . . .

"I heard you mention your children a while ago . . ."

> *. . . Just what I always say, one can never be too inquisitive . . .*
>
> *How right you are, I have always been very much of a . . .*

. . . Now she is not eavesdropping anymore; she seems interested; I have finally found a way . . .

". . . You know, Martine, I have a little boy, too . . ."

"Oh, yes, Nicolas. He is an adorable child. I saw him the other day when I went to visit Bénédicte . . ."

> *. . . I am also . . . Oh, no, not in the least . . .*
>
> *Anyway, she is not pretty enough to be stupid . . .*

"Isn't he a nice little boy?"

"A darling. He is between Jean-Paul and Rachel, isn't he?"

"I don't know . . . He is almost four . . ."

"A marvelous age!"

> *. . . It doesn't take him long, if you know what I mean . . .*

. . . How happy and gentle Gilles seems when he is talking about his son! What an amazing capacity to love there is in us, a surging, stammering, flood of affection, like nothing else in the world . . .

"Of course, Martine, even though I know very well that all parents . . ."

"Yes, it makes no difference. I have the same unreasonable conviction . . ."

". . . that my little boy is the most beautiful child that ever lived . . . and . . ."

> *. . . I agree, but somehow he seemed less . . .*
>
> *That, my dear, is simply because he doesn't show his horns in the evening.*
>
> *I was just thinking . . .*

"Their contented expressions . . ."

"The warmth of their little smiles . . ."

> *. . . Nothing goes on here, but life goes on . . .*
>
> *Did you make that up yourself?*
>
> *You are getting sarcastic . . .*
>
> *Touchy as ever, but you are charming, Bertrand . . .*

"When they are babies, yes. But after they grow up . . ."

"The same indescribable joy, always . . ."

. . . Now Gigi, please . . .

*Well, you can't try to tell me
that Léontine does anything for
nothing . . .*

"Inexpressible happiness."

. . . A perfection that would be out of this world if we
were not constantly frustrated, made to suffer for this
bliss that is so fleetingly given . . .

*Just like Edwige, yes, your aunt
Edwige . . .*

"When they are four, you can still fondle them sometimes."

"But I always will, Martine. I couldn't bear to stop . . ."

"You will have to, though. The time comes . . ."

"Just to hold our son gives us both such a feeling of
stability, of fulfillment . . ."

"It is the same with my little girl . . ."

". . . When I lift him from the ground, it is as though I
were carrying the exact measure of love in the palm of my
hand . . ."

*. . . After freezing all winter, I
need a hot summer, believe
me . . .*

*But Brittany, what about Brit-
tany . . .*

. . . Could Bertrand talk about his children with such marvelous understanding?

> *. . . Don't tell me about that*
> *. . .*
> *Then he said . . .*

". . . Yes, Gilles, I know exactly what you mean, the shape of their little bottoms, the trust in their little faces . . ."

. . . Luckily no one can hear us. How absurd it would sound, to someone who did not share these feelings, to hear bottoms and faces mentioned in the same breath, and in this order. Such things are hard to put into words . . .

> *. . . Painful but true . . .*
> *Absolutely. Believe me! . . . I*
> *was about to tell you . . .*

". . . How lovely it is to able to talk like this, Gilles. Only someone with small children can understand."

"To have a child is to be lifted into an entirely *different* level of human experience. A secret shared only by parents . . ."

"Our secret, Gilles . . ."

> *. . . all kinds of gadgets. Things*
> *with . . .*

"Maybe for a woman it is different. But I remember, when I was a bachelor, looking on parents as a distinct and frightening species, always ranting about their kids. Well, now I understand what they are saying even before they say it, and the simple reason is that I am one of them. I have been initiated into their secret society and the result is that I can now enjoy the conversation of some women whom I used to think were dreadful bores . . ."

"Thanks a lot! . . . Oh, I was just joking. You are perfectly right, those tedious children . . ."

"And fatuous parents . . ."

> . . . I find her just chaaarming.
> Well, my dear, all the better . . .
> And she said to me . . . So I
> said to her, "But my dear girl . . ."
> So finally she . . .
> Lucien Guitry (whom you
> never hear about anymore) used
> to say that he had the face of an
> old cab-horse . . .

". . . That is also the reason, Martine, why there is suddenly such a distance between you and me and the men and the women at this table who haven't any children (no matter how close they are to us in other ways). Just look at them, listen to them, all those strange creatures who haven't felt this incredible happiness. Another world, isn't it?"

". . . Bertrand, you are a man of tomorrow. You belong to the future. *An age is coming when the poles will become demagnetized; it will be the age of the fish . . .*"

128

"Why thank you, Gigi! I hope I can return the compliment someday. Did you make that up?"

"No, it's a quotation. Odon de Horvath . . ."

"Never heard of him . . ."

"You should have, believe me. He is one of your colleagues, a central European novelist. Hungarian, I think. He was killed in a storm just before the war, in front of the Marigny theater. A chestnut tree, uprooted by the wind!"

. . . An unnecessary death. But why is Eugénie giving Bertrand such a hard time? . . .

". . . Eugénie has a daughter."

"That's right. A daughter who has children of her own. It must be terrible to marry off one's daughter! Luckily ours is a boy!"

"Don't say that. Someday you will have to have a little girl. It is something entirely different . . ."

> . . . *No! Not him! I can't believe it . . . Although of course . . .*
>
> *You can't imagine how stupid he is . . .*
>
> *And after I had told him again and again: "All you have to do is . . ."*
>
> *Gigi, you are divine, simply divine!*

. . . Martine goes on talking and talking about her Rachel, and I am no more listening to her than I am to any of the other conversations. But I like this new intimacy between us. A sudden crack in her indifference. Indifference is not quite the word. Mistrust is more like it. When we danced together that night we experienced a different kind of intimacy, just as close, and so compelling that Martine, feeling the danger and knowing perhaps that she was more threatened by it than I, was on the defensive tonight, making herself as passive and neutral as possible . . .

"Gilles, you are not listening. I want you to understand. Everyday I am more grateful for the joy of having a little girl."

. . . No, I am not listening to you. Nor did you listen to what I was saying. The only advantage of this kind of conversation is that being among parents, one can talk without restraint about this very personal subject . . .

". . . Oh, but I *am* listening to you. The joys you are describing are familiar to me. I once experienced them—please don't laugh—in a dream."

"In a dream?"

>   *. . . But no! Wait a minute! If*
>   *you can believe it . . . And then*
>   *. . . Yes, my dear! every word! . . .*

"It was a long time ago. Long before I married Bénédicte. In my dream I had a daughter. A daughter. When I saw her, in the dream, an overpowering and undreamt-of force was released within me: paternal love. When I woke there was nothing left, and my unborn child was once again only an abstract idea in which I did not really believe.

So I have lived the miracle that you are talking about, before it ever took place. I also seem to remember that it was
more than a premonition of fatherly affection; it was not
just any child, but the daughter who has not yet been born
to me . . ."

"And who will be, someday . . ."

"You are right; it must be wonderful to have a little
girl . . ."

"Wonderful . . ."

. . . Last night, as I thought of Jean-Paul and Rachel, I
experienced love in its purest form. In the silent, empty
darkness everything extraneous was distilled, until they
alone, with their little faces, and their small, precious
bodies, filled my consciousness, existing not only as images
but as real, tangible presences, weightless and yet extraordinarily heavy . . .

> . . . But I'm telling you! It's the
> gospel truth!
>
> You must realize that when he
> defends the minor writers of the
> past it is only because he knows
> that he himself is one of them
> and hopes that some Jean-Claude
> Debrêt of the future will do the
> same for him . . .

. . . The uncanny feeling that possessed me this morning,
that distracted me from the preparations for our dinner,
was the presence of my two children, existing within me

as a single and indivisible whole. It was not just that I was thinking about them; both my mind and my body were pre-occupied by them, pre-occupied in the most literal, even physical sense of the word. My thoughts were not about them; they *were* my thoughts. And now, thanks to Gilles Bellecroix and his dream, I realize that every night, as I lie sleeping, Jean-Paul and Rachel take possession of me and I love them without identifying them or thinking of them as separate from myself. The overflow of emotion which I feel twenty times a day, everytime I hug Rachel, is love. Gilles is scratching his right ear and looking at me, with a tender expression . . .

"All the same, aren't they impossible sometimes!"

"Especially Nicolas, you have no idea!"

"You have only one. And neither you nor Bénédicte takes care of him. Mine are with me every minute of the day. But they are such a joy, if you only knew!

"But I do, Martine. You know I understand . . ."

. . . Sometimes the three of us find ourselves thrust together in the warmth of a single love. The nest. The archetypal family. The same primordial love that has existed through all the ages and for all the species. Sometimes I hold him in my arms and dance with him, holding his little face next to mine. Have I ever experienced such fulfillment? I, who have never been able to dance *cheek to cheek* with a woman? Except for Martine, my God, I had forgotten, with Martine who is right here, looking at me with an odd expression, not thinking about her children anymore, I imagine, but as to what she could . . . I wouldn't dare . . .

". . . I don't believe it! I was there, Gigi, and you told me . . ."

"I don't care what I told you! I know for certain that . . ."

"Very well, I'll take your word for it . . ."

"But we are all like that, you should be the first to admit that . . ."

"Gigi! if you please . . ."

"Don't worry about what the likes of us say, Roland. Underneath, you know, we are all . . ."

. . . Together we formed a little island of love, indestructible—but which someday will be destroyed. Yesterday evening, with the three of us squeezed into that armchair, like birds in a nest, I felt a realization of the concrete existence of our little family, of its weight, density, and location in space. Love is a fearful word, but it is the right word. Nicolas' round face, his light, curly hair, his very pink cheeks, his whole roly-poly being, I could admire them all day long if the miracle did not evaporate so quickly under my greedy stare. To allow this miracle to repeat itself, I have to go away, I have to leave my little boy's room and not come back until later. It is love, but of the purest variety—the love that makes me turn on the light at night to look at Bénédicte as she sleeps. Even this cannot last. Once again, I have to relinquish her face to the darkness . . .

. . . I remember Jean-Paul also in the very vivid and yet sharply abstracted form which he assumed in a dream I had not long ago. He was there before me, but somehow more real than in everyday life; each of his features was

highlighted and their symmetry was glorified. So handsome, so perfect. It was the very image of my love. The
next morning, when I compared his own face to the face in
the dream, the imaginary Jean-Paul was the more real of
the two. His appearance in the flesh was less forcefully
realized. It was fainter, less well delineated, of a vague,
less tangible substance . . .

. . . Martine definitely made a mistake. Her nose, though
a bit too long, was necessary to the overall balance of her
face, a face that was more human, and not so helpless as
now. Poor Pilou, she tries in vain to look aloof and inaccessible; all her defenses fell when her nose was shortened.
Gilles Bellecroix would never have dared to court her so
assiduously before. Her face is naked, offered to the world
like an open city. It embarrasses me to look at it. Bertrand
doesn't give a damn, I'm sure. Did he ever love her? . . .

. . . Poor Gigi is getting old and nasty. I wonder why
people still ask her out. Odon de Horvath, indeed! One
can't know everything. Since it is impossible to duplicate
in writing the object that is being described, and since one
literary convention is as valid as another, I prefer a com-
promise between beauty and accuracy . . .

. . . By covering the railing of my terrace with a blanket
maybe I could lie there without any clothes on but I
would have to make sure no one could see me from the
eighth floor what a shame I didn't think of it sooner but
with everything else I have to worry about next year will
be time enough and the spot on that curtain in the parlor
I forgot to call the cleaners again . . .

. . . Like Mallarmé, I don't enjoy books which have no
architecture. But I also agree with him that real books

134

have neither a beginning nor an end: *The most they can do is to make believe . . .*

. . . Yesterday Bénédicte said to me that I nuzzled my son like a mother animal her young. She is quite right, really. I love his smell. I rub my head against his, one pelt against another. This is a primary instinct, one of the basic joys of all creatures. How wonderful to feel within myself the same forces which quicken the animals of the forest. The smell of melted candles, Christmas when I was a child . . .

. . . Last night, I remember, my dream was even more precise. I woke up twice, and each time I thought I was hugging my little girl. Knowing her to be so close, in the next room in fact, I was not really disillusioned and besides, the tranquil happiness of this imaginary embrace remained with me in a most extraordinary fashion. Twice in the night, I lay there with my arms enfolding a child whose warmth, weight, and exact shape I believed I could feel . . .

. . . Paulo, that waiter with whom I lived for six months, may have made a prostitute of me while I was still not of age (several years short of it, in fact, but even so I was able to get out of Canada and into France) but if he did, it was only because that was what I wanted. After that redhead from Saint-Hyacinthe, with his clammy hands, no man could disgust me. My indifference was stronger than my disgust. And Paulo, I certainly fixed him. He got his, all right . . .

. . . The Novel. A *romance*, originally in the Romance dialects (sometimes in verse). Then, a work in which imaginary characters pursue marvelous adventures. That kind of novel will always find readers to justify its existence. But those readers are not the ones we are writing for anymore . . .

. . . In the same compartment, facing me, a gentleman is reading a newspaper. A little-known weekly, a kind of confidential gazette. In the trains, in the subways, everywhere, there are two kinds of newspapers, for two kinds of human beings, with news from two parallel worlds which have no common denominator. Those who belong to one look over the shoulder of the other, or figure out the words upside-down, trying to glean a few bits of information about the world next to them, from which they are excluded. That lucky man who is calmly reading about a society that knows no wars, no accidents, in which, (and why not?) old age does not even exist. To be able to join him, and leave the unhappy race of mortals. But no one escapes death. This is one of those hopeless daydreams which one elaborates in haste, before the mind, knowing that it will not be allowed to enjoy itself thus for very long, intervenes with the cool wand of common sense. Futile thoughts, worthwhile only for poets. I am a poet, though no one else knows it. I must tell them what a poetic trip I had coming back from Marseilles this afternoon . . .

". . . I've just come back from Marseilles . . ."

"By the way, Gigi, have you seen that cousin of yours from Marseilles?"

"Yes, I saw her at the launching of one of the new Spring Line ships . . ."

"Sydney Spring, I met him once at the Bötrels . . ."

"Oh, yes . . . A freighter with a few very pretty cabins . . ."

"A fine man. Immensely rich, too . . ."

"I would have loved to cross the Atlantic on a ship like that . . ."

"He certainly is. I also heard that he owns, or is about to acquire, a majority of shares in . . ."

"I would too. Ocean voyages are no fun without a little luxury . . ."

". . . a majority of shares in Handburger and Co. You can imagine . . ."

"I agree completely; just because one is traveling is no reason . . ."

"He has two daughters, I believe . . ."

"So they say. Actually, I once booked passage on the Spring Line, when I went to New York . . ."

"To New York. Well! They won't have any trouble finding husbands!"

"Armande, would you please help Madame Prieur off with her sweater. And please hurry . . . can't you see . . ."

. . . This is turning into a regular *strip-tease*. How many jackets and sweaters can one person wear? Huffing and puffing like an old . . . The two of them are chattering back and forth in front of me, which is embarrassing, for I can't think of anything to say. They are under the impression that they are talking about the same thing, but there is no real give-and-take. Eugénie Prieur and Marie-Ange Vasgne are each pursuing their own thoughts and only paying the barest minimum of attention to what the other is saying. A typical example of the simultaneous monologues which people call conversation . . .

"You can't imagine how beautiful New York is."

"Unfortunately I've never been there. I hope to go very soon, though. I would also like to go to Greece."

"I have an old, old friend in New York . . ."

"Did you know that Pauline Cruchet is living in Athens now? She would make things very easy for me."

"You can't imagine how hospitable she was when I was there . . ."

"Who?"

"Louise Branche, my friend who lives in New York."

"The notary's wife?"

"No, his daughter. The one who . . . She once told me that her mother . . . Well, as I said to her at the time, my dear girl, grandmothers are not what they used to be . . ."

. . . An imaginary child enfolded in my arms . . .

". . . Of course, if one could see the ruins in their original state . . ."

. . . Here we go; she is about give us her talk on the Parthenon. There is no stopping her now . . .

"Take the Parthenon, for example . . ."

. . . Just as I thought . . .

". . . with its columns painted in all the colors of the rainbow. It couldn't have been in very good taste, especially in the daytime . . ."

"When I was in Athens in 1937 . . ."

. . . Gilles Bellecroix looks surprised I shouldn't have mentioned the date he never would have thought that in 1937 I was old enough to take a trip to Greece . . .

". . . there was no paint left on the ruins . . ."

. . . Painful silence. Everyone is pretending not to have heard Mrs. Osborn. What a dimwit . . .

"I'm so glad you reminded me! I forgot to go see my notary, Maître Pincevault. He lives in Montmartre . . ."

"Montmartre isn't what it used to be. People just don't know how to have a good time anymore . . ."

"My first husband and I lived outside of Paris, you know, but we came to town very often . . ."

. . . Usually I came here without him, to the *rue de L'Abbaye* . . .

"I never knew your first husband . . ."

"I still see him once in a while. He lives on the avenue Matignon, near Rémon . . ."

"Do you have your clothes made by Rémon?"

. . . Here is a subject that may capture their interest, and spare us more of this disjointed conversation in which topics are grazing each other like billiard balls, then shooting off at oblique angles, perpetuating the momentum in a series of transitory encounters. The fragmentary nature of this conversation does not seem to bother any of the participants, each of whom is talking to himself in a kind of vacuum, without the least interest in what any of the others are saying.

. . . When you come to think of it, the books we are writing are not novels in the true sense of the word. Only the name stays the same, for publishers do not dare change the habits of the public. Even collections of short stories, and memoirs, are called novels. The so-called *new fiction* whose theories some of us are proclaiming, has nothing *fictional* about it, in the usual sense of the word. In this kind of writing the imagination is much less important than observation. Inventiveness is suspect. Our goals are closer to those of painters than of novelists. What we are trying to do is to show the surface of the world (and its inner reflections) exactly as it appears to us . . .

. . . There was a time, however, Marietta, when you almost succumbed to disaster. Those were very difficult days, when I lived near the Saint Denis Gate and Paulo tried to put me to work. I still didn't know my way around. Who would ever recognize me now in that snapshot? I keep it to remind me of a period of my existence which I cannot overlook because it helped make me what I am. It shows me and a girl-friend, standing in front of a badly-painted ocean . . .

. . . I took it all rather casually at first. It was such a relief to get rid of that shapeless little creature inside of me . . .

. . . Semi-precious stones, mounted in gold on my cufflinks. Opaque little cones which look dull against my very-white shirt. They fascinate me. When I am being dressed for my funeral, Martine will undoubtedly put them (have them put) on me, because I like them better than any of the others and wear them all the time. The thought is unbearable. How can I live with these little objects which will be sealed into my coffin, next to my decomposing body? What if I threw them in the Seine? Tomorrow. Better still, tonight, after our guests have gone and before I go to bed. I can say that I am going out for a little air. Then you will be destroyed, or at least you will disappear before I do, you evil little objects . . .

. . . When does one lose one's first memories? I must ask Bertrand. Jean-Paul is four and he still remembers walks he took and visits we made when he was a baby.

From time to time I will have to encourage him to dip back into his past, and help him to garner its treasures before it is too late. Find the diary I kept when I was a young girl and begin to write in it again. All the little incidents which he will forget would be priceless to him when he grows up. They will be his keys to a long-lost, distant past . . .

. . . No matter how low I sank, even in Montreal where I really hit the bottom of the barrel, I was still saved. I had escaped my village and the priest and all the rest of them. And my real chance, the beginning of my rise to success, was not far off. I owe it to a young man in dinner clothes who came to the brothel late in the evening and chose me, on a night when I was feeling blue. He did not give me any advice, unlike most of those well-meaning, salacious gentlemen. But his elegance, his manners, suddenly made we wish I were worthy of a lover like him. If only I could have seen Paulo's face, the morning I disappeared! The name of that customer who was so quiet and well-bred was René. I never saw him again, but I remember his name . . .

"No matter what they say, Rémon is still . . ."

"He just made me one of those little . . ."

"A suit?"

"No, one of those coat-dresses. Lined entirely with . . ."

"What kind of a neckline? A cowl?"

"Tailored, with flat lapels. You know. Three-quarter sleeves without cuffs. Large appliquéed pockets."

"It must be sensational!"

"A full skirt?"

"No, straight. Smooth in front, with darts over the . . ."

"And no belt. Oh, I can see it exactly . . ."

"It must be rav . . ."

"The hemline . . ."

"Sen . . ."

"Would you let me copy it?"

"Why of course . . . of course I would."

. . . For Lucienne Osborn everything is "sensational." But I am still one of them. I am condemned to be one of them all my life. Even if I were not so weak, how could I ever eliminate all traces of my birth and education? . . .

. . . I can see that Marie-Ange is furious in spite of her polite acquiescence. If Martine only knew that I was the one who bought Marie-Ange the dress she is talking about. The prettiest dress from the best collection in Paris. And expensive besides, very expensive . . .

. . . Bertrand looks annoyed. I could give him some better reasons to be angry. This dress which he begrudges me in his miserly fashion, was also offered to me by old Breillac. Rémon and I made a pretty good deal. He billed both of them and only filled one order. I get reimbursed for the other. Net profit from this last negotiation, not including the dress: two hundred thousand francs. But that old Ujanie has some crust. Why doesn't she go to Rémon herself? She can afford it . . ."

"I have a very pretty new dress. But Bertrand did not want me to wear it tonight . . ."

"What do you mean? I wasn't the one . . ."

"Now you know I asked you which dress you liked better . . ."

"So you did . . . And I said I liked this one better, but if you liked the other, you should have said so. Sometimes I just don't understand you . . ."

"Oh you don't? I am the one who . . ."

"Well, really. This is silly, your dress is ravishing . . ."

"Ravishing!"

"And let's not keep on boring everyone with it . . ."

. . . Even though Martine and I have been married for a long time, I have never learned to speak her language. She has a way of using words to disguise her thought instead of expressing it . . .

"I almost forgot the most important detail of all. (Without it the dress would be nothing.) There is a pleat at the bottom of each seam, an inverted pleat . . ."

"Those are very practical . . ."

"As long as they are well . . ."

"Some women really have no sense of . . ."

"The other day I ran into Lilian Decker . . ."

"Oh, Lilian. Now there is someone . . ."

"Her mother, old Madame Creux, is even worse. I must tell you a story about her. My sister and I once . . . But you know the kind of . . ."

"I met her a week ago at the Picquarts. She didn't . . ."

"They sold their villa in . . ."

"To buy one in Cannes. Will you go to . . ."

"There, or to Megève. It depends upon . . ."

"Yes, it's the same for us . . ."

. . . Here we are again, in the throes of a conversation which might be called telescopic because of the way the parts emerge one from the other, so rapidly that they never reach their full length. Bertrand seems more exasperated than anyone by this idiotic palaver. He is, after all, of a higher mentality . . .

. . . One cannot accept what she is saying at face value; one has to interpret. Pilou appears to express herself very clearly, but this is an illusion; each of her words is a cryptic reference, which I am able to decipher only because I am now familiar with some of her reactions, her tastes, fears, hates and desires. Like this business about the dress, so obvious, really, but I am caught every time . . .

"Were you at the Picquarts?"

"Wasn't it splendid!"

"There hasn't been a party like it for a long time . . ."

"Did you know that I wasn't even invited? Incredible, believe me! After all I've done for Simone . . ."

. . . Sometimes it is clear that she is only trying to convince herself, and not too successfully at that, when she exclaims *believe me!* in a voice that is far from confident . . .

. . . A burst of anger from Gigi, furious that she was forgotten. Like the wicked old witch who wasn't invited. Now that's rather amusing. Worth trying on my charming dinner partner . . .

". . . Just listen to her! She is like the wicked old witch who wasn't invited."

"Who?"

"Shh. Madame Prieur."

"Oh."

. . . What a moron, that Marie-Ange Vasgne. Now I can't try it on anyone else. Oh, well, Raymond Frôlet will appreciate it . . .

144

. . . The plates, which have just been changed, gleam in the candlelight. Lovely polished silver. In front of me, dark green stalagmites rise into peaks at the edges of dwindling candles. The affectation in these women's voices —"pure sixteenth century." Each voice has its own individual variations, but they are all in the same key, that of a whole *milieu* in which the little girls talk just the way their mothers do. Men, with only a few exceptions, those of the Quai D'Orsay for instance, and of course the *gay boys* who by some mishap are not represented here tonight, men do not adopt such a stunted, studied manner of speaking. I must admit that these inflections, whose outdated preciosity bears witness to a dying civilization, rather appeal to me. It would be hard to capture such voices in a film without falling into the stereotype of so-called "drawing-room" speech, which bears no more resemblance to the original than do the caricatured accents of vaudeville . . .

. . . Bourgeois. Worthy of further study, but no more than the members of the most primitive society. Bourgeois Parisians at mid-century, the last century of their existence. Customs, behavior, and habitat: all very instructive to an outside observer. But how can one acquire the proper perspective? I am one of them myself, more lucid, to be sure, but only because I am the youngest, not because I am any more emancipated . . .

"Did you go to the . . . on Wednesday . . ."

"Oh please! Don't even remind me of that deadly evening!"

"There wasn't a thing to eat, not a crumb."

"Let's be fair. They did serve drinks."

"Yes, champagne, but no Scotch. After all!"

"Of course, it's not as if she hadn't warned us. I saw her at the Peyresaubes the week before and she told me then, in her tone of make-believe vulgarity (which I must say is a bit too realistic, just too, too casual if you know what I mean,) 'Don't say I didn't warn you,' she said, 'There won't be a thing to eat when you come on Wednesday.'"

"That takes a lot of gall . . ."

"Imagine! When someone asks me for dinner two weeks in advance, and warns me that 'it is just going to be potluck,' I could simply boil, I'm telling you!"

"They haven't much money, you know."

"Well, she has her clothes made by Rémon. And a television producer, you know how much they make every time you turn on the set . . ."

"Besides, my dear, it is the poor who entertain most lavishly."

"The poor are never as poor as they are made out to be . . ."

"Haven't you ever eaten with working people? It's fantastic! They pile one plate on top of the other until you don't know what to do with yourself."

"Even savages have a sense of hospitality. To ask your friends over without offering them Scotch is an insult."

"Well, I took what you might call Scotch leave. Or as Marie-Ange would say, 'I ran for dear life.'"

"Do they really say that in Canada? How divine."

"It applies beautifully to the Benoît's party, don't you think?"

. . . Christian name or surname, I wonder? This is the

first time that they have called these friends, whom they are discussing with such exquisite kindness, by name. They understand each other perfectly. The secret rites of the clan. I haven't yet been initiated. And I am proud of it . . .

. . . Fortunately we had Scotch to offer them tonight. Pilou was right; one has to watch every detail when entertaining people like this. I don't think I will dare invite them again . . .

"Saccharine sweet . . ."

"Yes, but underneath she is as crafty as they come . . ."

. . . Wandering, exhausted, from street to street, from one part of town to the next. Vain expectations which always end in disappointment. Millions and millions of francs, of no use to me whatsoever . . .

. . . Roland Soulaires is smiling into the blue, showing off his very red gums. His head is tilted to one side, as though he were sad about something. I wonder what it could be . . .

"Will you be going tomorrow?"

"Tomorrow?"

"Yes, you know, the open house she has on Sundays . . ."

"Oh, of course! Why not? If I have nothing better to do . . ."

. . . Tomorrow morning there is very little on TV only Mass oh well it will be better than nothing three-quarter sleeves without cuffs what an odd thing to entertain Saturday night just like poor people I mean people who work during the week of course Bertrand runs a newspaper not a very interesting one either it has no horoscope . . .

"Is tomorrow Sunday? Already? Last Sunday seems like

yesterday. It is simply frightening the way time flies. At my age, you can't imagine how frightening it is."

. . . Poor Gigi, this time she wasn't satisfied just to express her silent thoughts with an occasional sad, croaking sigh. She spoke. Of death. After a certain age, everyone is to be pitied. I feel great compassion for mankind! And for myself, betrayed by the one I love. If I didn't have the children . . .

. . . Once, at the end of an evening like this one, at my mother-in-law's, or rather at the house of my future mother-in-law, not a dinner as I remember, but one of those *soirées* of which Irene was so fond, and which was swarming with women all as artificial as these, I suddenly felt an absurd desire for a more honest kind of illusion, and fled to make love with a very ordinary kind of girl, one I still sometimes see around the Saint-Denis gate . . .

"You just reminded me that the Visseaux asked me down to Cannes and I forgot to regret their invitation. But it would have been worse if I had forgotten to pay my respects to Pierre's mother."

"Pierre Blingaux? I wrote a letter."

"So did I."

"I went to sign in the book."

. . . The death of someone's mother, of a friend's mother, means nothing more than the necessity to sign one's name, to write a letter or to make some other polite gesture. Then death has no more claims. Or so they believe. Utterly lacking in imagination and compassion. And yet we all like Pierre. We like to think that we are fond of him. This is the moment for a little anecdote . . .

"... That reminds me of the story of my aunt Viget who once, when she was unable to attend a funeral at the moment, wrote a letter of condolence and added: 'I would also like to express the sympathy of my friends, Madame such-and-such and Madame so-and-so, who asked me to put their names in the book ...'"

... I made them laugh. Their laughter gives me pleasure. What hams we all are. But death, what about death? A very slight dislocation in the time sequence could make all funerals more bearable: another family could stand in for the bereaved in the funeral procession, bored but not unhappy, and the family of the deceased could postpone their ceremony for a later and less painful occasion. This is the kind of absurd idea which one's mind comes up with, left to its own devices, like mine most of this afternoon on the train ...

"I went. Because of Bertha. I really had no choice ... I've known her and Pierre for so long. They were both in tears. All the Blingaux are like that. They weep at every funeral like a bunch of schoolgirls ..."

... And yet Gigi isn't really stupid, or nasty, either ...

... How's everything down there?—as Raymond Frôlet would say. They can't go any lower than this ...

"Pierre Blingaux is an odd fellow. Do you know who his best friend is? A Negro."

"But Negroes can be very nice ... They are not like those dirty Arabs ..."

... I was wrong; the descent continues ...

... Poor Marie-Ange. Always on the alert, but unable to keep up a front on all sides. She was on guard about

Negroes, but not about North Africans. She has just admitted to certain hostilities and prejudices that she would have hidden, had she been better briefed . . .

"And the Jews? Have you ever noticed where their ears are located? And how they are attached to their heads?"

"You know, you have something there. Everyone always talks about their noses . . ."

. . . That is the limit. If what we are eating weren't so delicious, I would vomit . . .

. . . But I can't throw *everything* away, and die naked, without a suit or underclothes or anything. They will dress me. They will select a shirt and a coat and trousers from among those which I usually wear to dine out, to enjoy myself, and be happy. Who knows, I may be buried in the blue suit and the shirt that I have on this evening. Why do I worry about a pair of cufflinks? The trouble is, that even after living with Martine for a long time, one can never be certain of anything with her. Sometimes she actually means what she says. Not very often, of course, but just enough to keep me constantly perplexed. If black meant white and yes meant no in her vocabulary, that would be easy, but her language is capable of every shade and fluctuation of meaning and the fact that she uses the same words as everyone else makes her secret code all the more puzzling . . .

. . . Here comes the *plat de résistance*. At last. Exquisite little gamebirds. The waiters in the dining car this morning, in spite of their perspiring faces, their obvious weariness, and the worn texture of their humble, none-too-clean uniforms, did not seem mortal like the customers whom they were serving with such languid efficiency. It was as though they were not embarked, as we are, on the voyage of existence. Instead they appeared to be part of an endless relay, going and coming in clockwork precision, linking the world of the living with the world of the dead. Robots, somehow exempt from man's fate. Servants of the transitory mortal race, whose fatal destiny they do not share . . .

. . . If she feels like going out with me, she doesn't say so, that would be entirely too simple. In fact, she doesn't even answer in the affirmative if, sensing her wishes, I ask her to join me. I have to form a conjecture as to her true desires, according to certain faint variations in her expression of indifference or in her outright refusal; and woe unto me if I should make a mistake, like this evening, about the dress. She does not forgive my mistakes, on the contrary, she sulks for the rest of the day, and ends up by telling me, in the evening, "You know how much I would have loved to go out with you today . . ." I was wrong; it is important. The cloth will be destroyed, will disintegrate with my body, but these hard little stones will endure . . .

. . . What a relief to be done with that funeral at least they didn't linger on it will I be seen from the eighth floor I wonder the warmth on my skin and all through my body a man looking at my naked breasts what a bore not to be able to eat these little birds but my figure comes first just a taste couldn't hurt me with an inverted pleat it must be quite pretty how I wish it were time to see Léon-Pierre and feel him against me within me . . .

. . . It didn't take me any time at all to learn the ropes. I was soon at work, for myself, in the ski lodges and beach

151

hotels. Naturally I got the worst piece. Well at least not the best. I try to be polite and look what I get. I should have taken a piece of breast, like Ujanie. But it doesn't matter since I must eat as little as possible. Even a little is too much. If Roland Soulaires doesn't respond to that last look, it's back to Longe with you, my poor Marietta . . .

. . . She is flirting with me, imagine, (a woman as pretty as she is). One more girl flirting with me, like all the others who would have given themselves, at least for my money if they (at first sight) (although a bit stout) (a very little bit too stout) did not love me for my own sake. What an opportunity! To think that if I were like other men (I am like other men) (just slightly shy) this very evening, maybe . . . (*Would God* that I were like other men!) . . .

. . . Yes, we have learned from the impressionists, as well as the cubists and the abstract expressionists. Paintings once told stories. Now our stories are like paintings. Armande, my secret extravagance as a married man. Arousing and gratifying two of my oldest and most passionate cravings, because she is a chambermaid, and because her breasts are bare beneath the low neckline of her dress. Pleasures which are all the more rarified, in that I have never enjoyed them simultaneously. Tonight, however, she should have dressed properly. Of course Martine never notices anything. Which is as it should be . . .

. . . Eugénie is stuffing herself as though she had not eaten for several days and were fortifying herself for another siege of fasting. Since she is much in demand in the most "fashionable" circles, she often dines with friends whose cuisine is as good as ours. Why isn't she afraid of getting fat? An uncomfortable tingling, and burning sensation. Is that to be expected? I will telephone Doctor Chanuz the first thing in the morning . . .

"What about the film you made, Gilles, not the new one, you must tell us about that later on, but the last one?"

. . . Later on, when John Osborn arrives. He can talk about it then, to try to get me a part in it . . ."

"*Breathless*? Unless they change the title . . ."

"But *Breathless* is such a pretty title . . ."

. . . You, my dear lady, are the one who is short of breath . . .

"Yes, but they wanted to call it *The Saint of Pigalle*, if you can imagine . . ."

"How horrible, you mustn't let them . . ."

"Well it is not exactly up to . . ."

"How are you coming along with . . ."

"They haven't started shooting yet, but my work is all done. In the old days, I used to try to influence the director, to save my scenario. But now I know better. Without the screen writers, without us, they are helpless, impotent."

. . . Impotent. This word which applies to me, which I try to pass over as quickly as possible when my eye chances upon it, but which always lures my attention backwards to linger over its fascinating (excruciating) syllables; impotence, impotent (I don't feel safe until I have finally read far enough to be able to turn the page). But when it strikes my ear or enters my mind by itself, there is no escape possible. (No cheating.) *Impotent*, impotent, *impotent*, impotent, *impotent*, impotent. The engine of a car on the embankment, missing on one cylinder, thrums to the rhythm of my misery . . .

. . . An odd duck. It bothers me when my charms do not succeed. Ujanie is the only one who would be able to look too far into my past. Without, of course, having any idea of how I started. By some coincidence she was at Pyla the year I won that beauty contest, in 1956. How did she remember, and what conclusions did she draw? I can't tell, but of course she has told everyone in Paris. Though it hasn't hurt me as much as I feared. One, two, three, four, five, six. One, two, three, four, five, six . . .

"They can't begin to work, or even pretend to, without the inspiration we provide, but they distort our work beyond recognition. Except for Servingson, the directors with whom I have worked have been nothing but pretentious schoolboys . . ."

. . . Naturally. The only decent film he ever wrote was directed by the great Servingson. But the superior quality of *Royal Happiness* cannot be credited to Gilles Bellecroix. The original novel was not even written by him . . .

"Well, I refuse to work in collaboration with them; I deliver the goods and let them do what they please. If John were here he could tell you what troublemakers directors are . . ."

. . . I went a little too far that time; I betrayed the fraternity of creative artists to ally myself with the producers. I shouldn't . . .

. . . Out on the brilliant waters of the bay, a motor launch is purring, tranquil as the houseboats of Arcachon, and I glimpse the young breasts of an auburn-haired girl . . .

154

. . . Impotent, impotent, impotent, impotent, impotent, impotent. And yet I was cured. I am cured. But it is the same all over again. Like my nails, which I can never stop biting . . .

. . . He is looking at his stubby, nail-bitten fingers and fat thumbs. My own hands are so long and graceful and well-manicured. You were never made for the lower Saint-Lawrence, Marietta . . .

. . . I mustn't dunk my bread in the gravy, no matter how much I would like to. But why shouldn't I, since M. Soulaires is doing just that with his plump, ill-kempt hands. Anything goes with these people. They have a right to do as they please, and I don't . . .

. . . What if I gave them to Jérôme Aygulf? An excellent idea . . .

"Bertrand, what *are* you doing?"

"What has come over you?"

"Just a sudden whim, that's all . . . I would like this nice young man to have a remembrance . . ."

"Oh no, sir, I couldn't . . . You are too kind . . . Really I couldn't . . ."

"Yes, yes. Take them. You will be doing me a great favor. No, right now, this minute . . ."

"You are so *amusing*, Bertrand . . ."

"So spontaneous . . ."

. . . He has tied one on, no, here they don't say that, he is drunk, but it's not possible . . .

"That's his special charm . . ."

. . . A brief but deliberate plunge into his nostril, from which his fingers emerge, rolling an invisible little pellet, before they reach out to accept the cufflinks which Bertrand Carnéjoux is handing to him right in front of me, without even apologizing . . .

. . . What a shame. I always wanted those cufflinks of Bertrand's; they would be so pretty with a shirtwaist. Had I known that he didn't care for them, I would have asked him to give them to me. But he should have known . . .

". . . You should have known, Bertrand . . ."

"Known what?"

"Just known, that's all."

. . . What should I have known? Not what she said, nor what she may have suggested, or hinted, but the inmost thoughts that lay behind her words. I give up. Pilou could at least save her secret code to use when we are alone . . .

. . . A rapid exchange of words between Martine and her husband intended only for their ears like invisible arrows what a pretty thought I am really amazing tailored collar and no belt I should try to remember the heavy shadows and wavering beams of light the reflections of Madame Prieur's wine glass as she raises it to her lips eventually I will have to get new linoleum for the kitchen . . .

"I'm not saying this just because he is my husband; but everything he does, every last gesture, no matter how puzzling, is so elegant . . ."

. . . Dear Martine, how embarrassing it is when she talks about me like this. I enjoy her praise, but in front of all these people it makes me uncomfortable. I can't help beaming, which is ridiculous. All compliments have this physical effect on me, in spite of my attempts to react differently. All I can manage is a look of false modesty which is all the more absurd. My conscience, which parts company with the poor, vain joys of my flesh, makes my discomfort even worse. Only her love, which is as blind as it is passionate, could give my young wife such a reassuring opinion of me . . .

. . . Of course, men are useful; one could not do without them, and not only because of the money they give you. But the thing is to be able to choose them when and where one likes, not always to be chosen by them, anytime, anywhere . . .

. . . At last. My turn to be served. These little guinea hens look so good. Armande's perfume, mingled with their aroma, makes me feel slightly sick. Now I've done it: a spot. Why do things like this always happen to me? Hide it as best I can. This piece of bread will do the trick . . .

"Armande . . . Armande, now that you are through with the guinea hens . . . Would you go up to my room, please, and look in the green box on my bedside table . . . In there you will find some cufflinks . . . The gold ones that I never wear . . . Would you bring them to me . . . Thank you . . ."

. . . I did not hear what little Martine said so quickly to Bertrand a minute or two ago, but it sounded unpleasant. This silly public demonstration is probably her way of asking his forgiveness . . .

"I never get tired of looking at him. Go ahead and laugh, but it is true, I could look and look . . ."

. . . If only she would keep quiet! A blush could hardly be more humiliating. Instead of changing color, my face is swollen by a spontaneous inner combustion that my otherwise impassive features make all the more obvious.

"Swollen with pride" is a very accurate expression. Folk-wisdom often prefigures the discoveries of physiology. I am indeed swollen with pride, like La Fontaine's frog—which is perhaps where the words originated in the first place, not from popular intuition . . .

. . . Bertrand beams as he listens to the extravagant compliments which his young wife is lavishing upon him, in the innocence of her love, just as if they were alone. Why doesn't he sense how ridiculous this is, at his age? He is vanity personified. Am I as oblivious of reality when Bénédicte tells me that I am handsome? Of course I *am* rather good-looking . . .

. . . Why did Bertrand give me this present? My devotion makes me feel self-effacing, as though I wanted to recreate myself in his image, to be like him in every detail, in every thought, every feeling, to desire what he desires, to be exactly what he is, trying to anticipate his every reaction and correcting myself if my own personality distracts me, even for a moment. Why do I feel like this? Because he is well-known, because he has just given me a present and because we are all swayed, at one time or another, by power and prestige. As I wait for whatever reward is to follow the gift of these cufflinks (a job on his newspaper, a trip at his expense, a look, one kind look from him) I offer myself in friendship, as a girl would offer herself in love. Although I am not moving a muscle, this prostitution is physical as well as spiritual, for both my body and my mind are surrendered, are dissolved in his, into an intimate though impalpable union. Is it also because Bertrand Carnéjoux is so charming? Am I perhaps equally susceptible to masculine beauty? Yes I am, for my fondest wish is for him to accept me, to crush and overpower me and take over all my responsibilities, even my physical being. Because he is seductive. Because he is rich. Because he has written a book. Because even Raymond Frôlet . . .

. . . Disgust? Indifference? Sometimes I think so. The nausea which I feel when men desire me, following me in the streets. It is not that I would like to be ugly. (I wonder if this fat customer next to me, with the shrill voice and twitching face, really doesn't think I am pretty.) But I wish my beauty were neuter, or else invisible whenever I don't feel like using it. If men could just admire me at a distance, without wanting to contaminate me. Not just with their hands or their naked bodies, but with their eyes, their eyes which leave one helpless and defiled. How degrading it is to be a woman. But also how delightful, how delicious! Just thinking about these things, which disgusted me a minute ago, gives me a sensual thrill, makes me feel all warm and moist and open. I need a man, Bertrand would do, or that dark, handsome one over there, yes, him, but I shouldn't, not after all I have been through to get where I am, not a butler, even if he is attractive. Besides, tonight I can't. Why not the young man next to me? He is rather cute, with his red hair, even if he does still pick his nose. But no, only important men are worthy of me. Roland Soulaires, first of all; I really must get him over with . . .

. . . It would be utterly impossible for me to be unfaithful to Bertrand. It is a matter of cleanliness, in the literal and the figurative sense of the word, especially the literal sense, for it would be a rather dirty thing to do. I am really being faithful to myself, more than to him, when I avoid the contact of other bodies. I, who have never known any body but his, which sometimes strikes me as silly and unfair. It is not as if other men did not attract me, like Gilles Bellecroix, for example, with his bold blue eyes, though he is already so old, almost fifty. But I tolerate this desire, perhaps even enjoy it, only on the condition that it stays unsatisfied. And how little it means to me in comparison to the excruciating love that I feel for my children! If not excruciating, then at least consuming. I hold them close, I press their soft little cheeks against my own and I hardly know what to do with the hopeless excess of feeling that rises within me. What boundless love there is in my heart for these little bits of spirit and flesh . . .

. . . Happiness was brought to me by a marriage which I did not deserve, but which I recognized as my salvation. It began as a series of renunciations. First, and most painful of all: the sacrifice of every future *possibility*. My destiny was laid out before me. No more wild expectations. I now know that these dreams—which still haunt poor Bertrand though he, too, is married—were illusions, and that life, in at least one respect, has surpassed them all. In any case, nothing could have saved me from the onslaught of time. Despair—the despair that I might have felt, that I did feel—would have been even less bearable without a wife and child. I shudder when I think how it was only by accident that I met Bénédicte. How easy it would have been to have missed out on this one last chance of my life, which, I must always remember, was neither deserved, nor earned, nor even offered, but had to be thrust upon me when I did not reach out for it, thinking that it was impossible, that I was too old for such a young girl . . .

"Thank you Armande . . ."

. . . Try to put these cufflinks on without being observed. The parallel and complementary worlds of thought and sensation. Yes, one could sum up my goal in just such words. In my next experiment in fiction I will again attempt to confront these two elements, but this time I will explain what I am trying to do, in order to save time, to be understood . . .

. . . No, not Raymond Frôlet, with a big mug like his. Not really. And yet, sometimes, in his sad expression, in his weary voice, in his sudden exuberance when I least expect it, there is something, how can I describe it, some vague quality; well, the fact is that Raymond Frôlet is my friend, my only friend. I like him . . .

. . . The hard part is over with. Old Breillac is a good investment; he earns his living and mine too. Bertrand? A passing fancy. Take it or leave it. And besides, he is no longer the grubby journalist he was before his marriage; he is rich, and I did get him to buy me that dress, in spite of how stingy he is. Maybe this is the breast, after all. But it is still not as nice and meaty as the piece Ujanie got . . .

. . . I remember sitting with my back to the Van Gogh, where Gilles is tonight, one evening back in the days when the Belleuses lived in this apartment. I was thirty years younger; I was under forty. I was becoming fashionable. And yet I was not happy, no I was not happy. Have

I ever been happy? I felt old even then, when I was still so young. That gold necklace which Lucienne Osborn is wearing would be pretty against her tan décolleté if her skin were not so dry, withered by too much sun and the first wrinkles of old age . . .

. . . Marie-Ange is not only not saying anything, but it is apparent that she is not thinking either; she *is* the delicious taste of the guinea hen, just as Condillac's statue *was* the delicious fragrance of the rose. We still have a great deal to learn from the philosophers of the past, even from those of their theories which were considered the most far-fetched . . .

. . . A gap. Not just in the conversation. No one is thinking; only the blind clockwork machinery of digestion is at work within the ruddy darkness of the body . . .

. . . Everyone's mind is elsewhere, each in a different place. Mine is in Valromé, where are the others? . . .

. . . *These guinea-hen are marvelous* . . .

". . . We are eating the flesh of a young girl . . ."

"Roland, how ghastly! Please don't . . ."

"This younger generation is impossible, believe me! . . ."

. . . That is the limit! Roland Soulaires, who is over forty, a member of the younger generation! Of course the way old Eugénie said it was like a refrain, in a falsely casual tone of voice, out of habit, coy affectation, and courtesy, like a card player deliberately cheating in favor of his partner, in order to benefit from the same deceitful stratagem. Good Lord! The spot on my right is enormous. Try once more to hide it with a piece of bread. Poor old decrepit imbeciles, who are you trying to fool? Bertrand, though, old as he is, attracts me in a strange, rather disturbing fashion. Well, as Raymond Frôlet said, in the subway the other day: "Make way for youth." I must tell them about this and then say afterwards, in a blasé tone of voice: "Nice story, don't you think?" I like Raymond; it's as simple as that. Not so simple . . .

"Roland! Roland, please . . ."

. . . Roland, and Manon whom I loved and the other girls in the convent, rescued, thanks to her, from oblivion. At first I never knew whom I admired the most, that other Manon or Catherine. And little Noémie, young Ernest's unforgettable love. She tried to make herself ugly before she came to church, to hide her beauty, which was impossible. Ulysses, who taught at the Berlitz school in Trieste. Chasseboeuf, a ruin among ruins, who expired in fury at the thought of Napoleon. Another wing. (Wing?) The beautiful Noiseuse. Who and what am I thinking about? My mind is wandering. If it was not the beautiful Fosseuse, then who was it? . . .

"Do you mean to say that you have forgotten the Greek myth? About the weeping sisters of Meleager who were turned into guinea fowl and whose tears became white markings on their feathers?"

"I must confess . . ."

. . . I haven't ever heard of it, either. I know nothing; I never know anything. You still have a lot to learn, Marietta . . .

. . . So they were guinea-hens. But each taste is subtle and deceiving. Their peculiar flavor interferes with (without actually destroying) the pleasure which my palate anticipates. Knowing that they are such a delicacy, I am determined to enjoy them, in spite of the disappointment which comes with each new mouthful . . .

"Meleager the poet?"

"No, no. The hero of the Argonaut's expedition. The fatal brand. You remember."

. . . What brand? Roland Soulaires has a way of drawing attention to one's ignorance. I thought that I was going to exonerate my wife, poor Pilou, who had confessed her lack of knowledge and was looking at me with such admiration . . .

. . . Even if Geneviève hadn't told me about the night she made the mistake of spending with you, and which I happened to remember, I would have guessed what a faint-hearted lover you are, just by watching your behavior with Marie-Ange. Your shyness, your stationary flight, as though you were creeping back a little further into your shell every time she made an advance. And the only reason you have begun to talk so much is to avoid that look in her eyes . . .

. . . Afraid of the body of Lisbeth, clothed, but so near my own. And once more I lose heart and draw away. The misery of being impotent, when one is fifteen, then twenty, then twenty-five and cannot rely upon one's own body (nor leave it to accomplish the task on its own.) And now I am forty-three. (Forty-three!) *I am sick to death* of my feeble, ineffective self . . .

. . . You will be mine, Roland Soulaires. No matter what reasons you have for turning me down, you will still be mine. Sooner or later they all come around. Here I am with my first mink (a bit too dark but there will be others) and my first diamond (not big enough but Osborn or Soulaires, Osborn *and* Soulaires will be able to do better.) Oh, she will go far, that little Marietta from Longe . . .

. . . The train left Valence. I looked at a mountain, not a very high one, but far in the distance. My imagination wandered. I thought to myself: "What if Bénédicte were seriously ill, and to save her I had to reach the top of that mountain in an hour and a half, even if I lost my own life in the attempt." And, in my imagination, I was already running, looking for shortcuts, climbing so hard that I was out of breath. As I watched for landmarks at the edge of a pine forest, beside a vineyard,—as though I actually had to make this expedition, and not go astray, to bring it off at all costs—I asked myself, "Would I do this for my son?" And then, without deliberating for more than a minute, I was off again, this time to save Nicolas. I finally succeeded in putting an end to this absurd, imaginary race and realized that my egotism had been miraculously felled. And through the breach flowed humanity, pure, splendid, irreplaceable humanity. The humanity from which my exhausting quest for personal happiness had separated me for so long . . .

. . . A chance for me to shine a ploy of John's he knows them all . . .

". . . What is it that guinea hens say? . . ."

"I wasn't aware that they ever said anything . . ."

"No, the sound they make, what is it called?"

"Don't ask me, my dear lady. Do they cluck?"

"Or cackle?"

"No they gabble . . ."

"Well, if that isn't the shtrangesht thing . . . believe me! . . ."

. . . Strangest, Madame, the strangest. She is pretty far gone . . .

. . . I had the same feeling of being lost in time last July, when I spent the month at Valromé with my wife and the children. The oriole was singing the way it always sang, or almost, for each bird, or each generation of birds, Marie-Plum, has its own variation on the call peculiar to that species. The same turtle-dove was there. In the garden I picked a bachelor's button whose scent made the distant summers so vividly present that I wondered how I could ever have forgotten it, how I could forget it ever again; but it was soon gone; fragrances do not stay in the memory. There were a few new trees in the garden, but it looked the same. The most precious ones, I mean those which were there when I was a child, were still standing: the tulip tree, the cedars, the redwood (recently struck by lightning and dying, branch by branch) the poplar over the gate (so much taller), the elm at the edge of the meadow and, last but not least, the birch in whose branches we played The Swiss Family Robinson. René Duclost, who was severed by so many tragedies from his childhood, tells me that I do not know how lucky I am to be able to return and live in the very places where I spent my earliest years. But my own presence there is a fraud. The place is identical but I am different. Or, if I am the same as I have always been, then I find myself captured, alive, in the snare of the present moment. Each second that makes me what I am also cuts me off from the past, which itself, even when it was the present, was never more than a self-annihilating sequence of minutes, in motionless progression towards death . . .

"No one ever knows these things. Take geese . . ."

"Geese cackle . . ."

"Yes but wild geese honk. Ducks quack, cocks crow, (gobblers gobble!) and owls . . ."

"Owls hoot . . ."

"They ululate . . ."

. . . We all know about quacking and cackling. Ululation is from the Latin *ululare*, to howl, like a dog or a wolf, or to hoot, like an owl. Even natural histories are rather vague about some of these words, many of which are of imitative origin. I could be brilliant, too, if I dared. Good Heavens! I ate the piece of bread which covered that spot of gravy. Maybe my place-card would do. Not quite big enough. I must ask Armande for another piece of bread . . .

"You are perfectly incredible, my dear, really marvelous . . ."

"Oh, but I haven't finished yet! Finches warble, lambs bleat, crickets chirp, storks clatter, and jays . . . jays screech . . ."

. . . They are astounded I was sure they would be when John does this number an American well you can imagine everyone is even more surprised he knows it all by heart and picks the most unlikely moments I'm so glad that he isn't here tonight so that I can have my little moment of glory not just one cricket but a million of them chirp when Léon-Pierre and I make beautiful music at three in the afternoon . . .

. . . That Mrs. Osborn isn't as dumb as I would have

thought. Chirping crickets. Such fine words. None of us know our own language. We know that donkeys bray and the cat miaows. And I know that I am impotent . . .

. . . In a few days, after the first frost, the gulls will return and my son and I will watch them again through the windows in this room. Their melancholy cries, the white shell of their graceful bodies, marked only by the black porthole of an eye, lend a nautical atmosphere to our island. Jean-Paul and I watch them for hours, fascinated as they wheel above the swift yellow current, gliding slowly down-wind, and then rising upwards in effortless flight . . .

. . . As I was shaving earlier this evening, I heard the hoarse voices of crows, a sound that always surprises me when I hear it in Paris, which is not very often, only once in a while to the north of the Ile Saint-Louis, where our bathroom looks out. Incongruous rustic croaking, which superimposes images of lonely woods and hazy meadows over the outlines of town houses. Tall winter trees sprouting mistletoe and encircled by flights of thrushes, and endless fields with only the sound of a tractor and the black flight of the crows in the distance. Or a village belfry echoing their cries. Crows also nest in cathedrals, but there are very few of them left in Paris, only on our island where, it is said, they settled after the Bastille was razed and they were evicted from their secular habitat. Their croaking is of another age, and makes one's mind wander more in time than in space. The country landscapes disappear but Paris remains, Paris of days gone by, which is preserved not only in a few old stones but in these living witnesses to the past, these birds whom one hardly ever sees, but who can still be heard. It is as though they were not crows at all, but ghosts. Ghostly birds. Souls transformed into birds . . .

. . . Oh shadowy little room speckled with sunshine he does not coax me he forces me brutalizes me while outside the crickets chirp in the frantic rhythms of my desire then suddenly stop except for one who keeps up a dull throbbing like my still breathless watchful body suddenly a silence a brief respite and then the shrill madness of the crickets and my ecstasy rise together in one immense dizzy crescendo until the whole world . . .

"The only thing I know, dear Mrs. Osborn, is that crows croak."

"Well, you are wrong, Bertrand. Frogs croak. Crows caw."

. . . Bread, I must have a piece of bread. I can't ask the butler. And the maid refuses to look in my direction. And everyone is looking with scorn at the gravy which I so clumsily spilled on this beautiful table cloth . . .

"I never finished telling you about Meleager. He was the one who could live only as long as a certain brand kept burning. His mother, who knew of the prophecy, put out the brand and hid it. A nice story, don't you think?"

"Why didn't the child die?"

"I love fairy tales!"

"What a funny girl you are, Martine . . ."

"What about crocodiles, what do they do?"

"Fairies are of Celtic origin. They used to be found in our part of the world . . ."

"Oh, they are still found!"

"My dear, your imagination will be the death of you."

. . . Mrs. Osborn is hoping that someone will answer her question but no one is interested in hearing more of her glossary of animal sounds. Her foggy eyes are looking from one face to another, but in vain. They are like puddles of grey water in which nothing is reflected . . .

. . . Armande, standing motionless between the tall pedestals, her face emerging from the shadows, sees me at last. Her eyes take on a hard, inquisitive expression, looking right through me, invading me, taking possession of me with calm audacity. But mademoiselle, there has been some mistake, all I wanted was a piece of bread; I was only asking for bread. But my body silently cried out a different message, and your body understood. At last! What a relief. Now I can't see her anymore. I tore myself away from her mesmerizing stare which had captured me so suddenly, and looked in the other direction, cowardly as ever. When will I have the courage not to hide, to be aggressive, like Raymond Frôlet, Roland Soulaires, Gilles Bellecroix and Bertrand Carnéjoux who is so handsome, so seductive, even though he is already so old? How lucky Pilou is. She never would have been as happy with me, even if I had been faithful to her. Why does this man have such an effect on me? Why do I suddenly feel such a need for affection, for affection which only he, not Pilou, not even Pilou, could give me . . .

. . . Between the cables of the Eiffel tower, other crows are cawing, far away, high in the vertiginous shaft, so far and so high that their sad voices can hardly be heard, crows of the future, no longer of the past. Vertical flames, blue underneath, curving into pointed, sometimes slightly vibrating tips. The candles, which have melted unevenly, have a notched crevice near the wick through which the wax, white-hot near the fire, pours forth and gradually solidifies into hard green stalactites . . .

. . . And I feel my warm belly against my thighs. (The agony of the impotent male: all women are his and he cannot take one of them. He enters into each amorous adventure with an air of intrepid authority, deceiving everyone but himself, for he alone knows exactly how far he can go.) . . .

"I was just reading, in the *Notebooks* of Gerard Manley Hopkins . . ."

. . . Hopkins? Who could that be? I haven't the slightest notion. Ashamed of my ignorance . . .

. . . Hopkins John would know that's his department anything American . . .

. . . Hopkins? Who's he?

. . . Hopkins?

. . . Hoping to impress us all, Roland thinks up these obscure names and trumpets them forth in his shrill voice . . .

. . . Doesn't ring a bell here, as Raymond Frôlet would say . . .

. . . I met someone named Hopkins at the Peagsons, but it couldn't be the same one . . .

"Well, really . . . Hasn't a single one of you ever heard of Gerard Manley Hopkins?"

. . . Roland Soulaires couldn't be more delighted, and is prolonging the effect of his little coup by staring at each one of us with a roguish expression, or what he believes to be roguish, for his puffy face is actually contorted by a hideous twitch . . .

"When you come to think of it, the legend is perfectly consistent. Meleager's mother knew that her son would be safe as long as the brand was not consumed. That is why she extinguished it herself. When Meleager died, if I remember correctly, it was because one of his enemies, I forget which one, threw the brand into a bonfire . . ."

. . . With slow deliberation, accentuating each syllable, Eugénie follows her steady train of thought, even though we are now talking about something else, and continues an argument which the rest of us had abandoned five minutes ago . . .

. . . If I had ever settled, even once, for the piece on my plate, I would have been lost. It is only because I was never satisfied, and always wanted bigger and better servings, that I made my way along the hard road leading from Longe to Paris and from my mother's miserable hovel to the Ritz where I live now. No man has ever been able to resist the irresistible spark and velvety temptations of my eyes, or the fake but utterly convincing look of admiration which I can focus on whomever I please—just you wait, Roland Soulaires, you'll see—and which is now directed at Gilles Bellecroix who seems rather uneasy, and Bertrand, who, for once, is stealthily admiring my beauty. I must confess that the guinea hen is delicious, and I took too much, after all . . .

. . . Marie-Ange is a very pretty girl. What understanding there is in her eyes! But I am more disturbed than flattered

172

by the persistent way she looks at me. I have lost all hope in that direction. Only recently . . . but that is finished, finished . . . I yielded temporarily to the temptation, not of making love, of course, the thought has no appeal to me, only of tasting a few of my former pleasures: tender overtures, discreet caresses. But even before I attempted anything I found myself stiff and frozen, holding an astonished girl at arm's length. What is the meaning of such paralysis, such a numbing of my emotions? Bénédicte's presence is all the more compelling when she is not there . . .

. . . A look both of annoyance and distress came over Martine's face when she caught me staring at Marie-Ange. I am just guilty enough not to be innocent. I mean that there are too many reasons why I should not bring this girl to my wife's attention, why I should not hazard an indiscreet glance. If I was looking at her, it was only a mechanical reaction; she is sitting almost opposite me, to my right, and my eyes took in anything that happened to be in front of them. Their focus shifted soon afterwards, but not before Martine had caught me, *in flagrante delicto* . . .

. . . Marie-Ange is an impossible creature. It is all too easy to imagine why Bertrand insisted on inviting her. No one could miss the way she is flirting with Roland and Gilles, although, I must say, she doesn't seem to be getting anywhere. Men are certainly blind and Bertrand is worse than the rest of them, to be taken in by the wiles of such an obvious vamp . . .

. . . I am spreading myself too thin. But it doesn't matter; I will get down to serious business with John Osborn after dinner. Watch out, Martine is looking at me. Nice celery. How I miss the hashed-brown potatoes that we used to have at home. Bertrand is also looking at me. It's about time. He is more indifferent than he is cautious. I do not even exist for him when I am not in bed. As the red-haired young man on my right said before dinner, I don't remember what we were talking about: "It's all the same to me, but I couldn't be more annoyed". . .

. . . Poor Marie-Ange, she is like an insect being observed through a glass window. With her charms in constant rotation, from Roland to Gilles, from Gilles to Bertrand and back again, and her agitated little mind wandering from one subject to the next, she reminds me of a juggler who is spinning a dozen plates at a time and rushing to catch each one with a swift touch of his finger just as it is about to fall . . .

. . . Martine's rapid glances, the only kind of reproach I ever receive from her, and only because she is not able to hide them. Quiet, vague, and discreet. But although she says nothing, her thoughts . . .

. . . Marie-Ange, who is no longer paying any attention to you, is too young to understand you, to take you, or even to let herself be taken, without scaring you. If you would only look in my direction, if you found me even the slightest bit attractive (but you think that I am too old, of course) I would know how to help you get over your shyness. I helped so many boys like you, in the days when I was young and slim. But why starve all one's life? I will never get my figure back, never. You are not so cocky now, Roland Soulaires. You are not thinking about your Hopkins any more; we are still waiting to be enlightened about him. Your mouth and nose are twitching and your whole face is contorted . . .

. . . To *what serves mortal beauty*, yes, what use is your mortal beauty, Roland, *dangerous; does set dancing blood.* Danger, yes there is danger. But my blood is not dancing any more, Gerard Manley Hopkins, it is congealing, my blood is congealing . . .

. . . If only to be polite I had to take a little piece of guinea hen and now look how much I have eaten how terrible as a punishment I will not have any breakfast tomorrow you can insist all you like poor Zig I am determined I wish I knew my new horoscope those in the morning papers are worthless I will have to wait for the early edition of *France-Soir* but that is not for ages . . .

"And there were many other Meleagers, believe me! One of Alexander's generals . . . A king of Macedonia . . ."

. . . The subterranean course of Eugénie's thought has again bored its way to the surface. No one has been thinking about Meleager for a long time now, but it makes no difference to her; she is always quite happy to have her endless stories interrupted with a multitude of digressions, although tonight she will have a more difficult time because we are all silently agreed not to give her any encouragement, after those dreadful historical monologues at the beginning of dinner. If we were polite and let her have her way, the evening would really be too boring for words . . .

"Well, Roland, what about that Hopkins fellow?"

"Haven't you ever heard of him, Gigi? I thought you

knew everything. It is a fact, however, that almost no one knows about this English poet. According to Julian Green, even André Gide had not heard his name . . ."

. . . Green. What was it that I just read about him? Something quite important. But Gide, there is that key phrase in *Oedipe*, which I remember by heart. Alas, it won't be any more help to me here tonight than the poems of Gerard Manley Hopkins, many of which I also memorized. *For you must understand, my children, that each of us, as an adolescent, is confronted early in the game by a monster who presents us with a riddle which makes it impossible to go any further. And, my dear ones, even though the question asked by this sphinx is different for each of us* . . .

. . . When I tell myself again and again that I have not been understood and that in twenty years time I will be, I am playing a cunning game in which I am only half-duped. Instead of this partial lucidity I must awaken myself not only to the possibility of a temporary lack of success, but if, as it now appears, I have nothing to say and no talent to say it with, of complete and unmitigated failure . . .

. . . Even the most innocuous dance seems wicked to me, simply because I am holding another woman in my arms and touching a forbidden body. In the early years of my marriage I still allowed myself such pleasures, but I have now given them up completely. With one exception: that dance with Martine. But of course Bénédicte was there. If she hadn't been, would I have succumbed to that overpowering spell which I still remember with surprise? Marie-Ange Vasgne quite obviously has her eye on me . . .

*. . . you must realize that, in every case, the answer is
the same; yes, the answer to all these varied questions is
one and the same; and this answer is: Man.* For me, one
might say that the answer is always: Woman. How funny.
I can hardly help laughing!. . .

. . . Well! If André Gide . . . Tomorrow I will find out
about him. Gide, Geede. Green, Greener, Greenest. That
old bag taught me something, anyway . . .

"I certainly enjoyed *Brighton Rock.*"

"Why yes. Graham Greene is also a good writer . . ."

. . . Our host is very polite. He corrects Marie-Ange's mistake gently and casually, without drawing attention to what
he is doing. I know lots of things I could say about Graham
Greene. Light and frivolous things, like the rest of this
idiotic conversation. But do I dare try again? Pilou mustn't
get the idea that I am talking too much . . .

". . . I know a funny story about Graham Greene."

. . . What was it that I read by, or about Julian Green,
that seemed so important to me? . . .

"What were you going to say about fairies?"

. . . Odd. The delight I felt dancing with Martine. For
I am now indifferent to all women, except my wife, no matter how desirable they once appeared to me. A faithfulness
that began as a deliberate effort. But I have not had to
issue orders to my body for a long time now. Instead, my
body has become a law unto itself, warding off the inevitable treachery of my mind, which, at the approach
of old age, reminds me that it will soon be too late to
experience the dizzy ecstasy which the delicately dilated
nostrils, and wide, butterfly eyes of Marie-Ange Vasgne

177

promise with such brazen audacity. But this kind of girl leaves me cold. I meet too many of them in producers' offices . . .

"Parrots. What do parrots do? You will be surprised . . ."

"Oh yes, Roland, do tell us a fairy-tale."

. . . Oh well a parrot just talks but you are not interested any more see if I care it was only to amuse you but I would much rather sit quietly and think about my own troubles they are complicated enough as it is . . .

"Once upon a time a young ploughman, who had forgotten to take his lunch to the fields with him and was too far from his cottage to go back again, made a wish, as he plowed his field near a forest that was inhabited by fairies . . . Don't laugh . . . I am half-Scotch, on my mother's side . . ."

. . . Caithness was her maiden name and he would like more people in Paris to know this. I wonder if he cultivates that nasal voice of his, thinking it sounds aristocratic . . .

"He made a wish that the fairies would invite him to eat with them. Then he went on ploughing, without thinking any more about it. When he reached the edge of his field he turned around and followed his horse back again until he found himself at the edge of the same forest where he had made his foolhardy wish."

. . . That poor ploughman is going to find himself bamboozled . . .

. . . A train passing through the middle of a small forest could take away all the mystery. But not this afternoon, when I was in a train (only a few hours ago, near the end of my trip home from Marseilles). Even though I was looking at the only part of the forest that was disturbed by human hands, the mystery was still there. Pine trees with their ruddy bark glowing in the rays of the setting sun. Such peace, such complete solitude. Intimations of a perfection that is beyond our understanding, that is both exhilarating and frustrating. The ultimate in earthly glory. What more could one ask? But too perfect happiness brings pain. I feel a kind of anguish, a new disenchantment, knowing that never again will I experience the miracle of this afternoon, in that particular spot in the world, with those trees and no others, in that unique light, at the same hour of the same day. It is too bad that Bénédicte is not with me. Bénédicte is not here. I am day-dreaming. Around me are the sounds and smells of a Parisian dining room, of a dinner party . . .

. . . As I nibble this piece of bread, my teeth clamp down on the tips of my fingers, as though my body had taken it upon itself to bring my errant mind back to earth. Marie-Louise saved me. (She did not do a very good job of it . . .) Fearing that any attempts to try out my prowess on other women might endanger my new-found peace of mind, I am content to rest upon the laurels of this single daring (lucky?) adventure. The pellet which I have been nervously rolling between my fingers has joined the others which I will discover, stale and blackened, in my pocket when I undress tonight . . .

"What did he find, a full-course dinner?"

"How did you guess? But because he knew (like the rest of you) that if one eats anything prepared by the fairies, one is under their spell from that day forward, he did not touch this delectable repast . . ."

"So he outwitted them?"

"No one ever outwits the fairies. The moment he turned around he discovered that one of his eyes was missing, and saw it on the plate which the fairies had set out for him . . ."

"Like a fried egg . . ."

"Jérôme, how revolting!"

. . . My teeth feel as strange as that other part of my body which they are nibbling, my fingers. As the pressure which they are exerting becomes sharper, this slight pain reintegrates my body into the self of flesh, blood, and bone from which I had escaped, like a balloon into the sky, airborn but tethered, held captive by this corporeal being which the gentle bite of my teeth forced me to remember . . .

. . . M. Bellecroix is more interested in Martine than he is in me. I am not making a sou tonight. Of course I can't, I keep forgetting. It's annoying, because for once I feel like making love. Would Martine ever be unfaithful to Bertrand? That would be funny. Sitting still, with the least possible words or gestures, and a superb economy of means, Gilles Bellecroix is trying to seduce her. Elegant, poised, confident in his technique. How ludicrous men seem as soon as you escape their charm. One, two, three, four, five . . .

. . . There is nothing like being tan all over smooth and brown on the breasts the buttocks the top of one's thighs as well as everywhere else the groan of the elevator I need to make love is it because Marie-Ange keeps looking at my bosom or my neck maybe only my neck I don't know why it is but pretty girls always make me feel like making love and the continual grinding of the elevator I once had Bertrand but not the right way it is too bad and that odd chambermaid I can't see her right now but I can feel her across the room not very pretty I thought but with a young and desirable body . . .

. . . It is not the age of my partner on the left which bothers me, for she is still lovely, and I have always felt attracted by slightly overripe beauty. But it is a pity that she is so sunburned. A tan on women over forty only accentuates the years which they are trying to hide. The most feminine thing about Lucienne Osborn, her exacerbated and yet bridled sexuality, is physically distasteful to me. But I am not sure just what I feel. I would have to make love to her to find out. That shouldn't be too hard, and yet she seems to draw back when I come near her . . .

. . . With such thick walls, how is it that one can hear the elevator? We are so lucky to live in this lovely old town house, thanks to Mummy who paid for everything. When we were married, Bertrand was not yet editor-in-chief of *Ring*. Even now we would never be able to afford such a beautiful apartment. Our kitchen looks out into a labyrinth of walls and courtyards. It is the casbah of the Ile Saint-Louis, all shadows and mouldy poverty, quite another world from our sunny embankment with its ancient, luxurious mansions. Tangible evidence of the injustice in our society. A symbol of greater evils which I am unable to disregard and of which I have been ashamed ever since Jérôme forced me to open my eyes. It is so easy to forget the darkness that lies behind us, to look towards the light, to try to make a happy life for Bertrand though he doesn't do the same for me. It is not my fault, I never asked for this and besides, why is it any of Jérôme's business? He will be rich, too . . .

. . . When I am sure of myself (with Marie-Louise) the gestures of love are smooth and harmonious, falling into a single, unbroken pattern in the overall unity of the act itself. Quite the opposite is my lonely, gratuitous exaltation when I wake at night. Then I am amazed at my vain potency. The real prow of a phantom ship. Mine, and yet so overpowering that I belong to it. Making me feel, for the moment, master of the only thing in the world which matters to me, women, not one of whom, even Marie-Ange, would be able to resist such overpowering strength. Not even the beautiful Armande, standing so straight and still, in front of the Louis XV console, her breasts outlined against the thin black bodice of her dress. Armande, whom everyone here is staring at, consciously or unconsciously . . .

. . . A woman who is not intelligent enough to dominate her femininity. If Martine wishes to please me, she uses her sweet thoughtfulness, not her body. But her body is there. In its own place . . . foremost . . .

. . . Instead of idle talk, the way to rescue a man from his inhibitions is with gentleness and silence. Elizabeth knew this. But whether it was through laziness, fatigue, or hostility, she could not hide her tense expectancy. I would be so quiet and calm on our first night together that you would forget all your anxiety. I would be yours before you had time to think about yourself. The conversation has stopped. Everyone is alone with his thoughts . . .

. . . All my manly vigor has disappeared and I am again

reduced to size. Ashamed of the vain spectacle of my pride. How feeble are the reasons (the reason) for my outburst of confidence. Not bad, that console. Pure rococo. (Such delicate volutes.) Armande is not bad either, standing there, motionless, in front of that ravishing little piece of furniture. (Ravishing little piece.) . . .

. . . The sauce that is left on my plate, next to the well-picked bones which I have made into a little pile to one side, has congealed into strange images of men and animals. Botticelli once declared that a paint-soaked sponge thrown at the wall would create landscapes and trees. And Piero di Cosimo discovered scenes of equestrian warfare and other fantastic images on a hospital wall which had been spat upon by the sick. The cracked and peeling wall that Leonardo offered to his students as an inexhaustible source of creativity could just as well have been a dirty plate. Hamlet watched a cloud as it became a camel, a weasel, and a whale. Max Ernst found his inspiration in the grooves and scratches of a wood floor. His technique of rubbings and Dali's "paranoiac-critical camembert of space and time" stemmed from similar observations. The surrealists and their objects of concrete irrationality. My plate is a canvas, on which the arabesques of sauce reveal a variety of creatures, some ghastly, some beautiful. Are they the phosphorescent letters of *desire* read by Andre Breton? . . .

. . . The *porte-cochère* clangs shut. Some boys and girls burst forth onto the embankment, calling to each other. Their laughter is very loud. In the coffin, next to my putrefying body, are these indestructible gold cufflinks. Doors are slamming. Two or three drivers are racing their engines. The harsh stripping of gears. Brakes screeching on the La

Tournelle bridge. All this noise is swallowed up by the night, but my obsession, absurd as it is, will remain with me until I make love with Armande later in the evening . . .

. . . This is the last time that he will be invited. The flute-like quality of her voice as she talks to herself about the pictures in her little books, full of soothing onomatopoeia, with *mummy* and *daddy* emerging so lovingly here and there, the only recognizable syllables. Her sweet, desperate, little voice. But what is Armande doing, standing there like a statue in the flickering candlelight? An odd girl. Not very pretty. But not stupid, either. Forks sounding against plates. Again silence. Bertrand's mind is somewhere else, as usual. I cannot seem to think of a single word with which to disperse the sudden spell that has come over my dinner party. And it began so well . . .

. . . After so many years without any new victories, I am again beginning to be haunted (did the obsession ever leave me?) by the terror and the loneliness of the days when I had never had a woman (not even a whore). I remain uncertain as to whether this complex instrument of blind, impersonal forces really belongs to me. Nor prayers nor threats have any effect on it, and I can only hope to catch it by trickery . . .

". . . Why am I laughing? Nothing, really. Only a ridiculous idea which came to me . . ."

. . . Laughter that would be forced, Marie-Ange, were we in bed together. In a first encounter, one can never be sure of one's own prowess. In other words, at the moment when it is most necessary to be in complete command . . .

"What are those two talking about over there?"

"Come on! Out with it. Tell us all!"

"Whatever do you mean? We are being very well-behaved in our little corner . . ."

"I'm not so sure, Marie-Ange, I'm not so sure . . ."

"I'm innocent, I tell you! Besides, M. Soulaires is the one . . ."

"I assure you that I have nothing more to say."

"It's the fairies!"

"They've cast a spell on us!"

"Well, it is time to break that spell, believe me!"

. . . There are no impotent men, Roland, take it from someone with long experience in such things: there are only awkward women. I may be exaggerating, but only slightly . . .

. . . I thought it was a chance encounter. But no. Marie-Ange deliberately put her foot out to meet mine. With a look of complete innocence as she caresses my ankle. It is too bad that I cannot take advantage of such good fortune, such an honor. (How can I pull my foot away without appearing to be afraid?) Certain of the most prominent companies must have suffered heavy losses. Some of them dropped rather significantly when the market opened this morning. Only a few points, and certainly only a temporary phenomenon, but worth keeping an eye on, especially the oil securities. Royal Dutch, for one, in which I have a sizable investment . . .

. . . His leg has finally stopped moving. It is next to mine. But I can feel that he is still embarrassed. Such shyness is amazing in someone of his age and standing. We will see what can be done to make him forget it, unless everything gets off to a quick start with John Osborn after dinner. In any case, nothing can happen or even be decided tonight. The discreet and yet deliberately alluring glances which I am sending, every once in a while, in the direction of Gilles Bellecroix, without seeming to be aware of what I am doing, are not registering. This certainly isn't my night. Our young hostess seems to interest him more than I do. But of course none of this is of the slightest importance; John Osborn is the only one who can get me a part in that movie. After dinner I will make up for lost time . . .

. . . Their power cannot unfold if they are under scrutiny. But only those who have complete confidence are not on guard. A vicious circle, in which certain physically sound men can be trapped for a lifetime. You there, Roland, obsessed by your inhibitions, pay no more attention to Marie-Ange Vasgne; come home with me tonight, to the Avenue Foch. Let yourself go and you will be cured . . .

. . . Contact finally broken with the girl next to me. Why is Gigi looking at me so eagerly? It makes me uncomfortable. In the eyes of the women whose desire is aroused by his desires, the impotent man appears as the epitome of manly vigor. But to be really a man he would have to possess their bodies, and of this he is incapable. Thus his despair. Years ago, before I was cured (I am cured) (am I cured?) I looked with awe and envy upon the most mediocre individuals, only because they were lovers, or fathers. Oh! To harbor death at the source of life! I once knew a boy who turned to homosexuality because of his impotence. In the eyes of others, in his own eyes, he preferred such love to no love at all, and partook of pleasures that disgusted

186

him, in which he had to grit his teeth and close his eyes, finding sexual freedom the moment he no longer felt desire . . .

"Roland, has it been a long time since you have seen Elizabeth? . . ."

. . . What has come over me? This is mad, mad . . .

. . . That name! But Gigi could not know. No one can know . . .

"Oh, ages . . . But what are they discussing over there? It sounds fascinating. Are you superstitious?"

"Of course! Every one is. Yes, we must listen . . ."

". . . Luck, you know. There is such a thing as luck . . ."

"If I didn't believe in it, I couldn't go on living!"

"Maybe you wouldn't be alive."

"That's right. I have always felt somehow protected. My horoscope tells me . . ."

"So does mine."

"Don't tell me, my dear lady, that you . . ."

"Why of course, I . . ."

. . . In *France-Soir* where anyone can see them it is immodest such intimate advice in a public place but one has to be able to read between the lines to be initiated of course I know a little yoga and besides I am very sensitive I have a feeling about such things the pipes are hammering the whole house is shaking I like their butler his shoes are English the toes are turned up ever so slightly . . .

. . . My nose feels like a block of wood but all the rest of me seems to be on fire. It must be the champagne. Yes. The champagne. No more for me tonight . . .

. . . Her femininity, of which Martine Carnéjoux is all too

self-conscious, and which she keeps under constant control, glows brightest when she tries hardest to extinguish it. Thus inhibited, her sexuality bursts forth inopportunely. Hence my confusion. Confronted by a body whose connivance has been transformed into false indifference, my own body is caught off guard, and does not know how to react . . .

. . . Each new experience throws doubt on my past successes. A woman who does not know me thinks (perhaps) that I am incapable of acting like a man. Since the fact that I have already had mistresses (two) means nothing to her until she herself becomes my mistress (two, one more than Amiel, two more than Nietzsche), I must bring her the very proof which she believes that I am unable to furnish. Such suspicions make it difficult (if not impossible) for me to relax, and my sexual organs remain dormant, having lost the confidence which I myself lack. Once I have taken possession of a woman, I never again feel any qualms with her, and can take her when and where I please. But with only two exceptions I have always hopelessly bungled the first encounter. Meanwhile I stroke the soft hair growing in my ear. And I feel an electric current passing from Marie-Ange's ankles to mine, even though I have pulled them away, a current which does not stimulate my legs so much as my most private parts, bombarding them with invisible rays . . .

"I can find out everything I want to know just by reading the lines in the palm of my hand . . ."

"It is better not to know. To hope . . ."

"To hope for what?"

"Death would be nothing if it were not for old age."

"Sickness, suffering . . ."

"Death . . ."

. . . Such disenchantment, all of a sudden. Ill-concealed desperation. No longer the phony excitement of the earlier conversations. That was only a superficial game, into which everyone was drawn by a contrived but impassioned momentum, and whose rules include occasional flashes of irony or suspended disbelief. Now a fleeting transposition has taken place, the words are suddenly identical with the real thoughts, and the speakers find themselves caught up in a conversation in which their very lives are at stake . . .

. . . But they are mad they are insane it is dangerous enough without them interfering some wood quickly and in front of me of all people living as I do at the mercy of my body without knowing when or how it will be threatened some day they will say Lucienne my dear you must take better care of yourself and I will know then that it is already too late . . .

. . . In the eight dark rooms of our minds the same horror film is being shown . . .

"There is no such thing as death."

"How can you say that . . . I mean really . . . Believe me!"

"Only a paradox. Boris Pasternak. And like all paradoxes . . ."

. . . How can I explain this to them? The fact that we have no faith does not mean that we no longer need to read edifying books—or books which are therapeutic, to be exact. On the contrary. The words in which a writer confronts his own experience of nothingness with a maximum of lucidity are precisely those that can be of comfort when our feeling of self is most vulnerable. Among all the meditations that have replaced the Christian effort to grapple with death, Pasternak's writings stand out for me, in their convincing and beautiful simplicity . . .

". . . It is difficult to sum up his thought. An old woman believes that she is about to die. She asks a medical student to reassure her: *You surely know something . . . Tell me the secrets you have learned . . . Comfort me . . .*"

. . . Jean Rostand, and other writers lucid in their despair, brought me peace of mind . . .

"And so?"

. . . I am not worried about anything I am happy and yet maybe without my knowing it I am already stricken with a fatal disease the same old fixation daily obsession that haunts every hour sometimes every minute of my day I thought I had finally gotten rid of it with the help of the champagne and now these thoughtless words these clumsy allusions have awakened the evil spirits that are always waiting to torture me . . .

. . . I thought, though I could not be sure, that I heard a clock strike. Probably the church of Saint-Louis en l'Isle. Or Notre-Dame. What time is it? Already ten o'clock. While dinner lasts, we are outside of time, saved from this plunge towards death or at least under the illusion that we are saved, which comes to the same thing. Not that I haven't thought about the passage of time quite often this evening. But for some unknown reason I have the wild notion that I have succeeded at least temporarily in reach-

190

ing solid ground, that I am standing there, breathless, rescued by the ephemeral banks of a tiny island: this table that
is so well set and well served . . .

". . . He said, Pasternak that is, that the resurrection of
the body is an absurd idea . . ."

"What does he know about it?"

"You asked me what Pasternak said to that old woman,
and I am only explaining, or at least trying to explain . . ."

"If I had the slightest doubt about being resurrected . . .
Why it would be unbearable . . ."

"Luckily we are not all like that Russian; I, for one, have
a passionate belief in God . . ."

"And in the life to come. So do I . . ."

. . . So much the better for you, ladies. There is no point
in even trying to explain. Anyway I would have had a hard
time duplicating Pasternak's line of reasoning. What he
said was: *You who fear so much to die, who are you? What
part of your body feels to you like your real self? Your
kidneys? Your liver? Your blood vessels? Of course not.
All of you is projected outwards into actions which are
exterior to you and which define your being—you exist in
those you love. Our presence in others is our true existence.
This is what you are, this is your true immortality. There
is nothing to fear; there is no such thing as death.* When I
sum it up like this in my own words, Pasternak's arguments
no longer convince me. I must have lost the essence of it.
How could I help leaving out something? The inexpressible
quality that lies between the lines . . .

"We were born just a little too early."

"Why is that?"

"The day will come, very soon in fact, when everyone will live to be at least a hundred and twenty or a hundred and thirty, barring accidents of course."

"Won't that be simply sensational?"

"Horrible! I never want to be old."

. . . Silly, beloved Pilou, whom I have no right to love, you shouldn't say things like that, even in jest. But both of us are still so young . . .

. . . Everlasting life yes but in my own little apartment with all my belongings around me that is what would be sensational so we were born just a little too early only a few years I have all the luck imagine coming to tell me a thing like that tactless I would say . . .

"Do you mind if I ask Armande to bring me back my little jacket? Thank you. It is a pity, just the same, to miss the bloat by so little . . ."

. . . Once in a while even the intelligent and articulate Mme. Prieur—is it age?—uses the wrong word, lets an incongruous letter insert itself, causing a chasm to open over the depths . . .

. . . This gives me an idea. A story in which death is postponed. Marc and Gilles, let's say, waiting for an official medical verdict which will decide their fate. Meanwhile they discuss the joys of living, the tragedy of dying. Plain words. Commonplace subjects given their original poignancy. Hope for a reprieve blots out fear. How could I make such hope appear reasonable? A vaccine might just have been found to retard the aging of the cells. So that the average person would live to be a hundred and thirty, or a hundred and sixty. Two hundred, why not? The only question would be whether one is too old at thirty, say, or forty, to submit to the necessary treatments. Enter suspense, to quote the men in my profession. The two friends wait. Their hopes. The questions they ask themselves. The verdict is to be posted in the town hall. No, that is too idiotic; the radio can announce the results. Only Marc is young enough to be vaccinated against death. Marc, not me, I am Gilles; I am lost. Terror. The abyss. I am not going to die, no it can't be possible . . .

. . . For once they are right. Soon nothing will be impossible. That extra head grafted onto a dog by Soviet scientists. A handsome German shepherd with a pathetic little mongrel clinging to its neck, as though they were hugging one another. Beady little eyes with white circles around them, next to a large, trusting face with tawny jowls. Grafted to one body and alive, at least for the present, the two heads are independent. If each one of them is offered a bowl, they both lap the milk at the same time. But if only one of them is fed, the other one is oblivious of this, and goes happily on with its canine day-dreams, panting gently, its tongue half-extended, like any other healthy animal . . .

"It would only be a temporary reprieve. There would be the same anguish . . ."

"Another thirty years to live. I wouldn't ask for more . . ."

"But what struggles there would be between generations! Imagine the impatience of youth. Children of seventy or more waiting for Daddy to leave them the factory!"

"And with the population already exploding so disastrously around the world . . ."

. . . After a few moments of despair, Gilles comes to accept death, as the crowds rejoice in the streets. I see a young nun, her wimple blowing in the wind, her face pink with excitement. I see an old man sitting on a bench; he is slightly hunched and is drawing circles in the sand with the tip of his cane. And Marc, lucky Marc, I can see him clearly. He is running along the embankment, right in front of the Institute. He dashes across the street and is run over. So I will live longer than he does, after all. Well done, Gilles . . .

"Have you heard the latest statistics from China? A fantastic increase in population. Can you imagine what it will be like twenty years from now?"

. . . Of course, Roland Soulaires, we all know that collecting tinfoil for starving Chinese babies, though less effective, was a much more convenient method of dealing with the problem. The cheapest way to a good conscience. It is too bad, isn't it, that Chinese children are no longer dying in pestilences and famine or that they are not being killed, a million at a time. I can see what you are driving at: sooner or later we will have to face the situation. Perhaps with a hydrogen bomb, why not . . .

"What is happening, my dear Eugénie, is that Russia is actually becoming our ally. The time is coming when the West will have to stand united, . . . and act!"

. . . Here it comes . . .

"Or perish. How to act? That is the question. But it is not unthinkable that nuclear stockpiles, both those in the United States and in the USSR, could be used . . ."

"Another thirty years of life. That would be enough for me . . ."

194

. . . Eugénie was not answering Roland, but herself. Here is the kind of thing that must be observed on the spot and then transposed into literature, a new literature that will replace with its own conventions those of the past. All art must take sides, but it still is necessary, once in a while, to change the rules of the game . . .

. . . So we have come to this. It is not that Roland Soulaires is unusually despicable. He is like all the others, a true representative of his class—and mine. In all good faith, and with the best intentions, he suggests such atrocities as though they were the most natural thing in the world. The instinct of self-preservation? And if the world did become Chinese, what then? Or entirely interbred, with all the races mingled into one, into a new, peace-loving humanity . . .

. . . A new literature? The rehabilitation of the novel? Easier said than done. I now remember that Racine observed and made use of the psychological fact which I naively thought I had discovered listening to Eugénie. The earliest critics of *Andromaque* and *Bajazet* made note of this and admired Racine for his contribution to *modern literature*, pointing out in their footnotes that in such and such a verse Hermione or Roxane is not answering her confidante so much as her own thoughts. Racine being *the first writer who used the overpowering obsessions of human beings to dramatic effect* . . .

"I wonder if all this isn't exaggerated. Do you know how one of the most recent resolutions of the Central Committee of the Communist party starts out? 'Fresh as a sunrise over the boundless horizons of Eastern Asia, a new society is being born . . .' "

"China as it has always been, as it always will be. Such poetry . . ."

. . . Poetry indeed, as if they had the faintest notion of what poetry really is . . .

. . . There are not so many children suffering in China today. Not so many. But in India, what about in India? An intolerable thought, universally tolerated. Everyone says "All these children starving, how terrible," and then thinks no more about it. I don't think about it; I think about my own children. Of course I am moved when I hear about such and such a child who is sick or dying. Shocked. But I do not try to do anything, because it is not my child. We are condemned to such selfish indifference. Jean-Paul and Rachel, tiny vulnerable creatures who are not entirely separate from me, each of my five senses and others still not yet named find fulfillment in your bodies. You are sleeping peacefully. I know; I can feel it . . .

"You forget that even in the days of Stalin . . ."

"Besides, it would not be a political matter, but a strategic necessity . . ."

. . . Here we are, dining quietly, thinking about our own little affairs, while above our heads crackles a gigantic fuse that could blow up the world at any moment . . .

"Well, as long as our Europe is not united . . ."

"Our Europe, so provincial, partitioned into so many . . ."

"Yes, with boundaries of blood . . ."

"But there is always England . . ."

"And the ocean . . ."

"To wash away the blood!"

. . . I am probably being a bit glib, for Europe, after

all, our own divided, but precious, little Europe gave us Braque and Mozart. What our best writers today are lacking, because they belong to a generation which is too old—Bertrand Carnéjoux included—is a minimum of scientific knowledge. The books which I will write will not have the slightest taint of impressionism . . .

. . . Not so old as all that, believe me. With dreams like the one I had last night! A young man was courting me. The old enchantment returned, the feeling of being attractive, oh, much more than that, of being marvelous, fascinating—of awing and fascinating even myself. Must I admit that this happiness was only a dream? The giddy favors which I was offering, one by one, were my own flesh, from the first overtures to the final defeat, the final joyous victory of my body which was not just remembering and reconstructing, but reliving the love that has always been its due . . .

. . . But one must continue the hunt and go after these beautiful birds of passage, perhaps to bag a few modest specimens which have never been caught before—not even by Racine or Proust or Joyce . . . Silence. What are they all ruminating about? What chain of thought led them back to their own dreams and obsessions? Unless they have fallen into that visceral darkness which I have always found so terrifying and which has haunted me since childhood, projecting the same red whirlpools of fear into my mind whenever it begins to drowse. Or that young girl who has been sitting calmly, too calmly, in front of a train station in the country, sharpening the same pencil for forty years with one blade of the same pair of scissors . . .

. . . This is just fine, they have all stopped talking at once. I must find something to say. Anything. But inside me there is only a big black hole, a vacuum of stupidity. Poor Bertrand, he married such a moron. But he is day-dreaming too, and forgetting about the women on either side of him. This is definitely my last dinner party. It is too much of an ordeal. I am never going to entertain again . . .

. . . Roland is smiling, far off in the clouds . . .

. . . All these stomachs and intestines at work. Of course when it is my own organs I feel in close association with them. To think that the succulent morsel of guinea hen which I am now chewing (not without fully appreciating its melting tenderness and subtle flavor) could have been chosen and masticated by Eugénie Prieur. Gradually turning into excess fat, then filthy residue . . .

. . . Roland is looking at me with a distracted, and yet extremely penetrating expression which justifies my fondest hopes. I am not so old after all . . .

. . . Pasternak also said, *What is this state of consciousness which you are so afraid to lose?* And he said, *Wanting to sleep makes sleep impossible; trying to control one's digestion only interrupts it.* And, *Consciousness is blind.* He said it was like the headlights on a locomotive. To turn them inwards, he said, would be a catastrophe. But what do I ask of a writer, if not a light into my darkness? He said, *There is nothing to fear. Death does not concern us. It is none of our business. Death does not exist* . . .

. . . Not a bad plot, the one I just outlined. The trouble is that to make a film, it would have to be padded out. Bertrand Carnéjoux once had an idea that he said would make it possible for him to avoid these difficulties, which are the same for novelists as for screenwriters. This was to invent not only a writer but also, and most especially, his works. A commentary on a lifework that does not exist would have been a fine project. Fortunately he never got beyond the title: *Essay in Pure Criticism.* Since then, Jorge Luis Borgès wrote something very similar (tough luck for Bertrand). Writers are too garrulous, anyway. Why devote three hundred pages to elaborate a theme that could be expressed equally effectively in a few lines?

. . . I woke up happy and contented, convinced of my youth, an illusion which was instantly destroyed. All that was left to console me in my distress was the sweet, all-too-sweet memory of my dream, in which I gave myself to a stranger the way one would at twenty, in triumphant innocence. And now look at me, old, old, horribly old and decayed, but with the same inexhaustible, inextinguishable youth which I alone know and feel, and which does not allow me to hope for anything from anyone . . .

. . . How did I ever get by between fifteen and twenty, alone, under age, with all those men, without ever getting involved with the police? Somehow I committed very few indiscretions, knowing just what I was after, and pursuing it relentlessly, with stubborn persistence, never relaxing or allowing myself the slightest pleasures (almost never). Paulo, Bertrand, maybe a few others. Of course, when I say pleasure . . . The most intense emotion which a man can ever make me feel is a wild, futile kind of tenderness, almost maternal, which for some reason I now feel for this child, Jérôme, who actually disgusts me, just as the old fatty on my right disgusts me, the way he rolls the bread into pellets between his fingers and puts them compulsively into his pocket, one by one . . .

. . . Behind the crystal waterglass out of which she is drinking Marie-Ange's nose is suddenly white and strangely deformed watch out make no mistake astrology is a science my eyesight is not as bad as I thought since I can spot such small details on the other side of the table unless perhaps my nearsightedness is responsible for the bizarre look on the little Canadian girl's face but after all at my age I can't make a spectacle of myself wearing pince-nez like Madame Prieur Bertrand has nothing to complain about pretty apartment good furniture heavy antique silver quite a set-up he has here . . .

. . . Such a relief, such peace of mind when I stroll around my bachelor's apartment with no clothes on and my belly hanging out in front of me. Perhaps I should be a little more careful about money. If there is anyone who couldn't be called stingy, that person is me. Why I hardly even keep an eye on my budget. (Not enough.) The fear of having to do without (the thought of a destitute old age.) Eugénie once confessed to me that she sometimes had the same feeling, almost to the point of panic. Fortunately, I myself am not in such straits. I have considerable capital, and a steady income . . .

. . . I mustn't give in right away. The young man looks at me, smiles, takes me by the hand, his is so gentle and warm, and now our two hands are joined and clasped against my breasts, pressing close to them, caressing them, and then he holds me tighter and all at once every emergency bell in my body begins to ring, all the lights go on, I am blinded, deafened, I am lost, I am frantic, I am happy, my hand is outstretched towards the young man on my right, who looks at me with astonishment, in front of all the guests whose presence I had forgotten, and even though it is no longer the same young man, it is the same rude awakening as this morning . . .

. . . There is no doubt about it, the old girl is slightly gaga. Such deep, gasping sighs . . .

. . . He said, Pasternak said, *Death does not exist; your immortality is the life you live in others. Why do you care if, later on, it is called memory? It will still be you. And when none of our contemporaries are on earth any longer?* Pasternak does not answer. But he goes on to say, *Life is eternal. You there, so anxious whether you will live again, you have already returned from the darkness into the light countless times, without realizing it. Life is continually reborn, filling the universe, eternally renewed in endless combinations and metamorphoses* . . .

"I once knew an old peasant woman who told me, in spite of how sick and infirm she was, 'I would rather be a toad, sitting under a stone, than be dead . . .' "

"I know a teacher who murmured on his deathbed, 'Death has no meaning for me . . .' "

"Love redeems death . . ."

"He who has loved much will die easily . . ."

. . . We have come to one of those moments in the middle of a dinner party when champagne does away with modesty and all the customary inhibitions. No longer afraid to be ridiculous, each of us in turn gives voice to one of the eternal verities, recreating, in tones of sober conviction, its original freshness and depth of meaning. One of my Italian colleagues, Lucci, whose films are much too successful, told me a story which will fascinate them. It happened to one of his friends, but I will pretend that it was he, so that my anecdote will not seem to be second-hand . . .

". . . A friend of mine, an Italian screenwriter whose name you will allow me to keep a secret, was once deserted by the person he loved . . ."

"The person he loved . . . I have an idea what kind of love you mean . . ."

. . . Good Heavens! Was that a faux-pas? No, by some great stroke of luck, there isn't a single one of them here tonight . . .

. . . Love well at last they are talking about something interesting but death will they go on talking about death I am in good in excellent health my doctor assured me only three days ago not Doctor Bartet I haven't any faith in him any more Doctor Loubot but someone told me about a marvelous doctor I have his name at home I definitely ought to see him I feel so helpless with so many organs inside of me which I cannot keep an eye on maybe I am already stricken by an insidious ailment it is enough to drive you out of your mind at forty-two forty-two years old . . .

. . . The thought that everyone whom one loves is mortal makes one rebel, and turn to the selfish cowardice of contemplating one's own death, knowing or hoping that it will come before the death of those . . .

"There is only one kind of love . . ."

"How do you know about such things, Martine, at your age? Well, you are right. No matter what they say . . ."

"Someday people will recover from love just as they will also recover from death . . ."

"Well, it was love, no matter what else you might wish to call it. He loved. He suffered. And so, in order to find the boy again . . ."

"I told you so!"

"The word slipped my tongue!"

. . . Their horrible laughter. They were not even listening to Gilles. But it is much more interesting than the other rubbish they have been talking about. A slight modification in the nervous tissue of the brain and love is no more—nor homosexual love either. I don't give a damn about homosexual love! But love. Musset called it: *A disease which all of man's scientific knowledge will never be able to cure.* But he was wrong. A tiny little operation and Coelio will not think twice about Marianne. Nor I about Raymond. I am out of my mind . . .

"Well, to find his boy friend, you see I am not trying to cheat any longer, he went to consult all the mediums, all the experts in clairvoyance in Paris, where he was then living . . ."

"Was the boy French?"

"I think I know who it was!"

"Of course! There are so few of them!"

"They probably have their own special way of reproducing themselves!"

. . . More of their horrible laughter. Always *low* laughter.

Gilles Bellecroix has a habit of introducing each new statement with a subtly expressive "well." These interjections range from a shrill yelp to a low, evasive murmur, with only one thing in common, the way he scratches his right ear each time he says it. I usually pay no attention to such verbal mannerisms, until they suddenly strike me, as this one did just now. Perhaps it is not a habit at all, but some neurotic . . .

. . . Do we really matter? Of what use is it, and to whom, if one of us, or someone else, is living and not dead? Everyone of us wants to stay in the world forever! Everyone of us hopes for immortality! If I cannot think of any reason why Lucienne Osborn should deserve eternal life, then I must in all honesty conclude that my own survival is of little importance . . .

. . . I remember you on the boardwalk, my girl. You were not a social climber in those days, believe me. Miss Something-or-Other and proud of it. And tonight you are here at this table. It is only a beginning, you will be seen at others. You have acquired some manners. Although even then, I must admit, you had a kind of natural grace. And now, here you are, stealing my gigolos. It is unbelievable. Believable. A-ble. Blub, blub, blub, blub . . .

. . . Eugénie Prieur, staring into space, suddenly looks like a madwoman. The little red-haired boy won't be of much use. Watch out there, not too much to drink. I feel woozy already . . .

. . . The only part of me which I am aware of is my huge, monstrous, swollen mouth, and, far in the distance, my two gigantic, petrified feet . . .

. . . One of these unbearable moments when a human being is entirely helpless and exposed. All of Eugénie's secrets are spread out before us, under our none-too-kind scrutiny. So vulnerable, and alone, waiting desperately for something which will not come, like me with Bertrand, before the revelations of Naples . . .

. . . Eugénie, as though in perdition, is sitting with her eyes half-closed, without speaking, looking just the way she did a few minutes ago when she was listening to Roland, her body hunched up, her head leaning forward to hear what he was saying. Death is hardly a pressing problem for Pilou, or for me. I am not even famous yet. But these other old codgers might well be worried; they should be . . .

. . . My feet are right below my neck and there is no body in between. I put my hand on my stomach to reassure myself. But it does not help. I can feel my feet hooked to the bottom of my neck, filling the whole room all by themselves and bumping against the back wall of the apartment which cannot hold them. Now at last it is all over, all over. I am myself again. I hope no one noticed . . .

. . . Eugénie Prieur has pulled herself together and is taking a large swallow of champagne . . .

. . . The thoughts which go on behind conversations, yes, it would be interesting to try to do something with them in my next book. But the danger, to a certain extent inevitable, is that these thoughts would sound like theatrical asides. *Gadzooks! I'm hooked.* The stream of consciousness was actually used in Labiche long before Joyce came on the scene . . .

"Well you see, one of these mediums sent him to the Saint-Lazare station where he spent several days and nights searching in vain. Then one sent him to another part of town, Batignolles, I think, which he combed street by street. But he did not lose hope . . ."

"Why should he? I know what goes on around the Rue La Fontaine . . ."

"It wasn't funny. I met him quite often during those days. One could see that he was suffering . . ."

"Quite."

. . . I hate to hear the way Roland Soulaires answers "quite" in his high-pitched little voice. At home in Canada we always said "That's for sure." Much nicer . . .

"Well, it was Venus herself, or Eros rather. Don't laugh; the agonies of love are very real!"

. . . Even the pain of love, for someone as old as I am, doomed never again to enjoy its pleasures, would be a kind of happiness . . .

"Finally one of the mediums told him that he would find his friend in Canada. In Montreal, to be exact. Somewhat further than Saint-Lazare, to be sure. Nevertheless he jumped on a plane . . ."

"I don't believe it!"

"But you haven't heard anything yet! He had hardly been in Montreal for more than a minute when, in the lobby of the Hotel Windsor, he ran right into the boy he had been looking for, and with whom . . . Well, as they say, they lived happily ever after . . ."

. . . Hotel Windsor. The height of luxury. Now I would dare go in there; no one would be surprised to find me staying there. Except myself. In fact, if I ever went back to Montreal, I couldn't possibly stay anywhere else . . .

"Why that is sensational!"

. . . For once you have used the right word, Mrs. Osborn, if the story is true. But you were not aware of this; you only said it out of habit . . .

"Quite sensational. I tell you!"

. . . What a dimwit! Now she has picked up Roland Soulaires' "quite" and added it to her "sensational." How stupid can you be?

"Without knowing who your friend was, how can we . . ."

"Can you at least tell us who the medium was?"

"Or where she lived?"

"The story can't have happened. Someone must have made it up!"

"Oh, no, I can tell you things that are just as astonishing, even more so . . ."

"Rue La Fontaine, believe me . . ."

"I once met . . ."

"Let me tell you what once happened to me . . ."

"That kind of thing always happens to someone else. Never have I . . ."

"But I give you my word."

"And mine too! I . . ."

. . . They are all talking at once, carried away in a common burst of hope and excitement. Even little Jérôme, who has hardly opened his mouth until now. Every one of us is ready to believe anything which helps us renew our faith. I know the Rue La Fontaine . . .

. . . Our thoughts, or at least what we like to call by that name, are essentially alike. So similar that it would probably be hard to identify them if they were quoted anonymously. How can we be distinguished one from another if we are all the same? Interchangeable organisms whose presence is attested to only by brief signals, fleeting epiphenomena, flickering sparks of memory, emotion and fear. Why should our identities be differentiated, if we are all alike? . . .

. . . A lighted streetcar is moving along the opposite bank of the Seine, its windows flashing in silence. He goes away again, leaving another wake behind him in the clover; he goes away, pushing his bicycle, which rattles over the furrows. I was too surprised, too mauled, to hate him . . .

. . . With two exceptions. One of which was dubious. (That girl on the Boulevard de Clichy was as skilled as I was awkward.) That leaves Marie-Louise. (Not much, for forty-three years.) Foreign securities offer excellent values. Belgian and Dutch stocks in particular, which have held their own quite consistently, and certain gold mines. (It is incredible, just the same, to have to admit that I do not know whether I made love or not, in terms of what is properly called making love, with that girl on the Boulevard de Clichy.) . . .

. . . The drama and fiction of the seventeenth century insisted on the contrasts, the striking differences between one character and the next. For us, everyone is essentially alike. Differentiated one from another only by certain small deformities, like those which distinguish the nude bodies at the beach. Which one of us here is without his personal faith healer or medium? Probably only me, for even Martine goes, in the utmost secrecy, to visit a certain Madame Frau, way out in the eleventh *arrondissement* . . .

"Rue La Fontaine . . ."

. . . No one is listening to Eugénie Prieur. They are impolite. A woman as cultivated as she. Seen in the very best circles. Fashionable? I should say so! It is always a surprise to me when I find out that I care about such things. Just this morning I caught myself being outrageously snobbish. Had it been in Paris, at a salon, I would have avoided the woman who sat down at a table near mine in the dining car, so elegantly bored. Her slightly tired, beautifully made-up face, intelligent hands, impeccably-cut suit, and something in her expression that spoke of distant nonchalance, made her identical with all the other women in a certain society, in *society*, which I sometimes enjoy, and where I find myself this evening. Though she spoke only once, to order a half bottle of mineral water, and the racket of the train made it impossible for me to hear her, I could imagine the precise lilt of her slightly drawling, affected voice. I knew for certain who her friends were, in which houses she dined out. Her last name was probably familiar to me. And though this lovely lady in the dining car represented a class of society whose frivolity I find hard to tolerate, (even if I am occasionally weak enough to accept its hospitality) her affectations on the train this morning appeared to me more charming than ridiculous. The necessary distance and perspective were provided by the disorientation of traveling, and among such very ordinary companions, this lady seemed to me the height of elegance and refinement. I would have liked to distinguish myself from the others, for her benefit, by using, in the appropriate tone of voice, the passwords of her milieu, which is also mine to a certain extent, thanks to Gigi who once introduced me to it, and for which a trace of snobbery makes me still faintly nostalgic . . .

"I must tell you about the Rue La Frontaine . . ."

. . . The old witch made another odd lapse . . .

. . . If it became possible to feed electronic brains with the material which goes into our so-called thoughts, they would accomplish the same futile operations that we do, combining the elements at hand in a similarly haphazard fashion, choosing some kind of pattern out of all the millions of possibilities. The thoughts that resulted might be different from ours, but no worse or no better. Marie-Plum, discreet, reticent, and terribly determined. Silent, introspective, but with the dominating presence that goes with violent inner emotions which are very close to the surface . . .

. . . I might try raising some ghosts, just for fun. Mention the unmentionable name. Women are supposed to be scatterbrains, after all. It is very convenient . . .

". . . By the way, Bertrand, have you heard from Marie-Plum?"

. . . Have I what! What is she trying to do? She is out of her mind. Did I hurt her in some way? Just the other afternoon, when we were lying side-by-side in that hotel she spoke to me about Marie-Plum. She knows very well that I haven't heard from her . . .

". . . No, Marie-Ange, not in a long time."

. . . Marie-Plum who could that be Marie-Plum three minutes this way three minutes that way and I mustn't forget to do my sides three minutes on the right side three minutes on the left and the breasts the breasts are a difficult problem I only hope that I haven't got it impossible to leave before dinner is over all my pleasure will be spoiled . . .

. . . Bertrand is buttering a small piece of bread (toast) with a careful deliberation, as though he were only thinking of what he was doing, as though nothing (at the moment) were so important as the task at hand: buttering a small piece of bread (toast). But this make-believe concentration gives him away, even more than his anxious expression. The name which he pretends to be so casual about is haunting him . . .

. . . That does it. No one paid the slightest attention to the fatal name. My masterly poise and the fact that I had enough presence of mind to answer that bitch Marie-Ange without looking annoyed, made the brief ring of those dangerous syllables fall on deaf ears. No harm done. At least not this time. But she will pay for it, just the same. The look on Martine's face. My God, what a look! And the sly expression on Marie-Ange. I should have known better. How could I have expected to carry this off? Say something quickly, anything . . .

". . . Mediums, you know . . . I don't . . . I don't believe in them, that's all . . ."

"But there are certain instances. The story Gilles just told us . . . And others. Listen to this one and then try to tell me . . ."

. . . After a slight delay, the melancholy Mongolian profile of Marie-Plum makes an appearance, in answer to Marie-Ange's rash invocation of her name. It was not a faux-pas or the breaking of a taboo, but the heedless use of magic words which are so powerful that even the uninitiated can set them into action . . .

. . . Bertrand must have the same apparition before him as I do. It is as though Marie-Plum's pale little Chinese face were here before me, nasty, stubborn, and secretive, a hostile little mask . . .

. . . More than any of the other six people assembled here, Marie-Plum is monopolizing the dinner, not within us but before us, between the two of us, and although she is invisible, she is more vividly present than if she were actually sitting in one spot, at this table, instead of being everywhere at once, hauntingly omnipresent . . .

. . . She is here, between us, like the time, not long after our marriage, when he had the gall to ask her to our house. A cousin who was visiting Paris. Why should I have suspected anything? . . .

. . . The immediate and inescapable fascination of someone who is absent, the sense of a physical presence which is more compelling than anything our eyes and our hands are able to show us . . .

. . . She was there between us, almost where Marie-Ange is sitting tonight, not opening her mouth any more than I was, looking at poor Bertrand who kept talking, talking, looking at him in such a way that I suddenly understood their secret, the facts of which I confirmed later on, extracting the details with great patience from Bertrand, one by one, pretending not to be very interested, so skillfully that he eventually told me everything, and I had nothing more to learn about this relationship which the look in her eyes had, in any case, revealed to me from the start . . .

. . . Without thinking, she let the light from the match fall directly upon her, revealing a magnificent face, only slightly marred. To think that I had the chance to look at her, to touch her hand, to talk to her, and that I let these precious minutes pass by, without savoring them . . .

. . . At first one might have thought that the bomb Marie-Ange tossed so coolly was not going to explode. For a few seconds everything went on as usual, and then the silent explosion took place. It was as if the fatal name had only just been heard. Faces hardened, gestures were interrupted in mid-air, and voices became silent. And now we all find ourselves enclosed in the same block of ice and silence, inside which the vague, hesitant voice of Gilles Bellecroix is speaking, for some reason which no one can fathom, of death, trying to break the spell . . .

"Before dying . . ."

. . . Before dying? Protected by some mysterious charm, I found myself speaking out loud without anyone hearing, although the conversations have stopped. Yes, to my own astonishment, I said, in a loud voice, "Before dying." *Before dying.* It came out of me like a cry. Before dying I will at least have had a few minutes like these, in which, aided by the champagne and the more subtle intoxication distilled by the mind itself in such favored moments, I will have experienced, until I could hardly bear it any longer, the painful joy of existence . . .

. . . to break the spell in a falsely-casual tone of voice

which rings discordantly against the heavy glass dome
under which we are all choking, and which suddenly shat-
ters, freeing each of us from the enchantment, all except
Bertrand Carnéjoux . . .

. . . Marie-Plum. It is impossible to convey the extent of
her charm to those who did not know her. The figure of a
little girl. The animation in her Eurasian face, in her voice,
even in her silence. All the mysteries of her small body
which I alone knew, and valued . . .

"And the stars? My horoscope tells me . . ."

"How can stars possibly . . ."

"It is a well-known phenomenon, however . . ."

"Like the expression 'Thank your lucky stars . . .'"

"This celery is exquisitely prepared . . ."

. . . Their words are only a superficial probing into the
depths of truth. For the stars are indeed a serious matter.
Much more might have been said on the subject. (I was
born under an unlucky star.) But now we are back on the
slippery tracks of frivolous small talk. So the extraordinary
dish which I at first thought was potatoes prepared in a
curious manner, then turnips, turned out to be the vege-
table which I hate most of all, ever since I was a child
(when I was forced to eat it)—celery. Why didn't I recognize it, even disguised by this exotic sauce? Had I identified
it in time (investigated the vague feeling of disgust which
I felt) I would have pronounced the dish, or at least its
ingredients, inedible. Too late now. (It is always too late
for me.) . . .

"Like the concierge on the Rue La Fontaine."

"What concierge?"

"The one who is a faith healer. You know. Everyone goes to her, believe me!"

"Mme. Bonloird? She cured one of my cousins of the most terrible sciatica which no doctor . . ."

"A few magic words . . ."

"Tea brewed from willow bark . . ."

"No, birch."

"Why that's sensational! Tell us more . . ."

"One would almost like to be sick to be able to go to a woman like that . . ."

. . . Tempting fate asking to be sick Roland Soulaires is crazy every last word counts when it is a question of hope a chance for salvation which could be taken away at any moment Rue La Fontaine is not far from here but I'm not so dumb I have better addresses . . .

. . . Ever since that woman was mentioned the cynicism and sophistication of these apparently blasé socialites has been replaced by the most primitive, the most naïve faith and credulity. (Even in me, for whom Mme. Bonloird can do nothing.) A miracle worker has been found. Hope springs eternal. I myself have never had any reason to lose hope. It is just that my victories are limited; they affect nothing more than my relationship with the one woman over whom I have been victorious . . .

. . . They are all talking at once, carried away in a common burst of hope and excitement. Every one of us is ready to believe anything which helps him renew his faith. Only the young man with the red hair has kept his composure. He looks scornful, as he rubs the end of his nose. I must be very distracted this evening, for this is the first time that

I have noticed him. Until now this boy whom I have never met before was only real enough to occupy a seat which I would have noticed much sooner had it been empty. How could I have gone on for so long without noticing him? Now he has become a part of the tight little world of this dinner party. I cannot imagine it without him. Martine is so charming . . .

. . . What does he want, my photograph? The old goats are pretty eager this year . . .

. . . Seductive Gilles, with his silver temples. Bertrand. My children. I am happy, so happy, only slightly tempted by what I do not know—but my happiness is painful because it is threatened. Death makes it impossible to be happy. The more happiness one knows, the keener is one's anguish. Death would be nothing if I knew that those I loved were sheltered, invulnerable. An absurd but violent rebelliousness rises within me. Human beings are so resigned . . .

". . . Rue La Fontaine, you said. What number?"

"I don't remember. But I will call you tomorrow, if you like . . ."

"Oh thank you. But there is no hurry. In fact it doesn't matter in the slightest . . ."

. . . Probable translation: "It is urgent and of tremendous importance." (But why should Eugénie understand when I myself have such trouble figuring out what she means?) Dear Martine, she is pretending to be indifferent, but I can read the anxiety on her tense little face. Her mother, poor Irène, will never be cured of her neurasthenia. Although you can't ever tell about such things. The shadow of a pair of lovers together against the parapet.

216

From our second story window we can see everyone and everything that happens along the embankment . . .

. . . What we are really thinking is not what we are saying. Spoken words stand in for others that are kept silent. Everyone understands this perfectly well; words, except for a few stock phrases, are only symbols. Beneath this idle chatter about health is a deeper concern: eternity.

. . . An interesting conversation at last but I have my doubts about that woman she couldn't be as good as my medium certainly not I wouldn't be so stupid as to give out her name and address Mme. Frau 78 Rue du Temple it is a pity though that she won't allow dogs Rue La Fontaine is closer to where I live and of course a faith healer is not the same thing as a medium it wouldn't be as if I were being unfaithful to Mme. Frau I could go over there when I walk Zig and maybe that Bonloird woman would let me bring him in a slight feeling of suffocation but after all I ate only a tiny mouthful of fish because of my figure I must remember the recipe and a little bit of guinea hen Good Lord in Heaven I forgot the guinea hen . . .

. . . Potential invalids, listening to talk of a cure. But death is what they would like to be cured of. I am channeled along narrow steel tracks with a crowd of travelers who have been using this railroad ever since it was built more than a hundred years ago. A few of the living and an endless number of the dead are carried with me along the same path. Exactly the same path, within an inch difference. Here, and not elsewhere. Not down this slope, nor across that field. Living and dead, crushed together and driven along the narrow track. A railroad track. To the right, and to the left, despite one or two peasants working in the distance, the vast stretches of land are deserted. A feeling of panic seizes me. The desire to leave this moving convoy. This convoy moving towards death. To flee across these fields and take refuge under that solitary tree, where no one has ever died. Where I would be safe. Not only from the living, but from the dead. Especially from the dead. A little cemetery nested in a hollow, under the black tongues of three cypresses. No one escapes death. Not even in my story about Marc and Gilles. Their wild expectations. We are young enough, of course we are. Only thirty-three! Yes, but I am . . . How old am I? Forty-nine. (Or forty-eight? It's terrible, I don't remember.) No, forty-nine. That's right, forty-nine . . .

". . . My friend went only to humor one of his farmers whose cows were dying. This old medicine man was holding forth in Chartres and the farmer could not go himself because it was harvest time . . ."

. . . A single red roof stands out, in its brand-new ugliness, from the mellow uniformity of the brown tiles. Old houses gathered around the tall steeple and the bell towers. I can imagine the saints on the central portal leaving their rigid stone positions at midnight once every thousand years, coming to life, and descending in a procession to the street, from whence those who are then living would rise to take their places. In the torchlit darkness, the two processions cross. A young girl, brought to life, sees a boy moving upwards towards a niche in the stony flanks of the cathedral. It is the boy she had dreamt of in vain when she was last on earth. He sees her, and recognizes her. They understand each other. She follows him. And there they are, petrified one next to the other, hand-in-hand, for a thousand years of silence and love . . .

. . . Marie-Ange, with her head leaning slightly to one side, and the graceful curve of her neck reaching to her shoulder. Of her small bosom, I can see only a chaste roundness. Gilles is scratching his ear. Eugénie, on whose drooping eyelids blue eye-shadow and the blue shadows of age are superimposed but not blended, is burrowing in her oversized handbag. Roland Soulaires and his brilliant red gums. The circles under his eyes. And Bertrand, caught as he raises his arm in a sweeping gesture. The overhead light which was suddenly turned on, only for a second or two, left me with this amusing colored snapshot . . .

. . . The light, turned on by mistake, illuminated everything with stark, merciless rays, extinguishing the candlelight, throwing everyone's shadow against the dazzling white tablecloth, accentuating the magenta roses which I hadn't yet noticed, revealing a gigantic green plant until now hidden in the shadows, and making the Seine disappear behind bright reflections on the window panes. Crimson clover has a perfection that no other flower, anywhere in the world, can equal. One, two. Three, four. Five, six . . .

"What on earth are you doing?"

. . . The electric light, turned on for one ferocious, blinding instant. The butler has already turned it off . . .

"Are you crazy? Turn it off!"

. . . His reflexes were much faster than those of Pilou who barked at him after the error had already been corrected. If even someone like Martine allows herself to talk in that tone of voice to her—I hate to say the word!—inferiors, then sooner or later the unjust tyranny of money will be ended . . .

. . . Resigned rather than indifferent, the butler turned the switch back off again with the slightly ironic, superior, and impertinent expression of someone who deems it unnecessary to offer explanations to the madwoman with whom he is condemned to live . . .

. . . Safe and sound once again in the gentle twilight of the candles. Just so long as Gilles did not look in my direction! The mirror of my compact, in which I automatically looked at myself, revealed a face that had suddenly become thirty years older . . .

. . . The light which was turned on so unexpectedly (I don't know why) for a few seconds, took away and then gave back the mystery which thrives in the translucent shadows of this dining room, harmonizing with our euphoria. (My euphoria!) The Louis XV console is a superb piece. There are two armchairs, one on either side of it, which I had not noticed before. Their low backs are pure Louis XV but the feet seem to be Louis XVI. Of course. They are transitional pieces. Rather attractive, too. (But do they combine well with the very busy rococo carving on the console, which they are intended to complement?) . . .

. . . Still dazzled by that harsh light which revealed the weary lines of our faces. Next to Gigi's frightening mask were the fresh youthful features of this near-adolescent whose presence I am more and more surprised not to have noticed. But our eyes reaccustom themselves to the semidarkness. On the silver candelabra, teardrops and stars and

tongues of light begin to sparkle again. Behind the philodendron with its large, shiny, eyelet-patterned leaves, a
shadow has again appeared on the wall, its delicate outlines
multiplying and dividing more beautifully than the original, and rising upwards into a wide, semi-circular fan that
curves far above the tall plant, almost to the ceiling . . .

. . . Money is protection. But wealthy or not, I am still a
woman. I must never forget this. Another traveling sales-
man or even a wretched laborer might leap on me at any
moment, if I do not keep a constant watch. Love? Don't
make me laugh. The most beautiful, the richest women of
all are public property, like the rest of us. Females mounted
by males. I may have contempt for men but I am afraid of
them just the same. I have learned my lesson the hard way;
I am more careful now. If I can't escape making love,
damn it, at least I can be sure that I get some good out of
it. My skin. It is not as glowing as it should be. A little
pinch here, and a little one there. Once more. That does
it . . .

. . . I am short of breath all of a sudden it is very disturbing perhaps my health yesterday's horoscope the one
in *France-Soir* warned me about cramps but I didn't feel
any yesterday though it could have meant today the way
newspapers are dated ahead it is hard to tell very exaspera-
ting the trouble is that under Capricorn the health forecast
for today with tomorrow's date on it of course said constant
what will be constant the cramps they forecast yesterday
they should explain things better very slight pains in my
abdomen cramps just as they predicted everything always
turns out as they say it will I should have paid more at-

tention the pangs are getting sharper they hardly ever make a mistake all these little bones left over from the guinea hen Zig dear how sensational but dangerous I wouldn't have given them to you anyway what if I did go see that Mme. Bonloird one never can tell luckily I listened carefully for the address Rue La Fontaine but she didn't say what number Eugénie Prieur is a sharp one but I will find out the main thing is to know the name and the street that linoleum should last a little while longer they are talking about Tibet a country that is very far away even further away than Africa somewhere near Madagascar. Eugénie Prieur won't allow Bertrand to listen she is telling him another of her little anecdotes . . .

"I don't confide in just anyone, Bertrand, believe me. (*It is the same with me. Anything about Tibet has always fascinated me. Me too . . .*) But Mme. Bonloird is not just anyone. Someday I will have to tell you all about her; you would be fascinated. (*Yes, the living Buddha. But did you know . . . .*) Some late afternoon, in fact any day this week, I am not very busy. (*Oh no, Jérôme, if I may call you Jérôme . . .*) I will tell you things that I have never told anyone, well hardly anyone, believe me. (*Now wait a minute. Let Jérôme tell us about it. He knows a great deal about Tibet. Not all that much, really I don't. Science is more my . . . But precisely! . . .*) You see, Mme. Bonloird . . . but it is very hard to talk above all this noise. There is just one little fact, however, which you have to bear in mind, a mere detail, but very significant . . . (*Ultimately, religion, insofar as religion can be proved or disproved, will never . . .*) Are you listening, Bertrand? . . ."

. . . The focus keeps switching, as in the movies except that it is voices rather than faces. Different conversations come into the foreground. That faith healer of Gigi's is getting to be a bore . . .

"Bertrand, you must listen to me . . ."

"But I am, Eugénie, I am listening to every word you are saying . . ."

. . . And also to what Jérôme Aygulf has to say about Tibet, which I find much more interesting. It is a rather hackneyed subject, but there is always something more to learn. While Gigi, with her laborious monologues . . .

"First I must tell you about something which happened to me a long while ago, but which is an important part of the whole story, as you will see. Not long after the Liberation, I became very ill. None of my friends, not even my closest friends, knew about this. Even you, Bertrand, I doubt very much if you have any recollection . . ."

". . . That's right. Not just any little boy, of course. There is a different procedure every time. But if we take the fourteenth Dalai Lama as a case in point . . ."

"I suffered what might be called a severe depression, but this was a special kind of depression, for like anyone else, I had already gone through many . . ."

"It was in 1935 or so. The Regent had gone to the banks of a sacred lake . . ."

"Listen carefully, Bertrand. What I am about to say is off the record, just between the two of us: Mme. Bonloird was responsible for my recovery, but in a most remarkable way . . ."

"The Regent did not understand the syllables which

appeared on the waters, but there was also a picture, a monastery with carved towers . . ."

. . . This is fascinating, but I can't hear very well. Eugénie and her troubles are getting on my nerves. Unfortunately I have to be polite, especially since I am the host . . .

"A few traces of my breakdown still remained with me, nevertheless I had been cured, and in the most remarkable way, as you will see. I must tell you, however, that in those days I went quite often to a priest, a Catholic priest . . ."

". . . And all this, the monastery, the temple, the cottage, the road, and the hillside were clearly reflected on the surface of water, as though on a screen. One little detail captured the Regent's attention: an oddly-shaped rainspout . . ."

". . . I was unable to receive the sacraments, you understand. The priest made this very clear and it was a great blow to me in my condition . . ."

" . . . If you will excuse my interrupting, just for the moment, I would like to point out that this road, the one which appeared on the waters of the sacred lake, led, if I remember correctly, towards the east . . ."

"Yes indeed, sir, that is very important, for the embalmed body of the previous Dalai Lama had been mysteriously moved from one position to another, and the feet were now pointing in a new direction, towards the east . . ."

". . . For me, you know, priests have always had a most remarkable . . . well not all of them, of course, but a certain few like the abbé Préault . . . I will have to introduce you to the abbé Préault someday. It would be amusing . . . Well, in short, when I recovered, it was necessary for me . . . We must get together to talk about all this . . . just the two of us, don't you think?"

. . . Of course! Not on your life. Everything is *amusing* for women like her. Let's go see a priest—how amusing. They are all idiots, even some of the most intelligent of them . . .

". . . After searching for weeks to the east of Lhasa, the members of one of the expeditions who had been sent to the east and who, believe me, were not wandering aimlessly . . ."

". . . You *will* call me one of these days, won't you, Bertrand? So that we can . . ."

. . . He is not listening. Not only is he trying to avoid making a date with me, but he is not paying the slightest attention to what I am telling him, and it is so desperately important. I should keep these kinds of confessions to myself, especially when I feel such a need to unburden myself to someone. Am I really cured? Sometimes I feel some of the old symptoms, like tonight, and . . .

. . . My dear young man, I am familiar with your sole source of information. A book by Fosco Maraini. I know much more than he does about the subject. But you were tongue-tied for so long, and now you seem so happy to be able to say something brilliant . . . My pair of lovers has descended from the cathedral. They are there, under the street lamp, in a tight embrace, he leaning on the parapet, she with her arms around his neck . . .

". . . Everything was exactly as it was in the vision on the lake: the monastery, the temple, the road, the hillside, down to the last detail, including the oddly-shaped rain-spout on the cottage. And in that cottage . . ."

. . . They are all listening to me. How wonderful. How charming they all are. Bertrand above all. I have an absurd and overpowering desire to make the sign of the cross. But it is impossible. Except in my head. Without moving . . .

. . . All right, go no further, I know the rest. The only solution is not to wear cufflinks at all. But the buttons on my shirt will lie in the dust of what was once my body. There is no escape. In their tight embrace, they are rejoicing in the miracle of their *unique* love, so enthralled by the age-old attractions of the species, that they have not noticed that the last passers-by have disappeared, that they are really alone, if not *unique*, along this embankment where even the Sunday crowds, wandering back and forth, would remain invisible to them . . .

. . . In the name of the Father and of the Son and of the Holy Ghost . . .

. . . Any young man with any young woman. And they think that no one else was ever like them. They believe that no one else has ever known this stillness of joy, this dazzlement. Anonymous glands at work, the ancient and relentless instinct of the species, always the same no matter what fleeting names are given to this bearer, and that receiver of the seed. Bertrand and Marie-Plum, Bertrand and Amelinha, Bertrand and Martine. Any two people, it doesn't matter who, or whom . . .

. . . Outside, another light is shining. The blue neon sign lighting up the figure of a naked girl, in a hotel near the place Saint-Michel, near here, and so long ago. The unfurled body, the immense limbs of this prostitute reclining on a bed; they terrify me. Venus of the night. Night of

Venus, out of which three searchlights suddenly blaze through the windows, against the mirrors, projecting the shadows of the blackamoors on the ceiling, while a waltz . . .

"How marvelous!"

"Sensational!"

"It is only the *Bateau-Mouche*, the democratic old *Bateau-Mouche*. Martine and I offer this treat to our friends from April to October. But the season is over, now. The *Coche d'Eau* will not be making many more trips . . ."

. . . The season is over now someone else has said it no more sunbathing . . .

. . . These *Bateaux-Mouches*, whose sole reason for existing is to delight the tourists, and incidentally, to add such charm to our view, are in a different class entirely from the simple vessels which plied up and down the river before the war and which were methods of transportation like any other. One never met anyone one knew on board, and Edwige and I had our lovers' rendezvous' on them, without fear of being seen. This one, with its searchlights shining through the windows, is the *Coche d'Eau*, christened after the original vessels that used to travel up and down the Seine for centuries. In 1784 one of them arrived on our island from Troyes, with a young man named Napoleon Bonaparte, fresh from the military academy at Brienne . . .

. . . Bertrand is right, the *Coche d'Eau* and her sisters will not make many more trips this year. And as soon as the last *Bateau-Mouche* is gone, the first seagull will appear. It will skim over the yellow waters, alight, float for a moment, and then the white emblem of its fuselage and graceful wingspan will again rise and stand out against a cloudy sky. Maybe Rachel will be old enough to be interested in the gulls this year. From where Mummy lived we also could see the *Bateaux-Mouches*, and her parties were always illuminated by their searchlights . . .

". . . But there had to be further proof. The choice of the Dalai Lama is a matter of such crucial importance in Tibet. There had to be another omen . . ."

. . . In the name of the Father and of the Son and of the Holy Ghost. If I could only make the sign of the cross with my hand. Not just in my head. Marie-Ange is looking at me; she seems interested . . .

. . . I am bored stiff with his old Lamas. Babbling away there like a baby. He is cute, though, rather cute. A triple halo of light on the black water . . .

. . . The tall philodendron whose large, dark-green leaves rise in tiers next to the window, culminating in the pale, curly tendrils of a new shoot, shows how old-fashioned this party really is. Not that philodendrons are out of style. But they were already in style under Napoleon the Third. All of a sudden, I find that the sight of them, or maybe the waltz which is coming from the boat, the boat which is also of another era with its clusters of Japanese lanterns, carries me back to those days. I have the feeling that I am not just looking at, but am actually a part of one of those prints from the *Monde Illustré* of the Second Empire, which I used to pore over with Thomas when I was a child in the library at Valromé. The winter gardens of the Princess Mathilde, with accompanying violins, gave me a similarly exotic impression, not so much because of the tropical origins of many of the plants, but because of the desire to voyage into the distant past which the sight of them always inspired in me . . .

". . . It happened that the temple was dedicated to a god whose name began with the exact syllables which had appeared to the Regent on the waters of the lake. I-KA-PA, or A-KA-PA, I'm not quite sure. But in any case it was another sign. Just a sign. Not proof, you see, just another sign . . ."

. . . The sadness of waltzes. If we accept their melancholy, we can settle back and enjoy their easy rhythms. The vulgarity of music from the turn of the century dissolves into dust along with the flesh of the handsome men and women who delighted in it. Nothing is left but the skeleton of a sentimental melody, no longer an invitation to pleasure, but an exposé of its tragic deceptions . . .

"The leader of the delegation, who had disguised himself as a humble peasant, entered the cottage. Inside a tiny child was playing. As he approached, the child rushed towards him, crying 'Lama, Lama . . .' "

"It was he!"

"I beg your pardon, Madame, but you mustn't jump to conclusions. Further tests, further proof was necessary . . ."

. . . I never stop looking for evidence of the supernatural even though I am unable to believe in it . . .

. . . Lucienne Osborn's watery squint, as she tries to see the boat. Marie-Ange's enormous violet eyes, in which a thousand stars are twinkling. Violet, violent, violating eyes. This evening, as soon as I can find that photograph . . .

. . . Moving in the opposite direction from the boats on the river (I often notice this as I walk home with Bertrand in the evening) the shadows of the tall poplars whose branches have been lopped off until they look like gallows, glide slowly along the continuous façades of the houses, passing over the closed shutters, twisting and turning over the balconies and into the windows of apartments whose curtains, like ours, have not been drawn, sliding in constant metamorphosis over the sills, the draperies, the paintings, and the furniture which gently dismembers them, before they finally disappear (all too soon, alas), beautiful shadows which are more Japanese than Chinese . . .

. . . Projected on the walls and the mirrors, their mingled, multiplied shadows caught in a slowly-moving lacework of branches, elegant curved balconies, and the magnified arabesques of leaves from the *Monstera deliciosa*, the lovers on the Quai d'Orleans, trapped in this prison of branches and wrought iron, are a reflection of our love, Bénédicte's and mine. Not in the street of course; at my age I would not dare. But as soon as we are alone . . .

. . . In any case I would not have given him these bones certainly not I don't need any more troubles the pleasure Léon Pierre can make me feel is wonderful that and the sunshine are the only real things in my life I wish I knew how much John really doesn't keep me informed unfortunately I don't think he cares the least bit about income too busy watching the principal grow the old miser he never thinks of anyone but himself after his death however it will be a different story I will be what they call well-off it is annoying to be nearsighted I would have liked to see that boat for me it is nothing but vague blotches of light and shadow misty sunspots whirlpools of color rather pretty to be sure . . .

. . . Looming suddenly through the bay window, the searchlights fall on the mirrors covering each of the walls. This slow kaleidoscope of blue reflections eclipses the candles in a phantasmagoric play of light, and plunges our dinner party into bright and festive phosphorescence. Meanwhile our shadows, and those of the furniture, are turning and changing places in a kind of impromptu ballet . . .

. . . A distinct silence. They have not been listening very carefully, if at all, to what I have been saying for the last few minutes. But my story is a fascinating one. Not a story, really, or a fairy tale, but history, a quasi-scientific report on a contemporary miracle. Is it the champagne? Yes it is. My own voice sounds strange to me; it has a peculiar resonance and I am enunciating even worse than usual. I must get this over with, and keep quiet. Pilou herself seems distracted. But when has she ever paid the slightest attention to what I said or did not say . . .

" . . . The boy who was presumed to be the new Dalai-Lama was asked to select, among certain identical objects, the cups, necklaces, and canes which had belonged to his previous incarnation. Without hesitating, the child . . ."

. . . *But we all know that.* The trees are silhouetted with lacy precision against the blue, lightly-misted surface of the windows. Gliding, (in the opposite direction from the boat which can hardly be seen behind its dazzling searchlights) the shadows (on the wall of the apartment) duplicate the overlapping wreaths of the black branches whose quiet little leaves no longer rustle, and move slowly away (in the opposite direction from the *Coche d'Eau* which also disappears all of a sudden.). . .

. . . Then the last rays are seized and swallowed by the night, and the candles again surround us with a gentle, discreet radiance which speaks of the distant past. The distant past, believe me! When I desire a helpless young man, I always proceed (I used to, that is, for now I am old) slowly and systematically. When he has his first failure, indeed whenever he fails, I do not appear scornful, or confused, or make his inhibitions worse with wild, over-eager caresses; instead I relax my whole being, my mind as well as my body. No signs of impatience, or annoyance. Only a few soothing words, spoken with a composure that is genuine, because I know that this affliction will cease to exist the moment one stops considering it as such. I am perfectly happy at his side. I don't mind waiting. Given a little time, a man's organs will come to life most unexpectedly. When I desired a helpless young man. But all that is over, now. Not the desire. Nor even the pleasure. Only the happiness . . .

"Finally, before they could be sure that they had found the new Dalai-Lama, there was one test, a necessary and absolute proof, without which all the other pieces of evidence, no matter how convincing, were utterly worthless . . ."

. . . A room invaded by the garish lights of the nearby Place Saint-Michel (a neon sign immobilizing forever the image of that naked girl whom I didn't know what to do with). Vividly remembered minutes from my twenties, when I was ashamed of my big helpless body. (I am still ashamed.) And the empty eyes, like fish in the depths of the ocean, of a woman who lay with her legs spread apart. Another girl (Elisabeth Gréaumont) another failure (there were so many). My terror of a fiasco, from which each of my (infrequent) successes frees me, but only in regard to the woman I have possessed. *I run about the streets,* searching for some impossible salvation . . .

. . . On one of the walls, where their shadows mingle and dip into the labyrinth of mirrors, the palmate leaves of the philodendron form a clear-cut pattern. Like us, they reveal the continuous processes of life, the fabulous and infinite photosynthesis in which the sugar oxidized by animal organisms releases the carbon dioxide necessary to the growth of plants, which they in turn transform into the carbohydrates and oxygen which we need, and so forth, forever and always. It is marvelous to know this. Learning, and understanding such things is a great joy! Yes, this philodendron is a greater miracle than the story of the Living Buddha which I have been explaining for too long now, which I cannot seem to finish. Put an end to it, quickly . . .

". . . It was necessary, excuse me, my mind wandered for a moment and anyway I am almost finished, it was necessary to find on the body of the child certain marks, stigmata, you understand: a shell-shaped imprint in the palm of each hand, scars near the collarbone to show where the extra arms of the God should be, and I don't know what else. When they looked, every single one of these distinguishing features, all those I have mentioned, and others . . ."

"If only our religion offered us one-tenth as much proof . . ."

"Gilles! That is blasphemy! The abbé Préault has always told me . . ."

"But who knows if it was not all a hoax? The Regent . . ."

"Do you remember the pact made by Father Huc and the Regent?"

"Amazing, believe me! A game of truth, of metaphysics, so to speak. Each of them swore that he would become a convert if the other would bring him more convincing proof of his own faith . . ."

"That's a pretty good story, too. It is too bad that they were never put to the test, that Father Huc was sent out of the country before . . ."

"To go back to Greene, Graham Greene, if you don't mind . . ."

. . . But Julian, *what about Julian Green* . . .

"I myself do not believe in such . . ."

"The lines in your . . ."

"Quite. Let's say that there is some truth in it. Not in hands, but faces. When we meet a stranger, we can tell a great deal about him from his face . . .

"Well, the great talent of gypsies doesn't amount to much more than that . . ."

. . . Romanies encamped in a valley that is dry and barren in spite of recent rains. The black circle of a dead campfire. Half-naked children playing in the burnt-out grass. A birdcage hanging in the only window of a rickety green trailer. A man standing beside his thin horse. Why should it matter to him that he is always chased out of the villages; he has the power to make springs gush forth wherever he wishes. Where did I pick up this tiny and yet disturbing fragment of a fairy tale? *He has the power to make springs gush forth wherever he wishes . . .*

"Now Bertrand, how can an event which is accidental, determined by a series of chance occurrences, possibly be recorded in advance on the palm of one's hand?"

. . . I had better not answer Pilou. Watch out for those words which undoubtedly mean the opposite of what they say. On guard. I should find out the address of the very best palmist just in case she . . .

"But everyone knows . . ."

"There is no doubt whatsoever. And besides . . ."

"It is an established fact that my cousin . . . the one who was killed in an automobile accident . . ."

"Quite. But let me tell you . . ."

"Graham Greene . . ."

. . . I learned something very crucial from Julian Green, something which I did not fully appreciate at the time . . .

"The life line, it is true . . ."

"And the heart line, please . . ."

"Our own Gigi here, you know, is an excellent reader of palms . . ."

"Not really!"

"How fascinating . . ."

"I have to admit that I have a certain flair . . ."

"Here. Tell me what you see . . ."

"Oh please, my dear, mine too . . ."

"And mine, mine . . ."

. . . Not mine, with my nails bitten to the quick . . .

. . . Not mine, they are not very clean and anyway all this is nonsense . . .

. . . All these hands reaching across the table towards an old woman, whose heavy make-up and dyed hair make it too easy to imagine her sitting in a booth in a side show. Marie-Ange's lovely hand, with its perfect nails, her hand which caresses so well. Lucienne Osborn's blood-red nails . . .

"Not everybody at once! Here, Bertrand, since you are the closest, give me your hand. Ah . . . yes. I can see . . . In a word . . . But let me put it this way: your love of independence is too strong for your heart. You are, how should I say it, you are more thoughtless than you are wicked. That is it, exactly: you are completely unthinking. Also slightly selfish. Very selfish . . ."

"How delightful!"

. . . Momentary sparkle. Jarred by Mrs. Osborn's over-eager arm, one of the crystal water glasses next to Bertrand rocks back and forth. The rippling water slowly finds its own level again and settles into a small, transparent circle, parallel to the opaque white tablecloth where old Eugénie, awkwardly dropping her knife, has left a large stain. Well done. They are all waiting their turn. To think that this band of imbeciles has no idea of the masterpiece which I am capable of writing. *All I ask is to be admired by Bertrand.* The smooth, ash-blonde sweep of Marie-Ange's hair, the pretty forehead, immense eyes . . .

. . . Heavens, what if I do bite my nails, no one will notice, and besides, this is too tantalizing. Here I go . . .

"Roland? Are you next? Very well . . . How can I say this? You have not made the most of your opportunities . . ."

"You don't mean it! I find that very hard to believe, really I do . . ."

. . . How true, alas, how true . . .

"The ladies now. The ladies. Martine first. Let me see. Such a pretty hand. But too sensitive. A lack of confidence in yourself, the result of pride. Great potentialities, my dear, but, if you will pardon my saying so, it is written here before me, these potentialities have been nipped in the bud by a certain degree of laziness . . ."

. . . Eugénie doesn't say more than a few words about each one of us, but her analysis, spoken with an air of authority, is devastatingly accurate. Once, quite long ago, it was before I began to write my *Metaphysics of Physical Passion*, she looked at my palm and said: "It is absolutely necessary that you begin work on a large *opus*." Who knows whether her advice was not one of the incentives which finally gave me the courage to write my book, unreasonable as this may appear? But there were others, of a deeper, more decisive nature, in Brazil . . .

"And happiness, my sweet, I cannot deny the happiness which I see in your eyes . . ."

. . . I am lying. She has never seemed so listless, so far away from it all; not even sad, but as though she were beyond sadness. Pathetic, too, with her new little nose, the nose of a beautiful, happy woman . . .

. . . Happy? Yes, I am happy. This must be what they call happiness, even though Bertrand, (I am not thinking of his infidelity which is unimportant) even though he is not as tender with me as I might hope. The children are enough; with them I feel almost too much happiness. Happy, yes I am happy with Jean-Paul and Rachel, except that the very fact of being happy is so excruciating in this world which is not made for happiness . . .

". . . No, I am not happy . . ."

. . . As she drew her hand away, Martine murmured, in a tone of voice that did not sound serious, though it was: "No, I am not happy." No one but me paid any attention. Only me, the one who is responsible, the guilty one. We make each other suffer. And yet, and yet, Uncle Vanya, and yet, Martine, we love each other, we love each other . . .

". . . Now it is your turn, Gigi dear. No, not your hand, your face. Roland was right, faces are more revealing . . ."

"But you all know me too well . . ."

"Just as you knew everything there is to know about me. That did not stop you from . . . Besides, we are not dealing with the obvious facts. Not one of us really *knows* anything about the people closest to him. But faces, faces hide nothing . . ."

. . . I might have known it. She did not even glance at my hand. She forgot me. And it would have been so fascinating to find out if Longe and Hollywood were both written in my palm . . .

"They say that after a certain age a person's true nature can be read in his . . ."

"But of course. There is no question about it . . ."

"Even if you knew nothing about me, Bertrand my boy, you could see straight through to my soul, by looking . . ."

"So I could. On your face is everything which you try to hide: your goodness, your generosity, your modesty. And also your shyness. For no one else knows this, but you are shy, Gigi, dear . . ."

. . . I can't bring myself to go as far as Martine did earlier this evening, telling Eugénie, as she came into the living room, how beautiful she was, when she must have been struck, as the rest of us were, at how rapidly the poor soul had aged . . .

. . . I probably have a beautiful soul. But do I still have a beautiful face, or a beautiful body?

. . . It is not our souls which can be read in our faces, because we have no souls. A complete vacuum, empty of everything but our egos. Our faces betray us. Even the youngest of us, like me. So much cruelty and hypocrisy can already be seen on the pretty mask worn by little Pilou, which time has not yet spoiled. No soul, no soul. It is so easy to say . . .

. . . My fingertips stroke the harsh stubble on my chin, which is already beginning to grow again. It is not without pleasure that I caress these bristling contours. So many failures. Geneviève, not long ago. And the even greater number of women whom I never dared approach. That girl, when I was fifteen. (Nearly thirty years ago and I am still only fifteen.) What panic, sheer, overwhelming panic, when my (fat) helpless body gives in to defeat. *Quiet, quiet,* don't fret. Here in the dining room, even in the presence of three desirable young women (four counting

Armande), I do not have to prove myself. *And therefore*,
relax . . .

"Your charity work . . . Don't think we are unaware
of . . ."

"Only a drop in the bucket. Visiting the poor in my
neighborhood every Thursday, why it is the very least . . ."

. . . When Eugénie tries to be modest, it is too much
to take. Her coyness, her air of glorious humility . . .

. . . It would be nicer if she didn't boast about it. But
it's something, anyway, the old girl is trying, I like her
better for it. Most old bags like her . . .

. . . Charity which is heartfelt, genuine love for one's
fellow men. How beautiful! I can see myself, with Bertrand, visiting the sick and the poor. How pleasant, how
comforting. How nice to be nice. And how easy. Easy to
dream about, too; I know that only too well. As soon
as my inspiration goes, my sense of compassion, which is
really only sentimentality, will disappear, and I will be the
same selfish human being, the one Jérôme made me realize
that I have always been . . .

"You are right about one thing: I never do think of
myself. I live only for other people . . ."

"You are a truly wonderful friend."

"I don't know what I am. People tell me 'You are this,
you are that.' I don't know what to think."

"The main thing is not to think about oneself."

"God knows that I never think about myself. And I am
happy, I know that."

. . . Does Eugénie Prieur believe that she is telling the
truth when she says that she is charitable and good? In

any case she must know that she is lying when she says that she is happy. Her face is the living image of misery and loneliness. Suddenly, reflected in the centerpiece, I see the horrible face of a stranger whom I find it difficult to identify as myself. A stranger exposed to the scrutiny of everyone here, including my own, in all his weaknesses, his error, and depravity, a revelation which I cannot escape because, taken by surprise, I had condemned this stranger before I realized who it was. Martine, fortunately, is blinded by love as to my true nature . . .

. . . Eugénie was in about the place, relative to me, where Bertrand is sitting now. We leaned forward to see each other better, touched at meeting one another after I'm not sure how many years. It was in 1939, at the house of some friends whom I can't quite place. She was wearing the same emerald as this evening. I remember the aquamarine dress she was wearing, but not on her; it was lying over the back of a chair where she threw it, a few hours later, in a hotel in Fontainebleau. She held herself close against me. It was no longer what I had hoped for. How could it be? She was still beautiful, but approaching fifty . . .

. . . That couple is in the same place, petrified into a black, motionless flame of love. Speaking objectively, I am a scoundrel. To an outside observer, my depravity must be all too obvious. But I am never anything but indulgent towards myself; nothing can surprise me. Before Martine there was Irène, and the only reason I do not sleep with her any longer is that she no longer attracts me. Martine and Marie-Ange and Armande and Colette. All at the same time. And yet, as a young man, I was not like this.

Even today I am not so depraved that a generous thought does not sometimes pass through my mind, or that I do not sometimes act completely altruistically. Gigi was right, I am not wicked . . .

"The other night, at the movies, I found myself next to an indecent pair of young lovers; yes, believe me! indecent is the word, indecent and shameless in their innocence. They were so full of youthful rapture that they were oblivious of anyone else; they were completely unaware of anyone else's existence and held one another this way and that way until I must confess that I couldn't take it any longer. I thought to myself, 'This is the limit . . .' "

. . . The absolute limit, I am an old woman now . . .

. . . Eugénie did not say, "I will never again partake of such bliss." But that was the meaning of her words, of her nervous gestures, and of the silence which followed . . .

. . . She is trying to be funny, poor Gigi, but we all know that this kind of banter is only a disguise for the most immodest confessions, a veil of sarcasm which fools no one, but which preserves appearances and makes such daring intimate revelations acceptable and harmless . . .

. . . I haven't been to the flicks for a long time. Of course when I go to the cinema it is not as an ordinary spectator, but as a future actress . . .

. . . I myself am a part of this gigantic fraud, because I am living on my grandfather's money, money which should not belong to him. A large-scale conspiracy: it is agreed that there is nothing abnormal or undesirable about a system in which the many work for low wages, in order to make the few rich. But I benefit from this system, and I haven't the courage to repudiate it, so all I can do is to shut up about it. And at least avoid the hypocrisy of expressing leftist opinions while enjoying the status quo. Besides, Raymond Frôlet would not allow it. He would put me right where I belong . . .

. . . Men are timid. And cowardly. One, two, three, four, —five, six. There I go again! It is lucky that they are all cowards. They have no confidence in themselves. One, two, three, four,—five, six. They have so many fixations. Like me with the gold beads on this necklace. One, two. Enough! One, two, three, four. No more! Five, six. One, two,— three, four, five, six. They divide us into ladies, and those of us who are not ladies, instead of seeing us all as the women we are. They have made desire into a ritual. One, two. Men like Bertrand, who come right to the point without worrying about principles, are rare. That is what amazed me about Bertrand, the quick, casual way he seduced me. Three, four, five, six—one, two . . .

"Maybe you could tell me what news there is of poor Bibi?"

"Bibi? Bibi who?"

. . . As if she didn't know. As if there were more than one Bibi in Paris.

"Bibi Chartrettes, of course . . ."

"Oh! Bibi . . . No, not a word . . ."

"They say he is in Sainte-Anne's . . ."

"That is what I heard . . ."

"In Sainte-Anne's, but it's not possible . . ."

. . . Sainte-Anne's, of course, is for the poor, the sad ordinary run of humanity, not for them. Now, by some inexplicable combination of circumstances, one of them has landed in Sainte-Anne's . . .

"Well, what did you expect? He was asking for it all along."

"Quite. You remember his parties . . ."

"Oh yes, we always had a wonderful time at them . . ."

"That was ages ago . . ."

. . . Ages since he went bankrupt, and became ill, since anyone has seen him . . .

. . . This complete indifference, this calm egotism in the face of the loneliness, the suffering, and the despair of others. I like Bibi. At least I thought I liked him. But what kind of a friendship is it that can put up so calmly with sorrow, agony, and death? There are few people whom we really like. (Gold quotations may well ease off.) . . .

"His particular trouble leaves me cold."

"But the poor soul is suffering dreadfully."

"All he had to do was to stop drinking . . . It's his funeral. He had better not count on any sympathy from me. To go all the way across Paris to visit an old dodo in the nuthouse! It's his own fault that he's in there. After all. You have to draw the line somewhere. Believe me!"

. . . And she was the one who talked about living for other people! Bibi Chartrettes is paying for a life of drunkenness. He hasn't a cent. So there he is, in Sainte-Anne's, completely abandoned. After twenty years or more of close friendship. Or of the gossipy alliances and tired habits that pass for friendship in Paris. Complete and utter loneliness. I must go see him with Martine. I really should. Meanwhile Eugénie goes on sorting out the varieties of sickness, the kind she chooses to recognize and the others, the shameful, the disturbing kind . . .

. . . Dreadful selfishness. Bibi Chartrettes is someone I

244

am very fond of, someone who has always been kind to me; he even financed part of the film that was made from my first scenario. Now he is at death's door and I am thinking about my own death. I am somehow detached, twice-removed. As always, I am a spectator of my own feelings, out of reach and invulnerable. I watch myself suffer. Some-day, I may even watch myself die, with a feeling of detach-ment that will be stronger than all the pain, the despair, the regret of losing my dear, my beloved, my indispensable Bénédicte . . .

. . . This tingling sensation the horoscope this evening also said that I was very idealistic this oppression in all my feelings this burning of course idealism has always been my weakness it is getting worse the tingling the feeling of oppression the burning sensation I am afraid it is just what I expected and dinner isn't over yet unless perhaps it is a warning signal the beginning of the end . . .

. . . And yet there is such a thing as grace, even what I did could be pardoned. I am not lacking in repentance, nor in faith. It is just that it seems too easy. I have never been able to rid myself of the idea that we committed a murder . . .

". . . It is like the girls who are said, and rightly so, to have turned out badly . . ."

"The false romanticizing of girls who have gone astray . . ."

"Yes, of course, Dostoievsky's Sonia, and all the other novels on the subject . . ."

"Well, you may not believe it, but I have no sympathy for them, either. One of the maids I used to have . . ."

"Shh. Watch out."

"No, it's all right, Armande was just going out of the room. She is gone now. One of the maids I used to have, Lucette, do you remember her . . ."

"The albino?"

"No, she was dark. Lucette, you remember the one. She ran away, of her own free will, with a pimp who immediately put her to work in the streets. And I said to her, 'You can't say I didn't warn you, my dear . . .'"

"That never does any good. They have it in their blood."

"Yes, but this one had the crust to come sob on my shoulder afterwards!"

"Although I once knew some girls . . ."

"Oh you did, did you? And he tells us this with a perfectly straight face . . ."

"But of course, Gigi dear, we all have. And we love it!"

"Roland!"

. . . The vile language of those who are responsible for perverting these poor creatures. Almost as contemptible as the old man who was accused of corrupting minors and who said, to defend himself, that they had attained their *majority in vice*. Creatures. In my own mind I used the word "creatures." The corruption is everywhere, one cannot escape it, it is part of the very texture of the language, it *is* the language, or rather the connotations which words have taken on through usage; because "girl," "creature," after all, were originally sublime words . . .

. . . Flashing lights from the Place Saint-Michel, more than twenty years ago. (Devaluating the franc will continue the process of inflation, just as I had predicted in regard to the dollar.) With my chin in the palm of my

246

hand, and my thumb on my left cheek, my other fingers caress the stubble on my right cheek, against the grain. Little Jérôme Aygulf pokes his finger in his nose, then nervously rolls a pellet between his fingers, perhaps an imaginary one. Spread out on the bed in her bluish nakedness, almost translucent in the shadows, the girl . . .

"And do you know where she worked, my little Lucette? On the Rue Caumartin. Isn't that amusing?"

. . . I met her there one evening. We both pretended not to recognize each other. It is a part of the city where I like to wander at night, when I have the chance. Sometimes I catch the eye of a man who is looking for a girl. His glances seek out each woman who passes by, to see what is available, and the momentum of his search makes his eyes fall on me, old as I am. Of course the moment he has seen me, looked me over, and assessed me, the gleam in his eye disappears, but for one fleeting moment I have the illusion of being desired, as in days gone by, when I was young and beautiful. So beautiful, wasn't I, Gilles, so young, you remember, Jean-Jacques . . .

"In one of the cat-houses, excuse me, in a house of ill-repute, I met some . . . I will use an old-fashioned word so as not to shock you: some tarts, who were not at all . . ."

"Bertrand!"

"Yes, Marie-Ange, I mean it. You should try to put yourself in their place. People who have had all the advantages never . . ."

"Go ahead, insult us!"

. . . At home, cat-houses were where cats slept, and tarts

were to eat. But I don't make any such mistakes now that I am in France . . .

"I swear to you that in any bordello . . ."

. . . are girls who are every bit as good as you, and better . . .

. . . In bordellos and on the Rue Saint-Denis . . .

"Like the poor innocent girls who get . . ."

"Raped? There, Marie-Ange, I must disagree with you . . ."

"Wait a minute. Let me finish. That is just what I was about . . ."

"Well you are right. I can't feel very sympathetic there, either. You can't tell me . . . My shawl, where is my shawl? Oh, thank you . . ."

"I was just going to say that only those who are willing . . ."

. . . Who knows, who knows? Wild, the crimson clover is wild. So am I. Nothing could be more untamed than my innermost being. Was a woman ever freer than I am . . .

. . . I felt as though I were tainted. I needed to be cleansed. Since I had no father confessor, I went to the nearest church, in our parish. There, I believed that I would find a stranger, invested with the power to grant absolution, to listen to me. I even believed, in a rather cowardly and hypocritical fashion, that he might understand me. He would say the words which I wanted to hear. In a world where the infamy of a woman hiring herself out for a few thousand francs could exist, there was also a supernatural force capable of eradicating the sin that had been committed. I can still hear him clearing his throat. I can smell his stale breath and the odor of tobacco. "How many times, my son?" "Only once, I swear." There was a silence, then the muffled voice of the priest: "Think of the family which you will someday bring into the world, my son, a Christian family, which your rash error could permanently endanger. Disease is all too often the fruit of youthful indiscretions." He may even have said "shameful disease." The wretch! He was trying to make me afraid. All he wanted to do was scare me, and not with hellfire, which would have been low enough, but not as vile as the threat he used. To think of a priest trying to dismiss the disgrace of prostitution as nothing but a reason for certain faint-hearted social precautions! . . .

"All men like prostitutes, we know that."

"When they don't, it is a bad sign!"

. . . Why do I feel a sinister ache in my breasts also a kind of warmth not exactly burning but a warm sensation my stomach feels heavy as though something were going on inside of course I am digesting or else but how can one tell how can one make sure before it is too late . . .

. . . I have often felt like praying in the last few days. My silence, these days, has been a kind of prayer, hurled without hope into the void. They would never understand the very fine story which I know about Graham Greene; instead I shall tell them one which is more suitable to the occasion . . .

". . . I once heard a very curious story about Graham Greene, whom we were talking about a moment ago. One day he was walking with a friend, I think it was on the outskirts of London, yes, on the outskirts of London, and he suddenly pointed out the license plate on a car with tremendous satisfaction. Let us say it was number 278. His friend thought that the car belonged to someone in his family. But Greene hastened to explain that 278 was the number which he had been looking for . . ."

"What do you mean? What number?"

"Why was he looking for a number?"

. . . Pilou's shy young friend is high as a kite . . .

. . . My face in the mirror looks sensational I haven't lost a bit of my tan I never do lose my tan completely that would be all I need to lose my tan but I have to be careful keeping up a tan is hard work my hair really looks well Paul was right after all in suggesting that I wear it a little shorter oh if only one could have as much faith in one's doctor as in one's hairdresser this is much more becoming I must make an appointment with Harriet Ziem as soon as possible and also with the new doctor whom I heard about sometimes I feel that my poor little head will split with all these worries meningitis can come on so suddenly poor Zig all by himself *Tele-Faces* must be over by now I have missed it so there is no point in fretting about it any longer watch out be on your guard so as not to be taken unawares I am still a young woman sound healthy and strong but who can ever tell who can ever tell . . .

. . . Very often, through the day, I hold her in my arms. She puts her little head against mine and coos, and the touch of her soft, warm little cheek fills me with emotion. Have I had too much champagne? I feel relaxed, without a single qualm about the dinner. The pauses and silences do not bother me any more. A fleeting hallucination: the blue wallpaper between the mirrors in this dining room seems to turn into the pattern of garlands and geometric shapes —pink, yellow, black and white—that was on the walls of another room, on the Quai du Louvre, where I slept as a child. I saved a little fragment of that paper but it does not seem to match my memory of it while the clear picture that flashed through my mind just now seemed marvelously faithful to the original. My semi-intoxicated imagination probably recreates the poetry of childhood memories. Even though our private truths are not truth itself, the only reality which matters is the one which is within us . . .

"Greene's companion was every bit as astonished as you are. Then Greene explained, in all seriousness mind you, that for years he had been collecting the numbers on license plates in the city . . ."

"I've heard of people collecting all kinds of things, but this takes the prize . . ."

"It's not possible!"

"Before he could even begin his search, he had to find license plate number 1. Then he looked for number 2 (letters didn't count) and so on . . . He had reached 278 when . . ."

"Incredible!"

"It must have taken him years!"

"Years."

"An odd kind of game!"

"I guess he had a lot of time on his hands."

"But we all have our own little private lotteries, if not one kind, then another . . ."

"How right you are, sir. This was not just a game for Greene. He had two series of numbers going simultaneously, and had decided that if the second series reached 1000 before the first one, it would be a very bad omen. He had been keeping a double score like this for years, and had noticed that every time the second figure rose above the first one, some rather disagreeable, even sinister event, would take place in his life. He maintained that a catastrophe would occur if chance willed that the second series of license plates was completed before the first . . ."

"Well, you know what they say about the British . . ."

"No, I think it is all men, you and I and the rest of us, who are strange . . ."

"Graham Greene had come to the conclusion . . . He had decided . . . It seemed to him that . . . Well, in any case, he believed . . . How can I say it . . . He knew that there was no logical connection between the series of numbers which came to him more/or less by chance and the happy and unhappy events in his life. But, he said, in the beginning, there was also no necessary relationship between the signals of the Morse code, for instance, and the corresponding letters of the alphabet. Corresponding, that is the word he used . . ."

"This is getting interesting . . . Yes . . . Yes . . ."

"In short, it was simply a matter of establishing a means of communication, *of one kind or another*, between himself and the powers that be. Between himself and God. (Graham Greene believes in God.) Of course, once a particular means of communication has been chosen, it becomes necessary to stick to it . . ."

"A kind of code, then?"

"Exactly, a private code."

"Yes, but how does he know . . . that God is using the same code?"

"It is rather presumptuous on his part . . ."

"Don't be so sure about that! Haven't you ever suddenly had the feeling, a fleeting and illogical, but utterly convincing feeling, that a certain event concerned you directly, that *it had a meaning?*"

"Why of course I have, Jérôme. But how do you know that you are not interpreting the message in the wrong way? How can you be *absolutely certain* what it means?"

"Nothing is certain in this life . . ."

. . . The surprising juxtaposition of a human face next to one of marble gives Martine, on my left, a slightly unfamiliar appearance. As I looked in the mirror I suddenly caught sight of her profile, lodged in the graceful curve between the chin and the shoulder of a black marble bust. And Lucienne Osborn, whom I had first seen only as the wife, whom I had never met, of a husband who was missing, then as an undemanding dinner partner, neither pretty nor ugly, neither young nor old, just indifferent. Then finally, emerging from the haze that engulfs all women whose age or appearance does not invite favorable comparisons, her still charming face and desirable body are suddenly revealed to me . . .

"The beauties of nature, perhaps . . ."

"You and your 'breathtaking sunsets' . . ."

"That kind of beauty is devoid of significance . . ."

"But poets . . ."

"It is true that artists . . ."

"Proust wrote at length about this . . ."

. . . Is there enough cheese to go around? There are at least four kinds of goat cheese for it is Bertrand's favorite. But he forgot the Brie. My passion is both fulfilled and frustrated, with Jean-Paul and with Rachel. I know no more ecstatic pleasure than to feel the trusting face of my little girl pressed against my own, as she clings to my shoulder, and I carry her around, saying gentle little things in her ear, as she murmurs with pleasure. But at the same time, what a distance there is between us. They are both so fragile, so vulnerable! The Camembert looks about right. For that and for the wine, especially the wine, I can rely on Bertrand completely . . .

. . . The monotonous wail of fire engines. I feel an excitement within me. Nothing painful or unpleasant, just a kind of anticipation. Hopeful anticipation? How thrilled I would be to steal Bertrand's wife from him, if she desired me, if I desired her. But it has become impossible for me to betray Bénédicte, to whom I have never once been unfaithful. It has reached the point where I wonder if my fidelity has not been laziness, or cowardice, if the courageous thing would not be to make another sacrifice the way I did when we were first married, but in reverse: to force myself to make love to another woman, just as I once forced myself to make love only to her . . .

. . . A magnificent choice of goat cheese. Round, ruddy, dry little cakes of Chavignol, and the Saint Marcellin, a little less golden, next to the green speckled pyramids of Valençay, and the long unctuous wedges of Sainte-Maure, with their russet markings. Bénédicte has never shown an interest in cheeses. A man's business, she says, and rightly so. But I have so little time. Another treat in sight, the pungent Poivre d'Ane, from Provence, only just now uncovered . . .

"That reminds me of a passage in Barrès . . ."

"While we are on the subject of Barrès and Proust, I just read . . ."

"Barrès! Is there anyone today who has the slightest interest in what he ever thought or wrote?"

. . . Fire engines. It is someone else, always someone else who is in danger. I wonder what has happened to my brothers and sisters? Probably all married and settled in Longe. The most daring of them may have ventured as far as Chicoutimi . . .

. . . A magnum of Bordeaux. What a fine sight! I must remember to look at the vintage, when it is my turn to be served, next to last as always. The butler did not whisper the date and the château, as they do at my grandmother's. I can see the château on the label, hidden behind vines and white trellises . . .

"How amusing, Roland, I was also going to say something about Proust. There is a passage in *Amori and Dolori sacrum*, in which Maurice Barrès transfigures and then recreates the physical presence of Venice, which is worthy of the best of Proust. Now don't laugh . . ."

"But I must. The very thought that Barrès and Proust could . . ."

. . . No one can get a word in edgewise with Bertrand. Why do these fire alarms always seem to be warning of some disaster other than the one towards which the engines are racing? As though the siren were ringing for me; as though it were a special warning (telling me to watch out, to keep on constant guard.) . . .

. . . Like someone screaming and trying to catch his breath without stopping. The distance begins to quiet the sirens, and then in their wake another engine comes to relay their syncopated stridency, until it too dies away in some far-off part of the deaf city. Now she is like a little old lady, trotting around the house, touching this and that, chirping in her tender little voice about "Mummy," and I answer, even more lovingly, "Yes, my darling" or "Yes, my little angel" or "Yes, my precious baby" or "Yes, dearest heart." It is a presence, another little person in the house to console me when Jean-Paul is in school, and Bertrand is at the newspaper, or somewhere, I don't know where, I know only too well where . . .

"Barrès was describing the limpid sky reflected in the lagoon . . ."

"Technicolor! I can see it now . . ."

"Now wait a minute, please . . ."

. . . The melancholy sound of the engines at night. After forty-two years, they still give me a start. I was three years old. The alarm . . .

". . . The sky and the water merge together in such a way that the narrator . . ."

"The narrator! Now Bertrand, you are distorting the text to suit your own purposes!"

"Narrators, if you please, were not invented by Marcel Proust!"

. . . Leaving a sonorous wake behind them in the nocturnal silence, the fire engines, as they cross the city, are also racing down the long highway of my life, to the faraway avenues of my youth, to the gardens of my childhood, to Valromé where I still . . .

. . . The sad sirens of the fire engines fade away into the darkness and disappear three minutes on my back three minutes on my stomach I must be careful there is no time to think of anything else if one wants to make sure of a smooth even tan three minutes here three minutes there *Bertrand still finds me beautiful at last he is looking at me I am still attractive to him* . . .

. . . Pretty, yes, and still desirable. Not quite room temperature, my Pontet-Canet 1947. But what a divine year! My grandparents had a property in Pauillac. Valromé, this afternoon, the same as always, and yet *different* in an insidious way. Another season, another year. The disappointing contrast between what I see with such difficulty when my eyes are open, and so well when they are closed; the real Valromé, which I try in vain to describe to Martine, exists only within me. Dry, crumbly, and so deliciously acid, made from goat's milk . . .

. . . My problems are not of a metaphysical order; the fearful threat which hangs over me is physical. Free, unhampered by any restraints outside of the ones I create for myself, I feel compelled to find obstacles whenever and wherever sex enters into my life. Man cannot attain the simple innocence of animals. But those who believe that they are committing a sin when they make love are less hindered than . . .

. . . At home, after the evening when we had such a fine dance together, Bénédicte made a big scene, telling me that Martine was trying to take me away from her. Poor Martine, she is twenty-five; I am nearly fifty. But she does find me attractive. The lovers have returned to their niche in the portal. I never saw them go, but then I never saw them coming, either. Maybe I imagined them, along with . . .

". . . In such a way that the narrator had the illusion of floating in the sky. But now wait until you hear what follows . . ."

. . . The surface of the red wine, dropping, all at once, to a new level after I have taken a swallow, then rippling from side to side, sparkling with reflections and tiny glints of light at the edges. Martine is again avoiding my eyes. She forgets that any woman should consider herself fortunate to be desired. In love with her husband, she wishes to remain faithful to him in the very depth of her soul, and feels guilty if she momentarily forgets her passion, and desires the body of another man—my body. Yes, there is no doubt about it, this young woman finds me attractive . . .

. . . These feelings, which I dismiss, leave behind them a faint, distressing desire. Next to me is a man whom I know is in my power, but the presence of another man, to whom I belong, forbids me even to look at him, let alone to love him. Happiness is within my reach, at least of my voice, if not of my hands. I know the words to say, the gestures which it would be enough merely to suggest. Under scrutiny, however, I can only glance stealthily at this tempting, forbidden bounty . . .

. . . Cheek to cheek, for the length of one short but endless foxtrot, Gilles and Martine are again dancing before me. At first I paid little attention, only slightly surprised that they would do this in my presence . . . Pilou has always shown such convincing evidence of her love. It was such a fleeting impression. Everything resumed its normal course. Only gradually did the image begin to appear in a sinister light, returning now and then to trouble me, for reasons which even now I cannot understand. It has reached the point where I am suspicious of Gilles, and would never have invited him tonight had I known that his wife, whose presence neutralizes him, would not be able to come. But these suspicions are groundless. In all fairness, I cannot say that Martine has been anything but friendly and polite to this man who was her partner for the space of a short dance. A dance which for me has never come to an end . . .

. . . Bertrand couldn't be jealous, really, it would be too ludicrous . . .

. . . Little Martine certainly finds Gilles attractive. One would have to be blind not to notice that there is something between them. The attraction they feel for one another is very evident. As far as he is concerned, it is not surprising; she is so fresh and young. And there is still something alluring about him. Is it possible that Bertrand hasn't noticed? Not that he doesn't deserve it, believe me!

. . . Pilou, Pilou, you aren't going to let yourself be seduced by this old fop. Bertrand, your husband, is so much more attractive, so much more charming . . .

. . . The ridiculous advances of Gilles Bellecroix (whom I should nevertheless try to please if I want a part in his new film). And the feeble way that Martine Carnéjoux is pretending to reject them. In that blood-red field I was cured of love. I am perhaps the only woman who can look upon the hackneyed love-stories in books or plays objectively, and always take the part (I was surprised to notice this recently) of the woman or the man who is spurned, instead of the happy pair whose fleeting joys and pathetic caresses seem ridiculous to me. That young Jérôme is charming, and so shy; why he hardly dares look at me . . .

"But wait a minute, listen to what follows. The moment when reality seems to be surpassed by the magic of . . ."

"Magic . . . Here we are back again on our favorite subject . . ."

"The very words of the book, and I quote, are: "This immense magic." At that moment, some dark shadows began to appear, to take shape, to grow larger, and finally to crystallize . . . And then comes the Proustian anticlimax: *'These were the monuments of Venice.'* "

"We are not convinced!"

"I must say that I don't quite see . . ."

"Now really, how can you miss it! It is exactly the tone of voice in which Proust . . ."

. . . Of course to feel this one needs a certain minimum of taste. If they haven't understood, no amount of explanation is going to make them see the light . . .

"Did you know, by the way, what Barrès once wrote about Proust . . ."

"Yes, very interesting. But if you will listen for just a minute . . ."

. . . Impossible to get a word in. That Carnéjoux is a boor! . . .

260

". . . Just a minute, *please!* Have you forgotten the passage in *Albertine Disparue* describing the beauty to be found in the things which are the most prosaic, as well as in those which are the most exotic? Proust glorified Cambray before Venice . . ."

. . . Contact broken with Lucienne Osborn. My own fault, too. This was not the moment to try to take the floor and say something brilliant. I may as well give up my attempt to focus all the hidden forces of my flesh into my left arm, which is lying next to her right arm as it rests languidly on the tablecloth. It is not as though she has rejected my advances; I just don't seem to exist for her. Perhaps her body is animated by some other force of which I am unaware, but in any case it is not receptive to any magnetism that might be coming from me . . .

. . . What could Zig be up to right now the poor darling and Léon-Pierre luckily I will be seeing him tomorrow I feel as if I can't wait a minute longer why wait this young man across the table would do just as well but he looks timid boys of that age are always a problem they make such a fuss about everything Roland Soulaires is really a bit too fat I could go for Gilles but he seems to be interested only in Martine . . .

. . . I know that all men are my brothers, but I haven't the right to consider myself one of them. I know the meaning of truth but I have to live a lie. A lie that must be my truth if I do not wish to fall into an even more vile falsehood, that of setting myself apart from the society which supports me and relieving my conscience with occasional outbursts of mild criticism. Excluded, apart, dreaming of a harmonious future society which can only be created by exterminating boys like me. Looking forward to the day when I will voluntarily give up my modest worldly goods, perhaps even my life, in the name of the necessary, the inevitable, the hoped-for revolution . . .

"But when you get right down to it, (and this is the point that I wanted to make) Proust never said anything about Venice that Barrès had not already . . ."

"I think you are really exaggerating now, Bertrand . . ."

"Very little. Obviously Proust had to appear on the scene before we could recognize the prophetic nature of such passages in Barrès . . ."

. . . Gilles is becoming much too attentive towards Martine . . .

"While we are on the subject, I would like to quote something to you . . ."

. . . It is very frustrating not to be able to squeeze in my story. Carnéjoux has always liked the sound of his own voice, but now he has become insufferable. He has even forgotten to eat his cheese . . .

"Let me finish! One could go so far as to say that in Barrès, *and also in Anatole France* . . ."

"Anatole France! Now you are going too far!"

"You must be joking!"

"Do continue, but I am afraid that you have left us way behind . . ."

. . . The inside of one's arm is very difficult various gymnastics are necessary according to whether one is lying on one's back or on one's stomach I had forgotten about that run in my stocking what a nuisance . . .

"We shall see! Is there anyone here who has read *La Vie en Fleur?* No one?"

. . . To be within a budding grove, and terrified . . .

"Yes, I have . . ."

"Of course, so have I!"

"A sequel to the *Livre de Mon Ami* and *Petit Pierre,* if I remember correctly. A work of his later years . . ."

"Exactly, Gigi. Touching memories of childhood and youth . . ."

. . . *Souvenirs d'Enfance et de Jeunesse,* by Renan, one of the most beautiful books I have ever read . . .

. . . Last reminiscences, in the face of death. A tale told in a minor key, but with heights of eloquence, and sometimes great beauty . . .

. . . I am exaggerating a little. Within us all are overflowing reserves of admiration, attached to no particular object, waiting only to be let loose. We release them at the slightest provocation. Aesthetic delight which feeds on itself, blind enthusiasm, symptoms of what nostalgic yearning? . . .

". . . One must try to read with an open mind . . ."

"That is not the point. When Barrès says of Proust . . ."

"But yes, Roland, it is necessary to keep an open mind . . ."

. . . There he goes again. I will never be able to tell my story. Bertrand Carnéjoux will always interrupt, in that deep voice which he knows is impressive. If he would at least stop for a bite to eat. But no, he has completely forgotten that he is at the dinner table, in his own house. Oh well, I give up . . .

"Yes indeed, one must strive for an open mind! Writers like these have not been forgotten, they have simply been disregarded, which is worse. They have lost stature, one might say, to the extent that new generations have withheld their admiration . . .

. . . Even I am surprised by what I am saying. Conversation offers such opportunities to express, in a few, felicitously-turned expressions, the insights which have been unfolding slowly and secretly in some hidden part of one's mind . . .

". . . I am sure that the young man across the table from me, for instance, could tell us a thing or two about this particular kind of neglect, of disdain . . ."

. . . Me? I couldn't care less about Anatole France. Except for his political opinions, that is; he was on the right side of the fence; he was one of us . . .

". . . Don't ask me about Anatole France! . . ."

"Exactly what I was saying. A few minutes ago you made it clear that you are quite at home with Proust. But Anatole France means nothing to you. When someone like Jean-Jacques Limher is neglected, it doesn't matter. Limher does not exist, or rather he does not exist any more. That is to say he never really deserved his reputation . . ."

. . . You again, Jean-Jacques, you again. You who are now enjoying yourself with other women, you who are still so close to me. And they dare to say that you do not exist . . .

. . . The casual and irrevocable cruelty of literary judgments. Do I, Bertrand Carnéjoux, the author of *Sober Pleasures*, do I exist? . . .

"But Barrès, or Anatole France, that is a different matter, don't you think? . . ."

. . . How enjoyable to be admired. Jérôme, Gilles, and even Bertrand, they all come around sooner or later. It is not Jérôme, or Bertrand whom I would like to kiss me, but Gilles . . .

. . . This is no time to be funny or to tell one's life history or harp on the past now is the time to enjoy enjoy enjoy I don't know whether it is the effect of the champagne or of sitting next to Bertrand after so long but I feel more and more overheated burning up Eugénie is incredible she is helping herself to cheese as though she hadn't had a thing to eat of course with a figure like hers why bother . . .

. . . In my haphazard and probably inaccurate scientific reflections, what am I trying to find? A little bit of bread, a swallow of Bordeaux. If a few magnetized shavings of iron can point to the north and the tension of a hair can measure the relative humidity, would it not be possible for such a complex organism as the human body to be as infallible a guide to the supernatural? Claudel said this in almost the same words. He also wrote: *I had to study philosophy, but I found that in reality truth is a much simpler affair, as natural as the sun or cool water, as easy on the soul as bread and wine* . . .

"In the light of what has been written since then, their work appears in new perspectives. Proust was so dazzling, Dostoievsky, Joyce, and Kafka filled us with such wonder that for a while one could not see them clearly . . ."

"Quite. Just the same, however, Barrès once said of Proust that . . ."

"Exactly. I found a number of Proustian motifs in *La Vie en Fleur*, or rather, I don't want you to misunderstand me, themes which lacked only the Proustian orchestration, all the essentials, but not yet combined into the final score . . . And therefore . . . futhermore . . . therefore . . ."

. . . Martine is looking solemnly at Gilles, who is scratching his right ear. It is Pilou, and at the same time it is not Pilou. My love is not in gear with her new face . . .

. . . Suddenly preoccupied, Bertrand is looking at his wife and mumbling something about "therefore" and "furthermore" to indicate that no one is to take advantage of this brief pause and interrupt with words on Barrès and Proust. Staring straight ahead, his mind in a daze, he is filling this momentary gap in the conversation before picking up where he left off, after the last "therefore" which he has prolonged ad infinitum, lingering on its syllables as he commands silence with his raised hand. Bertrand Carnéjoux has always been rather garrulous . . .

. . . Gilles Bellecroix is still turning on the charm, while she, with her pretty face leaning over in his direction, is looking at him and smiling. Reserved, attentive, discreet, with a subtle mixture of shyness and poise in her bearing. Martine, Pilou, my wife. The same person whom I was watching less than two hours ago, as she dressed in front of me, aloof and graceful in her chaste nakedness, just as relaxed in my presence as though she were alone, revealing an intimacy which no longer surprises either one of us, but which now suddenly comes to me as a shock, and which I find hard to believe. My wife, my wife, she is my wife . . .

. . . There is nothing the slightest bit reprehensible, or even unusual, in his behavior. His eyes do not linger on me. And yet, under their brief, penetrating onslaughts, I feel helpless . . .

. . . Now would be the moment to tell my little anecdote.

But although Bertrand appears to be momentarily distracted, there is something so overbearing in the way he keeps repeating "therefore" that I do not dare disregard such an obvious warning. Soon, very soon, before I go to sleep, with the final quotations from the stock market in hand, I will do as I always do, and add up my fortune. A rough estimate, to be sure, but just to think about it comforts me. Troubles me. Fortunately the market did rather well today . . .

. . . Harriet Ziem or Nicholas de Perligny I must find out which one is better after John goes I will buy another dog maybe even two I will do anything I want to how ridiculous it is with him never at home but everything ready just as if he were I'm tired of his little whims he wants it this way he wants it that way I wonder where I should get my stretch-pants this year I really have too many things to think about and all his mistresses won't they be sorry when he dies all the money will come to me no more presents for starlets everything for Lucienne and for Zig except for what goes to Joan his first wife of course Joan and John how silly did I forget to give Zig his soup before I left and Bertrand I wonder if I can expect anything from him love is the only thing that is worthwhile anymore but not with John the few times he gets the urge poor Ivy Luck I feel sorry for her she certainly has seen better days yes many too many things to think about if I weren't so well-organized with such a good little head on my shoulders . . .

. . . Imagine what would happen if Bertrand were jealous of me. I could describe, in a film, the slow poison of this kind of incident in the mind of a suspicious husband. First he encouraged his wife and his friend to dance together, and was surprised only by the way she allowed the other man to hold his cheek next to hers. Then he thinks it over. Remembers that she did not seem displeased. What was at first only a hazy and innocuous memory becomes more and more unpleasant, grows clearer, takes on painful and insidious overtones, and finally turns into an unbearable obsession. Until the day when, three years later, the husband again meets his former friend, whom he has gradually ceased to like and has ended up by hating, and, in his delayed and of course unjustified jealousy, kills him . . .

. . . Marie-Ange is looking at me again and I am afraid. *One of those pure looks which are a woman's most terrible weapons.* I no longer desire to possess a girl, but would like the pleasure of abandoning myself to her caresses. Such passivity is not masculine. Deep circles under young Jérôme's eyes. Again I feel the oppressive inner urges of my inhibited desires . . .

"And therefore I maintain that in these writers the genius of Proust is prefigured, at a distance of course, and undeveloped, but nevertheless prefigured. And who knows whether Proust himself did not begin by using these writings as a kind of springboard? I mean to say that there is a reason for the narrator's great admiration for Bergotte . . ."

. . . It would be an insult to remind them of Anatole France's influence on Proust. They are supposed to know that. Thanks to Roland Soulaires, and also perhaps to Gilles Bellecroix (although he is not saying much this evening) our dinner has been a little less frivolous than those we are accustomed to. But perhaps I should refresh the memories of the ladies present, not Eugénie, of course, she knows everything . . .

". . . I was speaking of the early books of Bergotte, I beg your pardon, I mean Anatole France, not *La Vie en Fleur*, naturally; it appeared later, when Proust was no longer only the aspiring young writer who had asked France to write a preface to his first book . . ."

. . . He is brilliant. He knows so much. His voice is wonderful, so deep. But I mustn't behave like this, letting myself be fascinated by another man. A man. And Pilou's husband, at that. Unthinkable . . .

"My mother also used to say that Barrès . . . If you only could have known her. Once when I pointed out to her, I was very young, you see, but of course that was no excuse and besides I was not what you could call stupid, not at all, believe me. You never knew my mother, did you? That is too bad. She was a woman who, how can I say it . . ."

. . . buzz, buzz, buzz . . .

. . . It never fails. As soon as the conversation gets interesting, Gigi rushes in like a lunatic to tell us all about her mother, or something else that has nothing whatever to do with what we are talking about. Nobody gives a damn about her mother . . .

"If I remember correctly, *La Vie en Fleur* is the last book which Anatole France ever wrote. I believe it was published two years before he died, in 1924 . . ."

"Yes, it appeared in 1922, the year Proust died."

"So Anatole France lived long enough to be influenced by the writer whom he himself . . ."

"I doubt it . . ."

"Oh, but one could pursue this even further . . ."

. . . How eloquent I am tonight. If only I could record these improvisations of mine, word for word. They would hardly even need polishing. Why am I less intelligent when I am sitting in front of my typewriter? My *Metaphysics of Physical Passion* wasn't bad, but it could have been so much better . . .

". . . Even further. Certainly in the passages where Anatole France shows what time has done to the beautiful Céline, the aged model of the painter Gérard, his description is made more meaningful by Proust's revelations. Let us admit, for the moment, though I am not convinced even if it is chronologically possible, that Anatole France was influenced as an old man by Proust. But you are certainly not going to tell me that France read the novels of André Malraux . . ."

. . . Malraux! Carnéjoux' babbling has finally produced something worthwhile. I have found the clue which I have been hunting for all evening. It was a conversation between Julian Green and Malraux in 1930. (And it is even more important than I had thought.) I must try to remember the exact words, something like: Malraux told me that he was not afraid of death, but *of the impotence that comes at fifty and is already a sign of death* . . .

"I must read you the passage in which Anatole France prefigures Malraux. Perhaps later this evening. I knew you would be surprised . . ."

. . . It is not what he is saying that surprises me, but what he is. And what I am in regard to him . . .

. . . My look of surprise comes from the discovery which

I have just made, thanks to Malraux and Julian Green; not until this minute did I appreciate its extraordinary (miraculous) practical applications . . .

. . . Between Lucienne Osborn and me, as I talk, flows a series of swift, flashing, and what I used to call when I was young and innocent, aggressive glances . . .

. . . All hot and bothered again I had forgotten about it for the moment it must be all in my mind try not to think about it . . .

. . . I hope he doesn't think we are listening to him. Only Mrs. Osborn looks entranced. But what interests her is obviously the man, not his words. If I were Bertrand, though, I wouldn't complain . . .

". . . He was describing Gérard's *Psyche*, the one that was exhibited in the Salon of 1797, or '98, I don't remember. Maybe it was 1796. In any case France said that it was his masterpiece, but he also said that there was a study for it which was greater than the finished work. According to him, this sketch had a quality not to be found in the large painting which hung in the Louvre. I know what you are going to say . . ."

. . . Finish this as soon as possible. Except for Lucienne Osborn and Jérôme, no one is listening to me. It is interesting just the same. The preoccupied expression on Roland Soulaires' face is very insulting. He is the one person who might have grasped what I am saying . . .

" . . . Please don't misunderstand me! I am the first person to admit that any similarity or parallel between these two writers is purely coincidental. Anatole France is, by definition, the very opposite of Malraux . . ."

... My forearm, leaning on the table not far from where Lucienne Osborn has casually laid hers. No contact. Perfectly natural positions, chance proximity. No one could get the wrong idea. But now, between her bare flesh and mine, in spite of my sleeve, is a network of telepathy. Communication has been established, and we are sending each other messages, in the instantly decipherable code of desire . . .

. . . Bertrand is gazing silently at that little Osborn woman, as though the talk which he is about to resume were for her alone. He leans toward her slightly, with a serious, attentive expression. Handsome. And amazingly youthful. Is he aware of his other guests, or even of where he is? Nothing exists for him except this woman, who is still young and whom he is seducing in the presence of his indifferent young wife. So certain of his powers that it is humiliating for all the women at the table,—and also, by way of contrast, for me, alas, for me. He is content to sit and gaze at her. Slowly but surely he is bringing her under his spell, looking for all the world like some kind of bird, which tips its head to one side and stands absolutely still, yes, terribly still, and dangerous . . .

. . . There is no doubt that Lucienne Osborn desires me as much as I desire her. She and I are caught in a zone of high tension which no one else can feel. Like two packs of hounds, each held at bay; why hold them back? Already, though motionless and silent, our two bodies have leapt upon each other. Though at a distance, they are devouring each another, ferociously . . .

. . . The conversation is a blind. Is Bertrand interested in what he is saying? It seems as if a complicated plot were being woven beneath this protective cover of words, in preparation for some mysterious and imminent event from which I feel myself to be excluded forever . . .

. . . Eugénie Prieur is bubbling with agitation and excitement, the way she always was in the days when I loved her. But she is no longer *lovable*. Even when she keeps still for a moment, she can be heard vibrating silently, like the engine of the car which is idling below us on the embankment. Her eyes are sparkling with gratitude, as though someone had offered her the sympathy for which she has been begging all evening, as though she were thanking us in advance, in an unsuccessful attempt at blackmail. In desperate need of admiration, understanding, and support, not so much ignored by the other guests as deliberately and systematically rejected by them, she has us all under a kind of emotional radar, but has not yet managed to detect even a glimmer of hope. Even those who do not know Eugénie can sense instinctively that to offer her the least bit of encouragement would be to let loose a chain reaction of gushing sentimentality which it would be impossible to control . . .

. . . And Bertrand is at least twenty-five years older than I am! But what is happening to me, what is happening to me? He is morally so reprehensible—and physically so attractive. If to grow old is to betray, then I hope I never reach forty. Five or six years ago, at the time of his marriage, and the publication of his book, I was only thirteen or fourteen. I was already in love with Pilou. Yes, I remember the grown-ups talking about Bertrand Carnéjoux, and the new experiment in fiction which he had attempted. Such prestige, even then. And since that time he has become editor-in-chief of *Ring*. The operation threw Martine's face out of balance, even though it added a symmetry which was not there before . . .

. . . If physiological impotence comes at fifty (so soon, at fifty, is this plausible?) then one could say that I have only seven years before I pass from one kind of impotence to another . . .

. . . Like all the others, little Lucienne Osborn, you will escape me in a mockery of pleasure . . .

". . . One has only to remember his words: *Against the vestiges of an art* . . . No, *vestiges* sounds too much like Malraux. Anatole France is the one who is speaking here, after all. He must have said *the remains* . . ."

. . . How intelligent I am. What a memory . . .

". . . *Against the vestiges of an art unequaled in Antiquity, all else seems impoverishment and distortion.* It is the opposite of what Malraux would say."

. . . Bertrand is the most brilliant of us. But a bit long-winded. I have had enough . . .

. . . There is a strange aura surrounding this dinner. I can't put my finger on what it is, however. Everything has gone according to the rules. But even though nothing unusual has taken place, there are certain undercurrents. Perfectly pleasant, and yet disquieting. What causes these fleeting, invisible explosions which leave a poisonous fog lingering in the air? Bertrand Carnéjoux must be given credit for revealing, in his novel, the existence of this intangible reality. Nevertheless one could do better, one could pursue the matter further. I am much more famous than Carnéjoux. But though he is known only among a limited circle, it is alas, the one which matters most . . .

"They say that one should never mention what is on one's plate, that it is simply not done, but really, my dear, your dinner has been too marvelous. And the dessert! It looks sensational! Sensational!"

"An ice, my dear, just a simple little ice. As for all your compliments, undeserved, I assure you, I don't really know whether they should be allowed or not. But I can tell you one thing: hostesses adore them!"

. . . Why do I feel so uneasy? Neither Bertrand nor his young wife nor anyone else here has said or done anything improper. And yet I have the sinister impression that sensuality is slowly filling the air, a feeling which is unpleasant only because I do not feel a part of it, I, Marietta, in whose honor the dinner itself is being given . . .

"One minute, if you don't mind, and then I will be finished. In the words which I quoted to you, in spite of one expression which I now remember, and which dates the whole passage because it originated with the Goncourts, via Proust's brilliant parody, you remember . . ."

. . . They don't remember a thing, and besides, they couldn't care less. But this has such fascinating ramifications . . .

". . . The expression I referred to is the *manner*, that is, the execution of an artist, his style, his characteristic method, his idiosyncrasies or what have you. In spite of this, and I also notice (one has to be fair) a reference to emotion which is closer to the aesthetic of Diderot than

275

to that of the author of the *Musée Imaginaire*, nevertheless, one can find in this passage all the essentials of Malraux's analysis of Constable's painting the *Hay Wain* . . ."

"How curious . . . But I think Roland wanted to say something . . ."

. . . It's about time. But I have too much to think about now. Even though what Barrès said about Proust is quite interesting . . .

. . . It would be much better yes indeed it would be more convenient if John's first wife died too Joan is younger than I am but accidents can happen only three more months before I go to Megève I must be very tan when I arrive the stretch-pants which Rémon made me last year were sensational but I doubt if I will be able to fit into them again anyway they are probably wearing something else this year the best would be if they both died in an airplane he still sees Joan once in a while though I can't see why after all they didn't have to get a divorce but the two of them hardly ever travel together what a pity . . .

"One last word, if you don't mind, Pilou. We were talking about Diderot. I could find you a passage in Diderot that is pure Proust. Or pure Bergson, you might say . . ."

. . . Bergson, naturally. I am only repeating the obvious. My whole being is involved in this, but I can only graze the surface. To reach into the dark inner abysses of my mind would require more effort than I can exert right now. In my present state of passive well-being I hardly can find the energy to speak, in spite of the pleasant intoxication of talk. Aware of nothing but my presence among these silly people and of the words which are coming from my lips,

I sit here—with my real talents and the richness of my existence tucked away somewhere, but where?—as empty and destitute as though I had no past at all, and were reduced to the meager realities of a diminishing appetite and increasing intoxication . . .

". . . Diderot said the same thing, at length, and in a style that is as subtle and complex as anything Proust ever wrote: *Everything we have ever known, heard, seen, lived, conceived, everything we have ever looked at down to the smallest leaf on the tiniest bush or the very least of all the waves of the ocean, not excluding every note of the humblest melody, all this exists within us without our knowing it . . ."*

. . . I feel embarrassed to have talked so long and so didactically. Less certain now of my brilliance. Only the quotes were interesting. The rest? Air bubbles. The effervescent sparkle of champagne. Nothing more. Outside, along the deserted quai, a gentleman in his dressing gown is patiently walking a small dog who is taking his time as he sniffs his way along the uninspiring pavement. But he will have to make up his mind soon; a few drops of rain are beginning to fall . . .

". . . You have a dog, haven't you, Lucienne, if I may call you Lucienne . . ."

"Who else, my dear Bertrand, if not you? Yes, an adorable little dog named Zig. A purebred dachshund, you know. A lovely russet color. You can't imagine what a darling he is. A sweetheart. You know what dachshunds are like, don't you? Zig is so cute; I could tell you hundreds of stories about him. Do you know what he did the other day, when the two of us . . ."

"What about you, Gigi?"

"Alas, I can't have a dog!"

"But why?"

"Because I have no servants anymore . . ."

. . . Eugénie sighs in her weary, jaded, and rather noisy fashion, while Bertrand nods politely and that idiot woman joins the conversation for once, to tell us about her pooch. Imagine. Beautiful Marie-Ange with a far-away look in her big eyes . . .

. . . Here comes the rain. Luckily I can always find someone to take me home. It should be John Osborn, but his wife will be with him. Too bad. No, on the contrary, it gives Jérôme the chance to take me home. Though he probably has no car nor even any money. I will pay for the taxi; it won't be anything serious, just amusing. Besides I needn't worry this evening. Now, a little signal, a very little one, just to see how he will react . . .

. . . Good God! My knee just bumped into Marie-Ange's. I hope she didn't think I did it on purpose. Try to keep still. The plain, wholesome taste of bread. And what if she thinks that I think that she nudged me? That would be even more embarrassing . . .

"You see, Zig is a most unusual dog. He gives me a great deal of pleasure . . ."

. . . No one is even pretending to listen to me it is infuriating the conversation was finally getting interesting if I only knew what they were talking about Diderot indeed I don't see what is so interesting about a boulevard . . .

. . . Saved, I have been saved. I still have seven years, only seven years, but seven years is a long time (one can make love a great many times in seven years). Since the hostess actually asked me to speak, I will try out my little quotation after all . . .

". . . Yes, quite. Rousseau's periwinkle and the bit of ash which fell out of a letter in *Madame Bovary*, all this was Proustian, before Proust . . ."

. . . I don't try to embroider my stories. And I think too fast to be able to dramatize what I am saying . . .

". . . Quite so. All this anticipated Proust's *madeleine*. The periwinkle reminded Rousseau of his entire past and a flower in the new world (I don't remember what kind) did the same for Chateaubriand. And so it goes. Quite. We know all that . . ."

. . . Roland is so tiresome the way he keeps repeating quite, quite. Someone should tell him what a monotonous and boring habit it is . . .

". . . Well? What do you mean by 'all that'? Come on, Roland; you will have to explain yourself a little better . . ."

. . . Gilles irritates me the way he keeps saying *well? well?* Why did I ever get started on this literary discussion when I have just made a discovery that will radically change my life, or at least the years that remain of my youth. It is too bad that I look so much younger than my age! (If anyone had told me before this that I would someday complain about how young I look, I would never have believed them!) But I can always pretend that I am older, and say to the woman whom I meet for the first time: "You may not believe it, but I am nearly fifty . . ." I am

279

stammering. I must finish my story as quickly as possible . . .

". . . Yes, we know, quite. I repeat that we, we, we know all that. Where was I? Oh yes . . . Do you know what Barrès dared to call Proust, in the notebook which he kept at the end of his life, the very same Barrès whom you have been trying so hard to rehabilitate; for I agree entirely with our young man here—Barrès is permanently disqualified . . ."

. . . "Your young man" thinks you are a big bore. Barrès couldn't have been a more dreadful reactionary . . .

". . . Barrès called Proust, now brace yourselves, he called him *an observer in a vacuum*. And he added, referring to a phrase of Goethe's, which makes it even more incredible . . ."

. . . Say to her, or to any woman to whom I feel attracted, "I have made love so often and for so long that I have become impotent, it is my own fault . . ."

". . . So Barrès said: *In judging a work of art, the first criterion is its subject matter . . .*"

. . . Finished. Whew! By finding a valid reason for my impotence, I will be able to escape it. I can explain away my inhibitions; they will vanish. Why didn't I think of this before? I am saved . . .

"Think of Pascal and his ideas on painting. Or Goethe, whose theories on the subject were even more absurd. The imbecility of great men is in proportion to their genius . . ."

"A good book can be written on any subject . . ."

. . . Or a good film. Even this very ordinary dinner party would do. Why not? No subject matter is better than any other. Unfortunately, however, in writing scenarios, the public has to be entertained . . .

. . . Watch out, Marie-Ange. Your nose is getting red. How can I tell her to powder her nose? Martine Carnéjoux is really pretty tonight, with her brown hair and fair complexion, and her blue eyes—a rare combination which Bertrand has always sought and which he has sometimes found. But she is much too young to shine in a world where women only become fashionable with age. I predict a bright social future for her, but not yet. She will be in style in fifteen years. In fifteen years I will no longer be in style. How old will I be in fifteen years? At least seventy-five—I can't count any more—eighty-two years old . . .

. . . Maybe a wife and child would save me. Their well-being would come before a clear conscience. But I am still free. I could refuse to get married, I could give up my inheritance, and women—all women? I could go into exile, learn life the hard way, work for a living and also for the only happiness which means anything to me, the joy of communicating, communing, and uniting man to man. Marie-Ange is very sweet to look at me like this, with such a gentle, serious expression. Nothing from Bertrand, not the least sign of friendship. He doesn't even see me. I don't exist for him any more. I won't keep these cufflinks. When I leave, I will throw them in the Seine . . .

. . . Physiological impotence bears no stigma, while the psychological variety is ridiculed. This very evening, with Marie-Ange, why not . . .

. . . But you are out of your mind, Marietta, my dear girl. This young man has nothing to give you. You will throw away the results of years and years of effort. But I feel such a longing to hold him in my arms, now, right now, to hug him gently, not to make love, but for love . . .

. . . Symbols which exist only for the author's own pleasure. No reader will ever be attentive enough to notice them. Or to unravel their subtle correlations. Perhaps someday, one scholar, in an American university, maybe at Harvard, will understand, and this will be my reward, and my delight. These hidden facets of my work, although unknown to my readers, are the reason for its coherence, its necessity, and its beauty. And in my *Sober Pleasures* I have laid the foundations on which will be built the long-anticipated structure of my second novel, which itself . . .

. . . Darling Martine if only we dared . . .

. . . Gilles, Gilles, why not. (That dance, one night, with him.) Or anyone attractive. I have been too childish, too silly. As if a woman could devote her life to one man, even to Bertrand. Following his dog, a man in a flowered dressing-gown walks in the rain . . .

. . . I was trying to be worthy of that very young and very lovely girl. What if, in doing so, I became unworthy of myself? If, in being faithful to a woman, it was myself I betrayed? . . .

. . . For love? But what's coming over me? I am mad. Watch out there, Marietta, my dear, you are mad, mad . . .

. . . I will say to her: "My dear Marie-Ange, I can't guarantee you anything. I have made love so often (and with so many women) that I sometimes just haven't the strength. A physical weakness that is still infrequent and only temporary (if things don't work out with you, they will with someone else, I have no worry in this respect). But of course you know that Malraux said to Julian Green, in 1930 I think it was, (Julian Green was the writer we were talking about earlier this evening at the Carnéjoux?)" I must remember to say, in English, "*My dear* Marie-Ange . . ."

. . . A universe of sex stretched out before me, whose frontiers are unknown and probably also unknowable. Everything is possible, here and elsewhere, today and always. Every kind of discovery. Every kind of pleasure. Every kind of surprise. I cannot even imagine, with my still limited experience, the immense erotic potential that lies ahead. Disquieting, and yet prodigiously exciting. Such a long life in which to learn and to understand. Not long enough ever to exhaust its possibilities. But Bertrand, Bertrand with his hand on my forehead; no, it is unthinkable, inconceivable . . .

. . . The man in the dressing gown is still there, with his dog, but they will soon go back indoors for it is now raining very hard. Whatever is before me, I cannot expect to discover anything new. It is not that I am jaded, quite the reverse. But physical passion, no matter whom it is with, or where, or under what circumstances, is still only physical passion. At my age, knowing what I know, it is not possible, alas, or reasonable, to expect any surprises, as I did in the distant days of my youth when the shabbiest bordello was a palace of miracles. But pleasure, yes, this evening I can hope to give (and receive) pleasure to one (and from one) of at least three women here in this room who are mine—or still another, this Lucienne whom I do not know, which would be still better. Pleasure, which always surprises by not pleasing . . .

. . . But why do I need this confession of André Malraux? (A commonplace one, at that.) In a book I read recently, I don't remember the title, (*Faublas*, I think) there was a description of certain dissolute human beings whom death had stricken ahead of time, in their most sensitive parts. (What Julian Green and I found interesting in Malraux was his certainty as to the exact age when this is likely to occur.) . . .

. . . Youth, youth, my marvelous and inexhaustible and triumphant youth. Why is it that the men and women at this table seem so calm and self-assured, when they are already so old? Why am I the one to feel ill-at-ease, not that I doubt my own genius, of course, within myself I know that I am more intelligent, more sensitive than these numb, half-dead old fogies, haven't they all revealed what nonentities they are, even those among them who are supposed to be *successful*—what kind of a triumph is it to be as rich as Roland Soulaires, or to write idiotic movies like Gilles Bellecroix?—why must I doubt my own prowess, with men, and with women (especially with women) and feel like such a hopeless pariah, to be so weak when I am strong, so timid when I am self-confident, so insignificant when I am superior? Youth, youth, my tortured, miserable, terrible youth . . .

. . . Why are you looking at me like that, Pilou? The outrage of a woman who is loved but feels that she is threatened. Have you the same forehead, the eyes, the hair, the mouth, the breasts of Lucienne Osborn (not to mention those of Armande)—which neither your breasts, nor your mouth, nor your hair, nor your eyes, nor your forehead, incomparable as they are, can hope to equal? For every desirable woman is unique. You cannot be jealous of what is not you. But maybe you are only checking to see whether I am keeping an eye on you. That would be even more irritating . . .

. . . I don't care to know what is going on between Bertrand and the chambermaid. Things like that disgust me. *Faublas* and other novels of its kind are full of such coy, unsavory sexual pranks. ("Then I kissed Justine. 'Save that for my mistress,' said she with a pouting expression.") (Or: "As I closed the door on Justine, she gave me a little slap. But the Marquise did not notice.") . . .

. . . I am cut off from the other guests by tongues of fire, each with a nimbus of flickering light which penetrates the surrounding shadows. Even the candles are lost behind this spreading brilliance. Brightness which destroys all that is around it. Vague halos of sound vibrate at the edges. All conversations are engulfed in this absurd little universe of flame which bears no resemblance to anything in the world outside. But the spell lifts; before my eyes the reassuring shapes of the candles and their gleaming silver candelabra appear once again and recognizable words begin to emerge from the chaos of sound. I am becoming old, very old, poor Gigi, how lonely it is . . .

. . . I can't hear what she is saying, with all this noise. She has decided to break the silence and is talking in her own cryptic way. (*The country is nice, oh yes, but not alone* . . .) It is true that I had a hard time getting her to go to Valromé without me. (*Why of course, with . . . But I couldn't possibly . . .*) Just what could that mean? I can't hear what Gilles is answering. He is talking in a very low voice. (. . . *like certain books which one should not read alone, if you know what I mean . . .*) Martine advances in a conversation the way her mother does at a party, obliquely, veering this way and that way, but knowing very well where she is going . . .

. . . Pilou is charming. Virtuous, but restless. Tempted. If I were Bertrand, I would watch out. Quite a dinner they have served us! (Champagne with every course. Madness . . .)

. . . Bright blades of fire, like little red swords passing over the tablecloth: the reflection of the water and the wine. I am grateful to Gilles, although now I am not so sure that he attracts me. But I know that I was awakened by him. *Emancipated. One man emancipates me and makes way for all the others; I am ready for love.* Bertrand asked for it. Gilles? Maybe. Maybe tonight . . .

. . . Welcomed by a chorus of admiring cries, the *bateau-mouche* is making its return voyage. Falling into geometric patterns on the rug and on the ceiling, the reflections explode into myriad sparkling fragments in the burning mirrors. The multicolored lanterns of the boat, which I can just see against the dark river, are not so much eclipsed by the dazzling searchlights as they are dulled by the rain. Faint strains of a sentimental melody. The fleeting but vivid impression of another nautical celebration, more a dream than a memory: Venice with Marie-Plum. Venice in the rain . . .

. . . One, two, three, four, —five, six. Or else: one, two, —three, four, five, six. Or else: six, five, four, three, —two, one. Or else . . . I am getting really gaga. If only the dinner would come to an end! Then I wouldn't have this woman and her gold necklace in front of me any more. If only I could hug Jérôme, hold him in my arms; he would save me, would give me new faith. My little life is too heavy for me . . .

. . . A new complex of shadows, combining, overlapping, separating. Not a waltz this time, but a Brazilian song that was a hit several years ago and whose title I have forgotten; heard and loved in Rio first, it met me months afterwards in Paris, disappeared . . . and now here it is again, with its gaiety of another era that sounds so funereal. It no longer evokes the beaux and belles of 1900, but the shades of the women who departed after a certain young man was gone, the man who had loved them: myself . . .

. . . How pretty the river is, with the rain blurring the lights. I don't know what to do with such beauty. What kind of a game were we playing, Martine? Bénédicte is not here. Everything which I love and admire loses its meaning, its very existence, when it is not also witnessed by the person who has become an indispensable part of my life. So what could I hope for in the way of happiness with you, little Martine? Even this brightly-lit boat, when I cannot point out its poetry to my wife, loses its charm. This, you see, is love. From the moment I saw Bénédicte, I loved her for always, once and for always. How can I be deprived of anything when she is all things to me? . . .

. . . A pyramid of succulent pears. The film I would make

if I were given complete freedom. But censorship, censorship . . . To think of what could be done if . . . For instance? Well, this: a young woman carrying an armful of fruit, pears, or better still, peaches, which are slowly transformed into so many smooth, youthful breasts. A beautiful, heavy armful of naked breasts. Vain temptations. The young woman does not have your face, Martine, but Bénédicte's . . .

. . . Curled leaves floating in the transparent depths. Plants submerged in deep, quiet, blue water. Giant submarine foliage. A graceful stalk of maiden-hair curves from the vase to the tablecloth, which its delicate tip barely touches. I should not have given it a name, for now I can no longer believe in the metamorphosis which changed the air into water. Now it is only a slim fern, amidst the other dainty leaves surrounding the tea roses in the center of the table . . .

"What lovely pears!"

"Bertrand is a connoisseur . . ."

"They are sensational. Where did you ever . . ."

"Did you grow them at Valromé?"

"Alas, no. How could I? Such things can't be left in the hands of others . . ."

"We went there this afternoon, but the fruit we brought home with us was not even presentable."

"Here, let me recommend this one. It is not much to look at, but the taste is exquisite. It is called a *Beurré Superfin*."

"And this one?"

"The Baronne de Mello. This one has a curious name:

Alexandrine Drouillard. You should also try these Délices de Lowenjoul . . ."

"You are an expert!"

"He seems to savor each name!"

"What about Thompsons? Haven't you any Thompsons?"

. . . Thompsons are a cheap variety . . .

"I think they come later in the season."

. . . To sketch from life, not only fleeting reality but even that which is only an illusion, like the maiden-hair fern in its weird, submarine florescence. To render each phenomenon precisely and to be careful not to distort it in the process. Such was, such is still, my modest goal as a writer . . .

"And Chatelleraults?"

"Chatelleraults? I must confess, Eugénie, that I am not familiar with Chatelleraults . . ."

"Nor am I, you can be sure, but I've heard about them . . ."

. . . Chatellerault. As Eugénie spoke, my other dinner partner cast a myopic but deliberate glance in my direction. Of course! She is the one, the naïve little girl from the provinces, from Chatellerault. Lucienne was her name. Now I recognize her, beneath her newly-acquired sophistication. She is the one; of course she is. It must have been almost twenty years ago. She used to come to my apartment in the Rue de l'Abbaye, whenever she was in Paris. Not as pretty as she is today, in fact not even as fresh-looking—certain women seem to need a number of years before they come into their own. So inexperienced in those days, and so timid, so shy, which made her immodesty and sudden passionate outbursts all the more delightful. I didn't remember, though, that she was nearsighted . . .

. . . Now I've done it Zig my sweetheart no use pretending any longer there is no way out he recognized me Léon-Pierre if you care for me at all you had better watch out I am caught in the snare of memory oh my mortified young body my beautiful body not as beautiful as it is today for I was then so dreadfully white and pale my beautiful young body so long ago my body was frustrated by that mechanical love-making and yet Zig Zig why do I yearn for it again why can you tell me why . . .

. . . Infused with the sharp, cold air of early morning, these pears have remained cool from the time they were picked in a foggy orchard, in storehouses and wagons, on the platforms of stations, until dawn today when they were brought to the market. Taken from the crates in which they were packed like precious jewels, they were arranged in fruit bowls and served before they had time to become warm, remaining sweet and cool until they finally melted on our tongues. I enjoy the thought that Jérôme is also experiencing, at the same moment, this succulent delicacy . . .

. . . She never fled from my advances. Wisely, she refused to struggle in a match that was already decided, already conceded. Conquered once and for all, she omitted the unnecessary preliminaries. Wishing to avoid the humiliation of repeated surrender. She knew me as well as I knew her, but she remembered, while I, as she has come to realize, whether with amusement or sorrow I do not know, had forgotten her completely . . .

. . . He was so sure of himself and not once not once did I find satisfaction with him nor with anyone else in those days wilting in his arms on the very threshold of a climax just the same I wish that he knew that I knew oh now at last I understand today's horoscope not the one in *France-Soir* alas the one in *Paris-Presse* which is not as good said that today would be important for me in my relations with Aquarius I don't remember whether Bertrand is Aquarius I must find out . . .

. . . We haven't been quite so frivolous tonight. Not as scintillating as is customary at other dinner parties of this kind in Paris. Although one never knows. A person may think that he is being very witty when it is only his semi-intoxication which gives him the impression of sparkling intelligence. An illusion which becomes truth when all the guests share in it together for the length of one meal . . .

"Gilles, don't you remember the baskets of fruit which poor dear Saint-Palpoul used to send you? I don't mean to embarrass you or to be indiscreet . . ."

. . . These words of Gigi's made Gilles Bellecroix blush. It is both ridiculous and touching to see him ruffled, an old dandy who still, and he gave us some proof of his prowess this evening which I could easily have done without, still likes the girls, and little else . . .

"But Gigi dear, what have I to hide?"

. . . His color is back to normal . . .

. . . Why should I be embarrassed? No reason at all . . .

". . . Edouard used to come to meet us after the theater, Eugénie and me, with large bouquets of flowers . . ."

. . . My God, I am compromising Gigi. But it was so

291

long ago. Everyone knew about it. And besides, she was the one who brought it up . . .

. . . "Eugénie and me." How sweet, how lovely . . .

"Or else he would give them to me so that I could present them to the delicious Gigi."

. . . The delicious Gigi! What bliss . . .

. . . In the last euphoric moments of this dinner party, the two of them are proclaiming a relationship which they took such pains to hide earlier in the evening . . .

. . . Old Eugénie is lapping it up. How indecent! So it is true, then. Once upon a time, these two old birds . . .

"Now be honest, to whom was he really sending the flowers?"

"To me, Bertrand, to me, of course."

"That's right, dearest Gilles. You fascinated him. There was something rather touching about Edouard, beneath that self-possessed exterior . . ."

. . . Dearest Gilles, my own dearest Gilles, in the days when men belonged to me . . .

" . . . I hardly ever think about Edouard. I can't pretend that he ever meant very much to me. But not long ago, on the night of September 30 in fact, I dreamt about him, and he seemed so extraordinarily alive . . . I can't even begin to tell you . . ."

. . . What Gigi means is: "I can't begin to tell you what happened; it was too intimate, too important . . ."

. . . How could I tell them that he talked about Christ, he, Edouard, and in such strong, moving words . . .

. . . No one has registered any interest, but Gigi goes right on . . .

"Did you know who Edouard's best friend was? Forain . . ."

. . . Roland is nervously rolling his cigarette between his fat fingers. His red gums. His far-away smile . . .

"I knew Foraine quite well, you know. I'll never forget the day when I asked him, 'You were a friend of Rimbaud's, weren't you?' They were very close, and he answered, 'Oh, you can't imagine what an amusing time we had together!'—'How was that?'—'Well, we used to dress up like women and throw things at the people who went by. Calling them names. It was too funny!' "

"Yes, all that must have been rather depressing, once you saw it up close . . ."

"Sordid, I'd say."

"Pathetic. Really pathetic. Of course it still goes on. Poor Rico, you know, he doesn't get a cent, not one cent! When Zerbanian isn't home, he literally starves."

"Don't tell me about it! Many is the time I've had to take the poor soul in."

"But he enjoys it. It's all part of the fun."

"His masochism and Zerbanian's avarice make a good combination."

"Nobody, but nobody is stingier than Zerbanian."

"Yes, Coco . . ."

. . . and Roland Soulaires . . .

"Apparently she is crazy as ever . . ."

"Poor dear, she still wishes she were *en poste* . . ."

"But Léon retired ages ago. She must have accepted the situation by now!"

"Besides, she used to live in Paris."

"Yes, and Coco was never very popular abroad. Everyone knew that!"

. . . "Society," and its static little frame of reference. This conversation about Zerbanian's boyfriend and the gossip about the Ambassador's wife could be going on to-night, or before the war. Gigi is saying the same things, about the same people, and smoking the same cigarettes as twenty years ago. Roland Soulaires is still too fat. Gilles Bellecroix looks nearly as young. Unless it is the fact that we have all grown old together which gives this illusion. It makes me dizzy to compare this mirage of a timeless present with the actual number of years that have passed. Pilou was a baby—and we were already what we are now . . .

"But you know, she is very intelligent . . ."

"The person I envy is Lucine de Brouges. Now there is someone . . ."

"Coco, intelligent? Well, as someone once said to me, I forget who . . ."

"Lucine is a pretty name. There have always been a great many Lucines in the Montausier family . . ."

"Now wait a minute! Lucine, intelligent? She may try to give that impression . . ."

"Clever, perhaps . . ."

"But such a poor . . ."

"That sounds like a Hindu temple . . ."

"I beg your pardon!"

"Phonetically, I mean. *Suchapoor*, doesn't that sound Hindu?"

. . . Gusts of conversation are coming my way. Separate

waves of words, cries, and laughter break and mingle together, with moments of calm, silences quickly engulfed by
new surges of laughter, words, and cries. I am here, but I
am not here. Lulled by conversation in which I am no
longer taking part. The dinner has reached the point when
everything goes on smoothly by itself, and the host no
longer needs to intervene. My forehead is heavier than any
other part of my body, in fact it is the only part of me
that I can feel, except for my belly which is also oppressed,
though not by alcohol. My teeth ache after swallowing the
icy champagne. This is what is called being detached. I am
so detached that I have taken leave of myself, maintain-
ing only enough consciousness, though I am not drunk, to
be aware of this lack, this surrender, this absence. Where
am I? I am here. But there is no one here; only a pocket of
emptiness, me, myself. I. I, Bertrand Carnéjoux, whose
name no longer has any meaning except on identification
papers, where it looks so peculiar to me. Bertrand Carnéjoux, what does that actually mean? And to think that I
was once so afraid of dying. What could my wife be looking at so intently across the table . . .

. . . Now my nose is as warm as it was icy earlier this
evening. An unpleasant, prickling sensation. What a lot of
noise they are making! The children, my God, the children! They had slipped my mind. A complete blank, a terrible, unforgivable oversight. Usually they are foremost in
my mind, and in my heart, even when I am thinking about
something else, even when my feelings do not seem to concern them. Drops of wax on our best tablecloth. How
annoying . . .

"Penniless, you see, so she couldn't possibly hope to find a husband in Marseilles . . ."

"I must tell you a story."

. . . Not another! Nothing is more aggravating than someone who chooses the very moment when the conversation is rolling along in a nice haphazard fashion, to march in with his "little story" and monopolize the floor . . .

"I am a very poor listener, you know. Unless a story is very short . . ."

"Oh, this won't take a minute . . ."

"The weather is going to change. I can feel it in my bones. Like the concierges."

. . . Eugénie apparently doesn't think that she is made like other women . . .

"Concierges! They can tell for days in advance . . ."

"That concierge in the Rue La Fontaine, what was her number again?"

"I must tell you what my friend Raymond Frôlet once said . . ."

"Raymond Frôlet? Who's he?"

"A friend of mine. A very amusing fellow. One day I was riding in the subway with him. It was very crowded. Suddenly someone got up and left an empty seat. What do you think Raymond Frôlet did? . . . I'll tell you. He rushed forward, pushed an old lady to one side, and said, 'Make way for youth!'"

"So you think that's funny, do you?"

"Yes, I think it's a riot! What nerve, eh?"

"I could tell you a few things . . ."

"Do you know what I think of that friend of yours? . . ."

"Oh, that's *nothing!* It would take me all night to tell you about my friend Raymond Frôlet . . ."

. . . We really ought to be ashamed of the idiotic things which the rhythm and excitement of the evening make us say. The frivolity of it all strikes me for a moment, but then I am carried away like the rest of them. The intoxication of words and the euphoria of wine. Luckily this silly conversation vanishes as quickly as the smoke from our cigarettes, whose hazy blue arabesques have but a moment's grace. If Bertrand would only pay a little attention to me, just for one minute . . .

. . . To try to compare these two fires which burn within me, my affection for Jean-Paul and my affection for Rachel, is to divide the indivisible. The whole remains unchanged. Sometimes, from one moment to the next, one glows higher than the other. A fleeting incandescence. A brief red flare. But beneath the ashes, the coals burn with equal intensity. They will not burn out until I die. So many loves lie buried beneath the ground. As long as women have loved their children—and been loved by them . . .

. . . A teen-ager, really just a baby, and so cute with his red hair. Now that I come to think of it, the man on the bicycle also had red hair. No connection . . .

"Oh yes, he is a character, all right, my friend Raymond Frôlet. He doesn't give a damn about . . ."

. . . Jérôme is getting vulgar, and interrupting the grownups. I won't invite him again. That Marie-Ange, making eyes at him. I hope that we are not waking up the children.

I haven't been thinking enough about the children. But Gilles, what about the children . . .

"These pears are perfectly delicious . . ."

"Smoking is a crime . . ."

"He never has any parking problems. He leaves his jalopy right in the middle of the street where there is always plenty of room . . ."

"I've never found that cigarettes . . ."

"People smoke too much these days . . ."

"It's very easy for me. I can stop smoking whenever I feel like it. I've done it at least twenty times, believe me!"

"He just leaves a little sign on the windshield saying: 'Engine trouble. Thank you.' "

"And no one has ever bothered him?"

"Never! The fellow has real nerve, and mark my words, nerve is the secret of success . . ."

. . . That sounded awkward and pedantic. Fortunately Raymond isn't here. Alcohol makes the trivial seem important. Every opinion sounds convincing, every truth sounds fundamental. This is why we defend our current beliefs with such passion, no matter how insignificant they are. I, at least, have a sense of the ridiculous . . .

. . . It is meaningless for a mother to say that she loves one child more than another. Such emotions are impossible to measure, to compare. Each is a world of its own. Jean-Paul and Rachel are each *everything* to me . . .

"I don't smoke much anymore. They say that cancer . . ."

. . . That is madness pure and simple to say the forbidden word Gilles is crazy crazy cancer the word which I had succeeded not in forgetting for it is always tucked away in a corner of my poor brain but at least in avoiding even to myself but now I am done for my evening is done for finished I am done for we are all done for all threatened almost all of us will be stricken sooner or later . . .

. . . That word, that word which hurts so, but I am still young, with my whole life ahead of me. No, no one is safe, even at twenty-four . . .

. . . The year 1000 had its own great terror and we have ours. No one talks about it but no one thinks of anything else . . .

. . . Was it bravado or a slip of the tongue which made me say that word? I am at the dangerous age. We are all at the dangerous age . . .

. . . That *dreadful word*. Can silence exorcise its threat, or is it better to be courageous and say it out loud? . . .

. . . My old friend Raymonde died of cancer, but of course she always stayed up very late, not like me; even when I go out I always get to bed early. And poor old Saint-Palpoul. Yes, but he drank and Crespin smoked. Not I. But what about Angèle? She lived such a quiet life . . .

. . . I came so near to being arrested by the Gestapo. I probably would have been shot. I was never really afraid. But this . . .

. . . That millionaire who killed himself a few days ago. Suicide, without a motive, said the newspapers. Everyone had a different theory. But I know what it was: he must have had cancer and known about it. Which one of the guests here tonight has cancer? I am the youngest; I am not in danger, nor is Pilou . . .

. . . No one else seems to have paid much attention to

299

that evil word I must be particularly sensitive maybe I should see a psychiatrist oh but really come on now Lucienne I am sane and sound but for how long . . .

"Do you want to know something funny? I had no appetite at all when I sat down to dinner. I had to make myself eat and now, if you can imagine, I'm hungry . . ."

"Perfect timing, Gilles my dear . . ."

"Not at all!"

"Why?"

"Because dinner is all over, that's why!"

. . . This two-fold love cannot be divided. One love cannot take away from the other; each is complete in itself, each unique. This is my only joy and my only sorrow. Sorrow because each implies, indeed demands, an eternity which is denied. Oh! My poor helpless children, already dragged away by the ruthless hands of time! I would not mind having to go, if I knew that they were safe . . .

. . . As though the camera had changed its focus, the decor of this dining room settles into the background, becomes less conspicuous, without actually moving. An effect which keeps repeating itself. I haven't had too much to drink, only enough to put me in a pleasant mood. Our happiness is reflected in its purest and most intense form on Nicolas' face, when his mother and I are suddenly aware of the violence of our love, and kiss each other chastely but lovingly in front of him, and instead of being embarrassed, he, too, is carried away by this deep, serene, and wondrous emotion. We never argue in front of him and if he ever catches a note of irritation in our voices, even this is too much for him, needing as he does not only our understanding, but our complete and total communion . . .

. . . The philodendron seems even taller almost like a tree from the virgin forest where it first originated as though the warmth of this dinner party had made the room into a tropical hot-house where gigantic plants could grow new shoots in a few hours amidst sea-green shadows but this is all in my imagination the alcohol is distorting my already-feeble eyesight with a curtain of fire . . .

. . . A tree of faces, the like of which was never dreamed, even by Marcel Jouhandeau. A brief nightmare. Our seven heads grafted to the body of Eugénie Prieur. An octocephalic monster in which all identities are lost. Attached to her lascivious thigh, I would have the memories, the temptations, the desires and even the regrets of an old woman. They would not say: "He has lost his head," but: "He has lost his body." And then we would see which one really dominates, the head or the body . . .

. . . Bénédicte my beloved, soon I will be seeing you. Love is a refuge from other loves. A woman is a refuge from women. Possessing a woman from one moment to the next, even when one is separated from her. And possessed by her, for ever and always. Like Aragon, I could praise my wife's love, *the perfume you leave behind you, the rooms which tremble as you pass. And when you are gone, I am as forlorn as your mirror* . . .

. . . It took Lucienne almost twenty years to become pretty. Paradoxically, the years have made her younger, have given her time to find and to develop her own particular kind of beauty. In the days of our intermittent love affair, she was not ugly, (otherwise I would never have desired her) but thick, heavy-set. Not that she was fat, just awkward, ungainly, not knowing how to walk, or talk. Naked, she had even less idea what to do with herself. And I don't imagine for a moment that it was John Osborn who taught her this. Maybe I was the one, who knows, without being aware of it. I can't remember when, or how, I left her. Maybe I let her go too soon, abandoning her just when she had learned something from me, when she had finally understood love . . .

. . . As soon as he came near me chills went up and down my spine the very thought of his body sent chills up and down my spine even Léon-Pierre does not have that effect on me his hand on my shoulder made me tremble pleasure was so close at hand but the look of indifference in his eyes his mechanical gestures made me freeze and I abandoned myself to him without ever being able to really lose myself Bertrand was not the one who taught me how to enjoy love it was a friend of his I will never understand how or why but one night Bernard Freissane was kissing me behind the ear and I suddenly relaxed once and for all of course I have made a great deal of progress since then Bertrand will have to see how much I have learned luckily I am tan for him tonight looking my best I wonder if Zig the rascal will take to him he is funny about strangers but such a sweetie I wonder what sign he was born under could it be Aquarius . . .

. . . She was so young then. Barely of age. Not very intelligent, either, if I remember correctly. Married, I think, to a man who was more than twice her age. About forty-five. My age. Is he dead? Did she leave him? In any case she remarried. I had no idea that the pretty Mrs. Osborn whom people talked about would turn out to be the least memorable of my mistresses . . .

"It has been a long time since I have had faith. That is, if I ever really did believe, for I am not even sure of that anymore . . ."

"Roland! How can you say such a thing!"

"I couldn't go on living if I didn't believe in God."

"God. Yes, God . . ."

"God?"

. . . Sooner or later, of course, God had to be brought into the conversation, not disrespectfully, but with an unpleasant air of familiarity, a casual tone of voice that is all the more offensive when someone like Mrs. Osborn or Gilles Bellecroix, in answer to Roland's honest declaration of agnosticism, makes a game of proclaiming his or her piety. Marie-Ange's contemptuous smile. Eugénie Prieur, turning her back once again on Bertrand Carnéjoux, looks at me in silence, with a far-away, beatified expression.

"They have no idea what they are talking about."

"It is too bad, madame, but each of us says such things as best he can, when and where he is able to. Even at the end of a gay dinner party . . ."

"You are right, but . . ."

. . . I can't hear him very well. But it does not matter. I can easily imagine what he is saying . . .

"I myself lost faith in God years ago."

"You? Years ago? But you couldn't be a day over twenty!"

"It is not something which I boast about. On the contrary . . ."

. . . Why am I confiding in this frivolous old woman? . . .

"There is a great deal of difference, my child, between saying that you have no faith, and really having none. When you look deeply, in the bottom of your heart, very often you discover that faith is there, hidden but alive, believe me! . . ."

. . . Why is she saying this to me? Why should I listen to what such a silly old woman tells me? Silence is the best answer. Even so, there is now a secret understanding between us, while at the beginning of dinner we had nothing to say to each other . . .

. . . What a relief. (What a disappointment!) Marie-Ange is not paying any more attention to me. After careful consideration, I do not believe that there is anything to fear in regard to my oil holdings. (According to information which I have gathered, the volume of business is bound to rise.) As for financing the research projects, Bresval has assured me of complete cooperation. (I must keep on buying Royal Dutch and Sahara Limited . . .) Tomorrow, send eighteen red roses and three white ones to Marie-Ange . . .

"You are too intelligent, oh yes you are, don't be modest, too sensitive not to recognize, how can I say it, that in these matters there is an element of surprise. When one is most sure of understanding oneself, there is still room for the unexpected. Believe me. I know hardly anything about you, you know; you are not very talkative, and you never gave me the chance to read your palm. But Bertrand is right, faces are even more revealing, and yours gives me great confidence. I trust you. You will see. Someday you will remember what an old woman told you."

. . . No, she is neither depraved nor stupid. Better than I thought. What if she were right, if God will be revealed to me someday? Dear Mme. Prieur . . .

. . . All I can see of Eugénie, who is turned almost entirely toward Jérome, is a massive back covered with woolly wraps. What are they discussing, with their voices lowered and such serious expressions on their faces? I should be able to hear, for the room is relatively quiet. But now they have stopped exchanging secrets and I am reminded of a brief conversation which I had with a Brazilian poet, on the outskirts of Rio, one evening as we were riding beneath the trees of a murmuring forest, beneath stars that were equally melodious. We were rolling gently through the night, sitting with Amelinha in the back seat of a convertible. Through the tops of the tall, exotic trees, I sought and found the Southern Cross, framed by the over-hanging branches. Something was said at that moment which revealed a great secret to me, a secret which I have been trying to remember for a long time, but in vain. All that is left is a cryptic incident, which I have never given up hope of deciphering. That evening the same man told me something else, and this I have not forgotten: "You know, don't you, that I am considered a kind of prophet in my country? That when I have revealed to artists the work which they will create in the future, I have never made a mistake? Now I know, I am certain, I swear that you will eventually write a novel in which you will put into words something which you alone are able to express. And you, little Amelinha, you too will appear in this book." Lucienne Osborn is looking at me in an odd manner. Do I really desire her? . . .

. . . I remember the exact words of the horoscope it said that a relationship with Aquarius is very favorable you can expect spectacular results from a decision made in conjunction with Aquarius today or tomorrow you may outdo yourself I married my second husband because he was born on February second poor John without any spectacular results I must admit but with Bertrand . . .

"Tell me, Bertrand, I've forgotten—after so long—when is your birthday?"

"You want to wish me a happy birthday? How sweet. Unfortunately it is quite far off. May 15 . . ."

"That's too bad . . ."

. . . Too bad he is Taurus but then maybe someone else here is Aquarius to outdo myself that is a stroke of luck it doesn't seem as if this dinner will ever end I am getting very restless I can hardly bear it any longer but I mustn't speak about luck it is dangerous . . .

. . . Am I nearer Christ than I thought? In spite of everything do I believe in Christ, as Eugénie Prieur suggested a few minutes ago? All I have to do is put the question into words and I immediately have a negative answer. Though it is true that instead of praying I make the sign of the cross several times a day, very carefully and deliberately—and it always brings me an amazing sense of peace . . .

. . . How many times have these four silver candelabra illuminated dinner parties like this one? How many times have they stood beside a deathbed? The film which records this colorful story passes before me in accelerated motion. A Regency ball. A vigil. A *fête galante*. (I don't know why, but this evening has the aura of a *fête galante*.) A funeral wake. (I also don't know why I have thought about death so often this evening.) Another dinner. Another death. And so on, through the ages, from generation to generation. The master of the house hardly has time to set his glass of champagne on the table before his eyes are closed forever, and he lies with his face gently illuminated by the same candlelight as in happier days. If I were Bertrand, I would not enjoy sitting in front of the candles that will stand by my bed after I die . . .

. . . A woman who seemed to be all artifice, always playing a game, which is probably only her way of struggling against loneliness and despair. Now she is suddenly sober and sincere, showing an open, honest, and good side of herself which I never would have suspected. Speaking perhaps in behalf of God, although she believed that she was only telling me about God . . .

. . . Lucienne needn't bother looking in her mirror; she can't possibly powder her bosom in public, and the skin revealed by her decolletage, which was so smooth, in spite of her tan, is now rough and leathery. This sudden glimpse of enlarged pores and red blotches is a disappointment. In spite of it, I go on trying to be aroused by the partly despoiled nakedness of this woman who is less dazzling than when she arrived, but still beautiful. I would probably find her even less desirable, in the overheated state in which dinner has left her, were it not for the fact that bosoms have always fascinated me. Nevertheless, I can see that one hour of good eating and drinking have erased years of effort, the whole Parisian apprenticeship. Here before me, and recognizable only to me, not quite so young, somewhat more polished, but still a country girl with her rough shoulders and ruddy bosom, is my little friend from Chatellerault . . .

. . . Elegant tapers burned down to half their size. Impeccable make-up partly worn away. Now, in the last confused moments of the dinner party, you have reverted to your origins. Floundering among bloody carcasses, knee-deep in a swamp of meat and grease, the man of the Azores still slaughters his whale in the age-old manner; butcher of the oceans, carving up his kill on the beach, he tramples his harvest of flesh with his bare feet to extract its precious vintage for a famous perfume-maker. And his partners in the kill, ladies anointed with whale oil and the fragrance of entrails . . .

. . . Lucienne. This beautiful, desirable creature in full bloom has vanished, spirited away by a breath of the past. Nothing more to say. No advances to be made. The vanity, the futility of it all. Now I try just as hard to avoid her glance as I tried earlier to make her look at me . . .

. . . From Saint-Tropez to Megève such a long spell without any real sunshine every year the same problem although I must admit that I've done rather well in the past the trouble is that Léon-Pierre can only come on the week ends and even then he gets in my way if one isn't difficult to please there is almost anything right on hand I mean difficult to please in regard to intelligence because as far as physiques are concerned one couldn't do better than in ski resorts but I am intelligent enough for two . . .

. . . Have I had too much to drink? Or is it age, old age? I feel uncomfortable, my tongue is heavy, foul and sluggy . . . no, that's not it, the words are insidiously distorted in my poor brain. Sluggerish, that is the word, sluggerish. Try to relax, be neutral, as detached as possible so that death will not be able to find me . . .

. . . Eugénie's face, again fixed, petrified, as though of marble. After her spell of frenetic excitement earlier this evening, it is abnormal. Her dimpled little hands, lying on the tablecloth, rather pretty but with the liver spots of age . . .

. . . A lone woman leaning against the wet parapet. For whom could she be waiting at this hour of the night? Of whom is she dreaming? The nobility of her languid posture. It is not a pose. Although the rain has stopped falling, there is no one on the embankment to observe her. How lovely to see a woman's body silhouetted against the luminous night of Paris, a body that is heavy-set, but young and healthy and alone. It must be the champagne which made her appear to me, in the midst of a world as poignantly beautiful as she. On the other side of the Seine, the houses, perforated by light, thrust their tall, crenellated silhouettes against the pale brilliance of the sky. This too, although a prosaic, everyday sight, enchants me, as though I had finally discovered the beauty of the world and would never again lose the key to its mysteries. But it is the champagne, alas, only the champagne. The windows are too far away for me to see into them, even though the river is narrow along this side of the island. It has been a long time since I saw Edwige . . .

. . . Such a great, undecided future stretching out before me. Should I choose different courses when I go back to the university? But it is too late now. Or pursue scientific studies along with my other work? Or else forget about exams and start living as soon as possible? Become a parachute jumper and turn my military training into a real experience? Become an archeologist? A deep-sea diver? Or else a screen director, and make great movies, not trivial little scenarios like the ones Gilles Bellecroix writes, but the creative, revolutionary movies of the future which I already have clearly in mind . . .

. . . From the terrace of her house, where Edwige and I used to stretch out on our stomachs on summer nights, it was not the stars which we gazed at, while Uncle Charles thought we were watering his geraniums. With the binoculars, I could see deep into the open windows, into rooms whose every detail was revealed to me. The distance from any other windows as high as theirs put the couples completely at ease, going and coming under the eyes of the night, and ours, in their innocent nakedness, not so much to caress one another (after living together for so long did they even see each other?) but in the hope of a little cool air. I was a demanding voyeur, but it was something more than mere embraces for which I waited and which I feared that Edwige's eagerness for her turn would make me miss. To see her so demure, and well-bred, who would ever imagine the things that Edwige is capable of saying and doing? . . .

. . . Two of the candles continue to drip onto the table-cloth where the wax spreads in thick, light-green puddles. It will be quite a job to remove the spots. Fortunately dinner is nearly over. It didn't go too badly, except for that wait at the beginning which I hope Bertrand has forgotten . . .

. . . My slim fingers in the warm water with its slice of lemon. Oh, to hold you against me, Jérôme darling. A desire stronger than desire. This desperate tenderness . . .

. . . These nocturnal invasions of privacy are made all the more rewarding by the fact that they combine the advantages of being present with those of being absent. To be there or not to be there. Such is the question. For once I escape this alternative and can observe others in the intimacy of their private existence, an experience which is all the more moving when it concerns the dual solitude of a man and a woman. More disturbing even than the sight of her naked bosom, devastating in itself, is the way this strange woman is washing her hands. No matter how lacking the men and women are in any form of beauty (thin backs, flat chests, poor legs) my joy is undiminished. I feel like an indulgent guardian angel, full of such compassion that it never occurs to me that I could be doing something wrong. This elegant excuse does not convince me. The same old hypocrisy. As I watch, like an eager Peeping Tom, what is my hand doing? If only, if only, right at this moment, this very instant, I could put my hand on Edwige's bare breast . . .

. . . Petit fours, painted by Marie Laurencin. The dinner comes to an end. During the whole meal I have not had a single idea for a book or a film. Once again my mind has wandered fruitlessly. I will try to think of something during the evening. All the most passionate love affairs of my past are caught in the passage of time, while my love for Bénédicte is pledged to eternity. Even if we are headed for oblivion, which I do not believe, eternity still exists, *hic et nunc*. Time and eternity coexist in this life on two different levels. The realm of change and decay. The realm of the invariable and yet never stagnant present, volatile, incandescent, constantly renewed and yet permanent. Bénédicte gives me, in their complete and perfect form, the joys which other women have offered me only partially: youth, beauty, love,—plus a spiritual happiness which cannot compare with these pleasures of the flesh. Our life together. A child (a child!) and then this troth which is plighted until death, and beyond, this irrevocable step forward, for better or worse. A Sacrament which every day is revealed to me anew, of which every day I receive the grace . . .

. . . Come, Jérôme, wild clover is yours. She loves you. When I was a child they said I was a little spitfire. But I am not so difficult when someone loves me, you will see . . .

. . . The tinkle of a crystal bowl. A pure sound, prolonged in ever-fainter echoes. But I have drawn too much attention to myself already. Lukewarm water. Be careful not to splash the tablecloth. The spot in front of me is embarrassing enough . . .

. . . Bells and rooftops of Paris, have you nothing better than these wretched little memories for me? Dark rooftops, short red chimneys, wisps of blue smoke, pigeons, and the black caves of dormer windows. Rooftops in a reverent circle around the tall belltower, the ancient and massive lighthouse which the darting swifts seem to stroke with their wings and strike with their cries, in the early light over Saint-Germain-des-Près, one sacred morning of my youth, what have you taught me which I have forgotten, then remembered and forgotten again, which I always seem to be on the verge of rediscovering, oh night of Brazil, when I listened with a poet to the unforgettable music of the tropical spheres? . . .

. . . It would not surprise me if some of the gold mines were abandoned or sold outright. That does it! I mustn't eat any more sweets. And yet I am so fond of them (especially petit fours!) A burning pain shoots through my jaws, outlining their exact contours in a blueprint of pain. I must talk to my dentist about this. A bell rings insistently on the floor above us . . .

. . . Zig is a remarkably intelligent dog of course we live together so much even when Léon-Pierre and I make love he is there looking on with a happy expression as though he were glad that I was enjoying myself no one could be more intelligent than I am nor enjoy herself more I am not enjoying myself this tight sensation this oppression like a million tiny needles it is really time for dinner to be over it is over now I will take advantgae of the inevitable confusion when everyone moves into the living room and disappear for a moment no one will notice . . .

. . . To learn about death, not as something unjust or painful, but merely inconsequential. Moments of lucidity, in which I go further than a mere acceptance of oblivion,

313

in which life itself seems shocking to me, or at the very least, futile. At moments like this I feel a slight margin of security; since I am already non-existent—or existing in such a false, feeble, hopeless capacity—I look on my progress towards death with complete equanimity. What is left of the young woman she once was in the Eugénie that is here before me, clinging so desperately to the last days of an unhappy, useless and lonely life? This nothing-much, this residue, is this really what we are? These rare nuggets left behind in the sieve of time, are they worth all our laments? Old men sitting on doorsteps, warming their decrepit limbs in the sun, why are they so afraid to part with their poor carcasses? When they go, it will be no loss to humanity. None at all. The better part of wisdom would be to broaden this reasoning to include ourselves. To be wiser than they. Einstein mattered. Gide . . . perhaps not. Thus? . . .

. . . Martine is trying to catch Bertrand's eye, while, in the silence that has engulfed us all, we sit listening to a telephone ringing above us in an empty apartment . . .

. . . When has Bertrand ever paid any attention to me? Not even when he makes love; then I am only a body without a name or a face. Last night, he caressed me out of habit as he fell asleep. But as it was apparent that he was not thinking about me, I held myself back from feeling any pleasure, denying myself not so much the delights of the moment as the tantalizing possibility of future joy . . .

. . . A pretty girl, even a desirable one, does not mean anything to me anymore, or hardly anything, Martine, hardly anything. Women do not exist for me any longer.

Only my wife exists. As a mother, as a wife, as a mistress. Mine for eternity. I have learned to know the spirit which the body hides, and which gives it an added beauty. Everything seems to indicate that for each of us there is only one soul which we are destined to deserve, to possess. And I have been given this opportunity, unhoped for, undeserved, and yet destined for me throughout the ages. We cannot experience a greater happiness in this world, nor put our lives to better use. For happiness is made. Nothing is more sacred than the trust of a young woman who is given to you, before all men and before God. Kneeling at the altar I felt that I was responsible for Bénédicte, that someday I would have to answer for her well-being, that I could do nothing that would hurt her, no matter how slight. This utter, anxious tenderness, this feeling of moral and spiritual as well as physical responsibility, are the great revelations of marriage. I never received so much until the day when I decided to give something of myself . . .

. . . The truth came to me several times in the course of this dinner, but I did not recognize it, even though I put it into words myself, just as it was first taught to me, one calm, radiant morning on Saint-Germain-des-Près. *Death has not the slightest, not the slightest importance.* I cannot fear . . . But no, it could not last. The flash of illumination which made that early dawn so clear, so calm and reassuring, was too brief; the spell was broken once again by the shivering sound of a bell in a country railroad station, where a girl, a girl with a pair of sharp scissors . . .

. . . One, two, three, four,—one, two. One, two, three, four,—one, two. Little Marie-Ange, gentle Marietta, she of the crimson clover, she will be yours, Jérôme, tonight and every other night. Not just a woman, but your wife, your Indian squaw. One, two, three, four—one, two. One, two, three, four,—one, two. That shrill and fateful bell, upstairs. Why don't they realize that no one is home . . .

. . . I have never been so completely helpless, so cowardly, yes, cowardly is the word. Neither Julian Green nor Malraux can do anything for me. But there is another writer, whose words I like to repeat, like an ever-comforting exorcism: *I understood that my life was not my own, but the life of my wound,* Joë Bousquet whose life was ended at twenty by a bullet, though he did not die. I, too, in my own way, am gravely wounded, *and the only course to follow was in the direction of deeper and deeper understanding of this catastrophe which my instinct of self-preservation would always try to expunge from my memory.* Then, even more important: *You see, everyone has a great score to settle with fortune; together you can lay the foundations for spiritual health.* I see; I understand; I am saved. (It is certain that oil prices remain the determining factors in the market.) . . .

. . . A psychology in which nothing is fixed, and nothing is certain. In which no one is sure of anything—not even of himself. In which everything is relative. A disquieting thought: The permanence of the self, with its fixed frame of reference, always constant, denies the passage of time, which in turn denies our very existence. We think that we are alive when we are merely surviving. There is no progress. The same tiresome thoughts pass through our minds as we await destruction. We grow older with every minute.

316

And then we fall. What does Martine want? I can't even understand her when she talks, and when she tries to communicate in silence! Objectively, I have no interest whatsoever in the individual self, to which subjectively, I still cling. The telephone has finally stopped ringing. They must have hung up . . .

. . . Bertrand has not caught on to what his wife is trying to tell him with her glaring looks. He smiles back at her, happily oblivious . . .

. . . At other more frequent moments it is time which steals Martine from me. Slyly undermining her youth as it carries her—and me—away. Of course there will always be twenty-year-old girls, that is, as long as I am able to find and possess them. What does it matter to me if they no longer find me attractive? Money takes the place of youth. Nothing is more impersonal than sex. "To be loved for oneself" is a stupid expression. Nonsense. No one, ever, not even in the bloom of youth, was loved for himself alone . . .

. . . Bénédicte is present within me even when I am not thinking about her. How could I betray her? She is closer to me than my own self. This is happiness. No use looking elsewhere, or beyond. These are the farthest reaches of that precarious realm called happiness. I hope that her fever has gone down, that she will be asleep when I arrive home . . .

. . . Madame I have the honor and the unhappy task of drawing your attention to the official regulation which the legislature has found it necessary to pass in regard to sinister feeling that my inner organs are threatened my breasts my throat my brain but not my abdomen above all not my poor helpless abdomen so tender so soft and warm who is going to be happy to see his little mummy again Zig . . .

. . . Dead to myself, I am no longer vulnerable . . .

. . . The month is nearly over. And none too soon. I am down to my last penny and I owe quite a bit of money to Raymond Frôlet. If only Pilou had noticed the roses which I sent her . . .

. . . As soon as I get home I will look for that picture of Marie-Ange Vasgne, in the low-cut dress which revealed most of her bosom . . .

. . . If John Osborn doesn't show up I will be able to devote myself to Jérôme, without feeling guilty. It would be so pleasant, so relaxing. Let us hope that he isn't coming; I don't feel a bit like working tonight . . .

. . . My shoes! I thought I had lost them. Try to get them back on without anyone noticing. Then go home as quickly as possible, right after coffee. I am too tired. I need, I need so desperately to sleep. Impossible to wait any longer . . .

. . . Nothing more beautiful can exist in this world than the understanding between a man and a woman, the shared joys of love, the miracle of having a child. None of the pleasures which men seek, and which I myself have tried, can vie with this intimacy, this happiness—true happiness. I desire nothing more . . .

. . . Bertrand, oh Bertrand, it is time to get up from the table . . .

. . . And so life gradually fades away. Death should not frighten us, because we have never stopped dying. There are so few links between one era of my life and the next: the elementary, congenital satisfactions and frustrations, permanent traits of character, both qualities and faults, the knowledge of the little I am capable of accomplishing, of my essential limitations. Everything else, everything which adds charm and variety from one day to the next, disappears. When we reach the hoped-for joys of the future, there is only enough of ourselves left to insure an illusion of continuity. Well, it is over now; it is time to move into the living room . . .

. . . Bertrand, who has finally caught on to Martine's signals, rises, and Martine does the same. The chairs slide with difficulty over the carpet. We are standing . . .

. . . Eight napkins placed simultaneously on the tablecloth, all but one to the left of the plates, eight napkins still neat, showing their original folds, except for mine, which is crumpled and dirty and which I had to put to the right of my plate to hide the spot which I can finally stop worrying about. On my chair, the crumbs outline the shape of my thighs . . .

. . . White constructions, smooth, horizontal planes and sharp angles, shadows of white on white beneath peaks of well-ironed damask. But Jérôme's dirty napkin lies in a heap of messy wrinkles . . .

. . . And we will make love as never before, in a field of crimson clover, my little red-haired boy and I . . .

. . . As soon as I get home, I will make love with her, without her . . .

. . . Finally, a chance to kiss the children. No one will notice if I slip away for a moment . . .

. . . Just enough time I can find it by myself if only the

sun would make me healthy inside not just skin-deep penetrate me deeply purify me cure me but I am not sick not yet . . .

. . . Call Bénédicte, tell her I love her . . .

. . . If only I were sixty . . .

. . . Yes, but death . . .

. . . In the name of the Father, the Son, and the Holy Ghost. As simple as cool water and wine . . .

". . . To continue where we left off before dinner, I would say that liberty . . ."

DATE DUE

FEB 1 5 1984			
GAYLORD			PRINTED IN U.S.A.